HUNGER JOURNEYS

HUNGER JOURNEYS

A NOVEL

MAGGIE DE VRIES

HarperTrophyCanada™
An imprint of HarperCollinsPublishersLtd

Published by Harper*Trophy*Canada™,
an imprint of HarperCollins Publishers Ltd.

First published in Canada by Harper*Trophy*Canada™,
in an original trade paperback edition: 2010
This digest edition: 2012

Harper*Trophy*Canada™ is a trademark of HarperCollins Publishers.

HarperCollins books may be purchased for educational, business, or sales
promotional use through our Special Markets Department.

HarperCollins Publishers Ltd.
2 Bloor Steet East, 20th Floor
Toronto, Ontario, Canada
M4W 1A8

www.harpercollins.ca

Library and Archives Canada Cataloguing in Publication
information is available upon request

ISBN 978-1-55468-580-6

Printed and bound in Canada
10 9 8 7 6 5 4 3 2 1

To Lin, my mother-in-law: your story inspired this one

PROLOGUE

FEBRUARY 5, 1945
UTRECHT TRAIN STATION
OCCUPIED NETHERLANDS

The two girls froze. The area had been deserted when they came up, but suddenly the train platform was alive with German voices and stomping boots.

"Have you checked the cars?" said a voice, almost right beside Lena's and Sofie's heads.

"Schultz and Biermann started at the other end. I'll do these three. Here, jump up with me," a deeper voice replied.

A grunt of frustration. "Can't get this door open. Hey, help me, will you?"

Lena gripped Sofie's neck and leaned to speak into her ear. "They're searching the cars. We've got to find our bags and dig right to the back." She felt Sofie nod just as the door to the next car opened with a loud creak.

"You take the far end, Rauch, and dig deep. I'll start here. Any hideaways in here, we'll flush them out like rats."

Lena's body went rigid. They know we're here, she thought. Of course they do.

CHAPTER ONE

"Lena! Lena, come!"

Lena turned from the basin of lukewarm grubby water, dirty plates and knives and spoons forgotten. Her brother stood just inside the kitchen doorway, his face alight.

"Come," he said again, stepping forward and grasping her wrist. Lena felt a rare smile take hold of her face. She followed.

Piet did not speak again until they stood outside, with the front door of their apartment building closed behind them, parents and siblings shut away inside, and a bit of wartorn Amsterdam open to their gaze. "The British must be coming," he said at last. "Look!"

But Lena had already seen: people clustered all down the length of the street, doors standing open, German soldiers ignored. And the buzz. Somehow, even though voices were

3

muted and no one was close, the air hummed with energy. Two soldiers on the boulevard actually looked nervous, speaking into each other's ears and glancing over their shoulders.

Lena almost danced on the spot. Could it be true? Could British armies be crossing the border into the Netherlands right at that moment? More than four years had passed since the Germans occupied her country. Food grew scarcer by the month, and the war just went on and on. Could all that be about to change?

Piet's voice was low. "I told you about the rumours last night. I heard it all on the radio."

Lena glanced around at the word *radio* to be sure no one was listening. Radios had been illegal for years, but Piet went to his friend's house every day and listened to the broadcasts from the exiled Dutch government. Radio Orange from London. She felt a familiar rush of fear. If he was ever caught . . .

"And Prince Bernhard is our new commander," Piet continued. "Do you know what that means? He's the new leader of the Resistance. He said the Dutch soldiers should 'restrain themselves . . . even if the hour of liberation is near.' That's what he said. 'The hour of liberation is near'! And now rumours are flying fast."

"You're babbling, Piet," Lena said, but her fear evaporated and her smile turned into a grin. What could be better than her younger brother's bubbly chatter joining the buzz that ran the length of the street and surely the length of Amsterdam as well— even of the Netherlands?

She had felt this same excitement not long ago: the landings on the Normandy beaches, just three months earlier, in June. As she thought back to that time, doubt clouded her mind. Back then, she'd felt certain the Allies were coming. She had taken the old school atlas from its spot at the back of her classroom and peered at the map of Europe, tracing with her finger the path from those French beaches to Amsterdam. Later, she and Piet had imagined the troops, marching steadily onward, dispensing freedom as they came. Surely the tide had turned, they'd thought, and it would be only a matter of days or weeks before the German occupation ended.

But days and weeks had turned to months. Lena had lost interest in maps and gone back to her daily labour of preparing heaps and heaps of potatoes—that and trying to ignore the mounting misery in her own household.

"Maybe I'll bring more news," Piet said, breaking into Lena's thoughts. She tried to rally the grin, but it dropped from her face. He was already halfway down the steps, abandoning her once again.

Lena knew where he was going: down the street to see the man with the radio. Meneer Walstra had lived on the Hoofdweg, a wide boulevard in the western part of Amsterdam, as long as they had, which was forever. They had not had much to do with him in the past, but Piet had spent half of this most recent summer over there, and he had invited Lena to go with him only once. Mother had kept her home that time, deep in her kitchen drudgery, and Piet had seemed happy enough running off on his own. He had never asked her to join him again. Lena was glad that he came back with news, but lately, with his mentions of the Dutch Resistance, she had begun to wonder what he was up to.

She had begun to worry.

Resistance was all very well. Someone needed to do something about the occupation—the Dutch army could not fight openly, like the armies of the unoccupied Allied nations, but there was much they could do underground, in secret. Lena agreed with all that, but she did not agree with encouraging a fifteen-year-old boy to get involved, especially when that boy was her own brother—her only brother.

She took a deep breath. Maybe she need worry no more. Maybe today the British troops would put all her worries to rest.

* * *

Piet strode off down the street, and Lena wandered back inside, finished the supper dishes and collapsed on a kitchen chair, an unread book clasped in her hand; even from the back of the apartment, she could hear the excited sounds from the street. They washed over her. She had no idea how much time passed before Piet slipped back into the room with none of his earlier ruckus. Lena started out of a doze and sat up abruptly. She had been sitting there waiting for him, she realized—for his news.

No one else in the house seemed to be all that affected by the mayhem in the streets. Lena's older sister, Margriet, was putting Bep to bed in the big bedroom. From the kitchen, Lena could hear the rise and fall of her voice as she told their little sister a story. Father was out, as he so often was. Mother was in the dim study, unravelling an old sweater in her endless, and largely futile, attempt to keep her family decently clothed. Lena was glad they were all out of the way. She jumped to her feet and, for the second time that day, slipped outside after her brother. Slipped outside and stopped. Doors on either side of her stood wide open, and people—the men hatless and jacketless, the women still aproned and in house shoes—crowded into the street, shouting and laughing. The city that earlier had buzzed with excitement now sang with joy.

A big bubble of hope lodged in Lena's throat. She swallowed hard and looked to Piet for an explanation. "'The hour of liberation is here,'" he shouted at her. "That's what he said. The prince. Our prime minister. From London. On Radio Orange. 'The hour of liberation is here'!" Then he stood back and looked at her.

The hour of liberation is near. The hour of liberation is here, Lena thought, her grin as wide as her brother's. She made no attempt to speak. There was no need. What a glorious journey it was for a day: from "near" to "here"!

"And in the morning," Piet went on, his mouth back beside her ear, "we will go to welcome them. To welcome the troops!"

They made their way out of the crowd and back to their own steps, where they could speak more easily. "Mother and Father will say no, Piet," Lena said, hating the meekness of the words even as she spoke them. "What about school?"

Piet glared at her. "Oh, Lena! There'll be plenty of time for school later. But if we miss this, we've missed it forever." His voice was edged with anger. "We'll just go. We'll be gone before they're up. No matter what happens after, it will be a day to remember. Are you going to let them take that away from you along with everything else?"

Lena flinched as she met his eyes. She was almost seventeen years old, and he, though barely fifteen, was so strong and determined. She lifted her chin a tiny bit. "Yes," she said. "We'll just go."

* * *

Light came early on that fifth day of September in 1944, war or no war, but Lena and Piet rose earlier. Lena slid out of bed, leaving Margriet snoring gently, and dressed in the dark without making a sound. Then she settled in to wait. Long before dawn, Piet tapped on her door, and she picked up her shoes and her coat and shadowed him down the hall. The front door greeted them, solid and locked. Lena held her breath while her brother fiddled. She twitched at each click and clenched her teeth as he eased the door open.

Leaving it unlocked behind them, they paused on the stoop to slide their feet into their shoes and shrug their shoulders into their coats; then they looked up and took in the goings-on, more through their ears than their eyes. The street was dark: no streetlights in wartime; every window blacked out. Stars glittered in the moonless sky, and the street was thronged with moving shadows, at least as many as the night before.

Walking down the steps and entering that ghostly multitude frightened Lena. Despite their energy and excitement, the bodies didn't feel quite real to her. She held tight to Piet's arm. At any moment, she could lose him entirely. German trucks or guns could tear into them from either side; a child could lose her way and plunge into a canal.

Piet felt no such fear, apparently, for soon he was deep in conversation with a young couple, and Lena soothed herself by listening. She was greatly bolstered by what she heard. Last night, late, on the BBC, according to the young woman, it had been reported again: Breda, a Dutch town just north of the Belgian border and about seventy kilometres due south of Amsterdam, was liberated. German resistance was rapidly collapsing.

As Lena listened, her fear diminished and the sky lightened.

The joy in the streets grew and grew, nourished by the strength-ening rays of sunshine as dawn turned to morning. Where all the flowers, marigolds and others—many in the Dutch colour, orange—came from, Lena never knew. But when smiling stran-ger after smiling stranger bestowed small clutches of blossoms upon her, she collected them eagerly and did not let one drop in all the hours of that strange and fateful day.

They walked in the street, making their way south and then east, over the broad, straight canal that led north to Amsterdam's harbour and alongside the ruins of the once beautiful Vondelpark. Lena pushed aside the memory the dev-astated park tried to force upon her and marched on, relieved that they didn't have to enter the park itself. Eventually, they reached the Singelgracht, the southernmost of the five canals that ringed central Amsterdam. They would follow that canal to the Amstel River. Many, too weak and tired to make the jour-ney themselves, leaned out their windows and gathered in their doorways to watch the procession go by.

They passed German vehicles too, and soldiers, lots of them.

The first time, Lena froze in shock. Three men in grey uni-forms were bundling two women and a small boy into a car, one of the strange ones with a wood-burning generator mounted on the back. Every part of the car was laden, with bags tied onto the top and even attached to the tank behind. The crowd moved aside to let it lumber down the street, crossing their route, barely containing the six humans and all their possessions.

Those were Germans. Next they saw a group from the Dutch Nazi Party—the NSB, collaborators with the enemy—hustling wives and children ahead of them down a side street. They were on foot but also laden. Lena tossed a marigold in the air and caught it again, revelling in its orange beauty. The enemy armies were fleeing! They were taking their families and fleeing!

The route they chose took them well south of the central station. At every cross street, they were caught in a tangle with enemy men and their families pouring north toward the trains, using every conveyance imaginable, including their own feet, and laden with suitcases, parcels and odd collections of household possessions, just as the first groups had been.

"They've all gone mad," Piet said, echoing the words of the crowd. Lena tensed. What if violence broke out between the Dutch celebrating their freedom and the Germans and their supporters running from what that same freedom might mean for them? She need not have worried; each group continued toward its destination in joy or fear, as suited its circumstances.

Once they reached the Amstel, the Dutch crowd turned to follow the river's west bank to the southern reaches of the city, where everyone seemed sure the British army would arrive. It was a long journey, and as the hours passed, people began to wilt. Fathers and brothers hoisted toddlers to their shoulders; flowers were trampled underfoot. Hunger set in. Still, Lena saw no one turn aside. And while most voices fell silent, hope prevailed.

On Lena and Piet walked.

As they drew closer to their goal, the crowd swelled. Local residents, already filling the streets, happily absorbed the thousands upon thousands who poured in from the rest of the city. At last, the river curved to the right, and a wide bridge spanned it. They had arrived at the vantage point from which they could await the troops. The crowd surged onto the bridge, filling it from end to end and overflowing onto the road behind and beyond.

They settled in to wait. Those at the highest point of the bridge could see south some distance. Amsterdam was behind them. The long road stretched ahead, thirty kilometres straight to Utrecht and from there another forty to Breda—surely the route the armies would take. As soon as the first tanks were spotted, word would spread through the crowd.

It was eleven o'clock in the morning, almost six hours since they had closed their door behind them. All they had to do was wait.

Lena spent the hours in silence, staring into the distance, filled with hope and wonder at what it meant to be a part of this enormous gathering and this terrible war. Piet turned to a pair of boys who were more talkative than his sister. The hours passed.

Two o'clock. Still waiting.

Three thirty. And the mood changed. Lena saw the news make its way through the crowd. Faces turned from south to north. Bodies turned from hope to hopeless; children clambered down from shoulders.

She turned to her shorter brother, wishing she didn't have to be the bearer of this news. "It's over," she said. "Word is spreading now."

It took a long time, though, for the tangle of bodies to unite in the desire to go home, and for those on the northern outskirts of the crowd—and the last to have their hopes dashed—to make way for those in the centre, and they for those in the south. Exhaustion slowed the process even more. Exhaustion and despair.

The details reached Lena and Piet at last. "They knocked on doors and found someone with a phone," a man said. Lena stared at the tracks that tears had made on the dusty sagging skin of his cheeks. "He called Breda. It's not free. The British never came. Belgium, yes. The Netherlands, no."

Lena wanted to sink to the ground and weep. Her chest tightened, and her eyes stung. They had all endured more than four years of German occupation; they had all suffered hunger and loss, fear and frustration.

And the people of Amsterdam had left their homes that morning sure that it was over. They had waited on the bridge for five long hours to see a line of British tanks approaching.

Now they had to turn back from that hope and return to their miserable lives.

* * *

The journey home was long.

Piet turned away from his newfound friends, and he and Lena left the river almost immediately, seeking smaller roads where the crowd was thinner.

An hour into their walk, Piet stopped in the middle of a barren park. "Let's take a detour," he said. "Let's go see what happened to all the people we saw fleeing this morning. They must have been going to the station."

Lena drew in a breath. Where did he find his spirit of inquiry after their recent crushing disappointment? Her legs were ready to collapse under her. Her feet, in their shoddily repaired, hand-me-down shoes, were pinched and aching. Her head was heavy with misery. And he was suggesting as much as an extra two hours of walking.

Then a thought came to her unbidden. When did she ever get to do anything like this? She reached out and put her hand on a lone tree trunk in the middle of the park. I am here, she thought, and she felt the bark, grubby but alive beneath her palm. Really felt it. I am beyond their reach. All of them.

Soon enough she would be back in her proper place as student of the sixth class and Mother's captive potato peeler, but now, this minute, even without the British army, she was free. Sort of.

"Yes," she said. "Let's!"

It took them another hour to reach the station, but Lena soon forgot her tired legs, so stunned was she by what she saw. She had not been into the city's centre since early in the war, and the destruction and the misery shocked her. People were poorer here, and the war had hit them hard. She saw more buildings in disrepair, more signs of German occupation, more men and women in rags. A young boy had bare feet and stick-thin legs protruding from shorts that must have grown shorter over the years. It was early September, but it still felt cold for bare feet, and the streets were filled with hazards—broken glass, twisted metal, sharp stones—that called for wood or thick leather, not naked skin.

Lena had no food or anything else of value to offer, but she handed out her marigolds, one by one. They were not edible, but they were as Dutch as Dutch could be. Even the starving boy seemed to appreciate his. He tucked the bright orange flower behind his ear, and his cracked lips formed a small smile.

Then they passed the Jewish Quarter. Lena knew what it was, even though she had not been there when thousands of Jews were crowded into it behind a wire fence, more than two years before. The wire fence had tumbled now, and many of the buildings were in use, but Lena averted her gaze. She hurried to

13

catch up with Piet, who was walking much more quickly all of a sudden.

Shame washed over her, but it was too late for that. Much too late.

She squeezed her eyes tight shut, opened them again and made her legs pump faster in pursuit of her brother. She did not want to think about Sarah right now, though she was sure Piet would be.

Nearing the station, they were both distracted from their memories by the growing crowd, a crowd that slowed and stopped as they reached the large open space in front of the station entrance. Excited murmurs rippled back to them. Lena fought forward on her brother's heels, eager to see, to hear, to shove the Jewish Quarter and what it meant out of her mind and heart. At the edge of the jostling bodies, they stopped short. The space in front of them was filled with a jumble that should have convinced them they had all gone mad.

Lena didn't know what to look at first. A sewing machine. Prams, lots of prams. She counted three . . . no, four . . . no, many more than that. Typewriters. An antique writing desk. A large bird cage, its door open, bird flown. Out of the corner of her eye, Lena saw a woman dart forward and grasp something. A chicken. A live chicken! There were several small chicken coops, she saw then, one of them still holding three chickens. And there were bicycles. Heaps of bicycles.

The fleeing Germans and NSBers had taken what they could and abandoned the rest. The pitch of the crowd's response rose. A man ran to the edge of the mound and tugged a bicycle free.

"They stole from us. Let's take it back!" he shouted. "Freedom or no."

Bodies forced past Lena and Piet. Lena grabbed Piet's arm and held on tight. Piet pulled forward. She pulled back, filled with certainty and strength for once. "We must go," she said. "We do not want to be a part of this."

"But they took our bicycles," Piet said. "I really need . . ."

"The British didn't come, Piet. They didn't come! How do you think the Germans are feeling right now? At any moment they might arrive here. Some may have fled, but those who are left will not stand by and watch a mob pick over their possessions." Urgency took hold of her. "Come!"

Piet stared up at her, surprise in his eyes. But he came, lagging a bit, peering over his shoulder every few moments. It was hard getting through the crush. Fear stirred in Lena as she urged her brother on. The crowd, peaceful through the whole day, was turning into a mob.

Much later, but without further incident, they stopped outside their door. It was growing dark, and the door was locked. Piet knocked smartly, no apology in his fist's connecting with the wood.

Mother let them in and led them to the kitchen, where she dished up some stew that had been waiting on the stove for hours. Blackout paper covered the window, and the single bulb that hung from the ceiling cast a harsh light. Lena chewed and swallowed. Chewed and swallowed. The meal was mushy and gritty, its ingredients unidentifiable. Mother had been a poor cook when food was plentiful, and growing scarcity had not improved her skill in the kitchen.

She stood over them as they ate, one hand gripping the edge of the table, the other pressing her apron to her body. "I've got enough to worry about without you two off who knows where," she said. But she did not seem to expect a response, nor did she seem interested in where they had been.

Lena paused mid-chew. Before the war, Mother had taken pleasure in feeding them, she remembered, and in hearing about their exploits. Sometimes, if Father wasn't home, they had laughed over meals at the kitchen table. Sometimes the food had even been tasty! She stared into her bowl, shoulders taut under Mother's cold gaze. That pre-war mother had deserted them years ago.

Without further words, Lena and Piet finished eating and went to bed.

CHAPTER TWO

Four days had passed since their hopeful journey, and Amsterdam had settled back into its dreary pattern of waiting in both hope and despair while scrambling to survive.

On Saturday morning, Lena crawled out of bed while Margriet was still sleeping and tapped on her brother's door, waking him for their regular journey in search of wood. The two slipped out together into the dawn, light seeping into the battered streets and warming the tumbled brick and stone, the torn pavement, almost giving the illusion of spring.

The sky, the sun, the seasons were not touched by war. A thin beam of sunlight found its way into the road, and Lena reached out and grasped Piet's arm.

"Let us find more wood than ever before," she said, her voice quiet but glad, just a little bit glad.

Piet looked at her and grinned. "Yes, let's," he said. "Vondelpark, here we come!"

Vondelpark. Lena's joy slipped a little. Couldn't they go west instead, to the fields? No. It was all right. She could go there. The park was only a few blocks away, and the streets were almost completely deserted. They saw several people out scrounging like they were, but no soldiers, which was a good thing, because collecting wood was forbidden. Since Tuesday's mad panic, the soldiers' presence had not been quite as strong as before. Lena couldn't help hoping. Surely the British had to come soon.

She tugged on her brother's arm and smiled a hopeful smile at him as they crossed the broad canal. Minutes later, they were there, facing the sign that announced, as similar signs did on all entrances to all parks in the Netherlands, *For Jews Forbidden*. The sign had been new just three years before, but now it hung crooked and faded.

There, the excitement and determination Lena had been clinging to evaporated, replaced with a sickness in the back of her throat. She let go of her brother and tried to fight down the nausea, along with the memory that had brought it upon her.

She did not succeed.

* * *

The war had taken so much, but the worst thing, Lena thought— the very worst—was what the war had done to her one and only friendship.

Lena had not been blessed with friends in her life. Until Sarah. Sarah had come to Amsterdam partway through the last year of elementary school, almost six years ago. Her family had moved from Germany. Lena had given that no thought at first, but soon she understood. Germany had become a bad place for Jews by then. Many Jewish families had fled, and Sarah's was one of them.

Sarah had been assigned a seat next to Lena's. Lena helped Sarah with her Dutch, Sarah helped Lena with her math, and the two girls became friends. Sarah, her father, mother and sisters lived with a cousin's family in a three-bedroom apartment much like Lena's own. Even in that crowded environment, Lena remembered the warmth of Sarah's mother's welcome after school, the delicious snacks, the laughter over homework and games, and the delight of lying in the sun in the park on weekend afternoons, talking and talking and talking.

Pushing aside the memory of what happened later at the entrance to that same park, Lena thought back to the shock she received the one time she had brought Sarah to her own home.

She had not expected her own parents to be as welcoming as Mevrouw Cohen, but neither had she expected rudeness. Mother and Father were both in the kitchen drinking tea when the two girls arrived. Lena had known Sarah only a few days, and she had not yet told her parents about her new friend.

"Mother, Father, this is Sarah Cohen," she said, smiling as she introduced a real friend to her parents for the first time in her life. Her smile froze as she watched their eyes, all four eyes—could that be fear she saw in them?—travel over Sarah's body, while their lips set in thin lines.

Mother managed to speak first, twisting those thin lips into a shadow of a smile. "Hello, Sarah," she said, but she looked at her husband as she spoke.

"Hello, Mevrouw Berg," Sarah said.

Lena watched in horror as tears formed in the corners of Sarah's eyes.

"Ah," Father said, "a German accent. Have you only just arrived in Nederland?"

"Yes," Sarah said. "I . . . I . . ." She turned to Lena. "I'm sorry, Lena. I forgot. I'm expected at home." And she almost ran from the room. A moment later, Lena heard the front door close.

Lena turned to follow, but Father grasped her arm. "It's best if she goes, Lena," he said. "You don't want Jewish friends right now, especially not those who can't even stay in their own country. Nederland's got enough Jews of its own."

Lena stared at her father. He had made a comment or two about Jews before, but never anything like this. "But, Father, she's not—"

"There are a lot of problems in Europe right now," Father said, "and the Jews are no small part of it."

Lena turned to Mother, only to catch her nodding. "It's not good for our family to be mixed up with them," she said.

At that, Lena ran into her room and slammed the door. Father wrenched the door open instantly and ordered her out again. Pretending meekness, she walked back into her room and left the door ajar, as instructed. No children behind closed doors in Father's house. Lena curled up on her bed, huddled against the wall and wept.

* * *

Lena pushed the memory from her mind, straightened her body and followed her brother past the dangling sign and into the travesty that Vondelpark had become.

The ground was beaten down by countless feet, by truck tires, by years of occupation and neglect. Ponds and waterways were dried up or scummy with rotting vegetation. Not a swan or a duck to be seen. Dinner for someone, Lena thought, and saliva rushed into her mouth as she thought of a roasted duck on the table.

Some trees remained, but matted brown grass and scuffed-up dirt were all that was left where flowers should have grown. A city's rubble might receive a moment's grace from the first light of day, but that same light revealed the park as it truly was: stark and dying.

Lena and Piet did not speak of it. They did not meet each other's eyes. They passed that first site of devastation and made their way deeper into the park. It took them half an hour to collect a small armload of wood each, taking low branches that they convinced themselves had no more life in them and part of a tumbledown fence.

Sweaty, filthy and exhausted, they stopped for a rest once they had their wood in a heap, and Piet chose that moment to share his latest news.

"The Germans launched a new weapon yesterday."

Lena looked at him. What was this? He seemed excited somehow, as if he were telling her something good. "What sort of weapon?" she asked.

"A rocket. There's never been anything like it before. I heard it on the radio last night. They can shoot it all the way to England!"

Lena tried to ignore his expression. "Where do they shoot it from?"

"The west. From the dunes near The Hague. The rockets are huge. They carry them on train cars."

"Piet," Lena said slowly, searching for the right words, "they sound like terrible things, these rockets. I thought we were about to win this war, and now you say the Germans have new weapons that come straight out of comic books. And"—she paused—"you seem excited, somehow."

Piet's voice rose. "How could I be excited? These rockets are killing machines, and the Germans are happy to use them. How can you say that to me?"

Lena didn't answer, but she felt a small tug of satisfaction. Her brother was not so perfect. Typical boy—obsessed with the enemy's weapons, no matter the destruction they caused! She breathed deeply. "Let's go home, Piet," she said.

They emerged from the park, walking well apart, one behind the other, dawn now past. The city was coming to life. They were almost over the canal and about to turn north toward home when the alarm sounded.

"Halt!" a voice shouted. A German voice.

Lena glanced back and saw the soldier. He was close enough that she could make out his face, distorted with anger. He broke into a run.

But Lena and Piet were already running. Even as she was turning to look behind her, her legs were pumping. Wood clutched to her chest, she took off, with Piet matching her stride for stride.

"Halt!" the soldier shouted again, this time breathlessly.

People on the sidewalk stepped aside to let Piet and Lena pass, ignoring the soldier's shouted order to "Stop them!" Moments later they skidded around the curve to the right and stopped. They were in their own street now: the Hoofdweg. Wide and bare, it offered nowhere to hide.

"Here," a voice called, quietly, urgently. A door was open, and a man beckoned. Feet pounded behind them, just out of sight around the corner.

Lena almost fell over her brother as she pushed to get the door closed behind her in time. All three froze in a strange tableau: waiting, listening. A moment passed, no more, before they heard the soldier's boots pound round the corner. Another moment and the feet, soldier attached, had passed them by.

Deep breaths all round.

The man was kind but nervous, with a scraggly face and a sweater full of holes. He smiled and offered them bread. Piet shook his head fiercely at that, then tried to give the man their biggest piece of wood. The man shook his head right back, though not as fiercely, and pushed the wood into Piet's arms. As soon as they were sure the soldier was gone, Piet and Lena thanked him again and made their way home.

They did not tell Father or Mother about the German soldier, but they received angry words nonetheless for coming home in broad daylight with arms full of illegal wood. What were they trying to do—get the whole family arrested?

Piet disappeared out the door soon after, and Lena settled down to steal an hour with a book before someone claimed her. Had she and Piet returned bonded by the chase, she wondered, or pushed apart by their strange conversation about those terrible rockets? She could not tell. She hoped they would not have to return to that particular park for a long, long time.

* * *

Lena had Sunday dinner on the table at the stroke of six, just as she was supposed to. She had hardly set eyes on her brother since their dash home the day before. Now, her jaw clenched and her shoulders raised themselves up around her ears as she waited for him to come through the door and join them for the most important meal of the week.

"God bless this food and drink," Father said, without warning as usual, and everyone's heads tilted forward obediently, eyes squeezed shut, hands clasped.

The front door clicked open and then closed. Lena breathed a sigh of relief as Piet slid into his chair just as Father firmly voiced the next line of the prayer. Peeking through her lashes, she saw Father's eyes snap open and glare for an instant at his son, while

Mother's worried gaze fixed on her husband. Piet's eyes remained closed. He looked calm as calm. Lena admired that, but she hated it too. Maybe it was all right that he didn't care about Father, but what about her? What about what his absence had put her through? Didn't he care about that? She knew exactly what he was thinking: that he was going to help save people—he and Mr. Walstra. What did a missed prayer matter to him?

Lena opened her eyes again to find Piet looking at her. He smiled. She snatched her eyes away.

"How do you manage to cook food so it's raw and burnt at the same time?" Margriet said.

Tears pricked at Lena's eyes. When had her older sister grown so mean?

"I think it's tasty," Bep said, reaching for Lena's hand.

It was all Lena could do to hold still and let Bep's fingers rest on top of hers. She looked over at her little sister and managed a small smile.

Despite the crunchy bits, Father ate eagerly as always. Greedily, Lena thought. She fixed her eyes on her own bowl and tried not to flinch as he slurped at each spoonful. She fought to stop her teeth from gritting as she listened to her father mash his dinner around in his mouth.

"Your mother's got news for you all," Father said between bites.

Mother's head reared up and she stared at her husband. "I don't . . ." she said to him. "I didn't . . ."

"You do," Father said. "And you did." His words were mysterious, and his voice had a tone to it that Lena had never heard before. She did not like it.

Mother's knife made a sharp click as she put it down. She laid the hand that had held it flat on the table, fingers splayed.

24

Her other hand went to her belly. Lena knew before her mother spoke what she would say.

"I'm going to have a baby," Mother said. Her eyes slid up from the table and rested one by one on each of her children before coming to a stop on Father. "There," she said then. "Now they know."

"A baby!" Bep's face had opened up with joy. She was out of her seat, leaning up against Mother, her hand on that pregnant belly. "A baby sister for me!"

"Or a brother," Father said.

Margriet and Piet, side by side, both looked serious. "There's not enough food," Piet said, his voice low. "The war . . ."

Mother had her arm around Bep, and they were whispering together.

"Well, this war can't go on forever," Father said. "The baby's not going to be born tomorrow." He paused. "He's not due till February or March, actually. And there will always be food in the country, even if it runs out in the city."

"What good is food in the country going to do us?" Piet said. "Besides, who knows what the Nazis will do next. All they have to do is burst a dike here and there, and . . . no more farms."

Father glared at him. "Enough of that talk, young man. Finish up your dinner." His gaze took in the whole table then. "All of you."

Bep disengaged herself from Mother's arm and went back to her place, but her glow did not diminish. Mother went back to eating silently. And Father wolfed the rest of his food and left the table.

After dinner, when Lena and Margriet were left alone to clean up, Margriet dropped the dishtowel suddenly and leaned her head against the wall. Lena stared at her.

"Are you sick?" she asked.

Margriet ground out her response through tears. "No, I'm not sick," she said. "I'm tired. Tired of this house. These people. I'm nineteen years old. I'm finished school. I should be off living my life, not starving slowly in this house, with them . . ." she trailed off.

"But you . . . you . . ." Lena was too stunned to form a reply.

"And now there's going to be a baby." Margriet picked up the dishtowel again and dried fiercely, stacking the plates together violently.

Lena flinched at each clank.

* * *

After that, it was as if Mother's pregnancy had never been. Even Bep seemed to realize that she shouldn't mention it if Father was around. Father was angry at Mother for getting pregnant. Lena had realized that immediately. He had forced her to announce it as some sort of punishment, but now he didn't want to hear about it.

The news had frightened Lena. Babies were so vulnerable. And Mother seemed so weak and tired.

And it had unsettled her. She was almost seventeen— almost a woman herself—but she didn't know how babies were made, or how they got out of their mothers and into the world. She had a vague idea, but it all seemed so dreadful and unlikely that she had tried not to think about it until now.

September's midway point came and went.

On September 17, the British and the Americans failed once again to penetrate the Netherlands north of the Rhine. Maastricht, the southeasternmost portion of the country, had

26

been liberated the week before. Piet vibrated with excitement as he shook Lena awake and pestered her until she joined him outside to watch the planes pass overhead. Dozens and dozens of them crossed from west to east, their heavy hum almost drowning out his cries to her to "Look, look!" All up and down the street, people rushed outside. Piet shouted his report to her of an upcoming battle at Arnhem, something to do with bridging the Rhine.

Planes or no planes, Lena's doubts were a match for her brother's excitement, for the crowd's. She planned never again to have her hopes dashed as they had been two weeks before. The news that spread in the latter days of September confirmed her doubts. The battle at Arnhem had been a rather spectacular failure, apparently. She watched her brother's disappointment and congratulated herself on her own cynicism. This time it had kept her safe.

Now, Piet said, the Dutch leaders had issued orders from the safety of London, to which they had retreated four years earlier, when the Netherlands was first occupied. ("Cowards," Father had said at the time.) Dutch railway workers were to go on strike. They were no longer to help the enemy by operating the trains. That meant thousands of railway workers would have to go into hiding.

Lena felt the emptiness in her own eyes as her brother rattled on. What did she care about railway strikes? What did she care about anything, for that matter?

Annoyance flushed through her; she looked at Piet and slowly, deliberately, raised her shoulders and let them drop.

Piet's eyes flashed at her.

"We'll never be free if everyone just gives in like that!" he said, almost shouting.

"Like what?" Lena said.

He opened his mouth but seemed to find no words. After that, he was absent even more, if that was possible. He spent his time talking or running errands with that man, Meneer Walstra, Lena knew, or running errands for him. He didn't bother to tell Lena for days that in response to the strike of the railway workers, the Nazis had shut down all transportation in the country, including shipping.

When he did tell her, he was brusque about it. "Prepare to be hungry," he finished, and turned away.

The rest of the family was more and more absent as well, even when they were right there in the house.

Margriet was kept busy lining up for less and less food, ordering Lena around in the kitchen and cleaning everywhere else. She was lucky to bring home any food at all. It turned out that contrary to what Piet had said, food in the country *could* help those in the city, and people were starting to go in search of it, so many people that the dangerous trips got a name: hunger journeys. "Journeys," Margriet scoffed when she heard of it. "Begging, I'd call it." And she got up earlier and earlier to be closer to the front of the endless lines.

Piet often didn't come home until hours after school was dismissed, using the house just for eating and sleeping. Father shouted at him sometimes about homework, but Piet did not appear to be bothered by a bit of shouting.

As her belly began to jut out from her shrinking body, Mother fussed over ration books and guilders and gave orders that were mostly ignored.

Father did mysterious things at his desk, or went on unexplained outings. Pretending to work, Lena thought. She had long ago stopped worrying that Father would be picked up by the SS and shipped off to Germany. He was over the age limit, for one thing. She knew of other men too old and boys too young who were taken despite their ages, but Father somehow seemed immune.

She had also stopped wondering how he managed to bring home money. Before the war he had been some sort of businessman, though exactly what he did had always been a bit unclear. Since the start of the war, money had become scarcer and scarcer, but he still managed to get his hands on some. Lena suspected him of involvement with the black market. But whatever he was up to, he wasn't very good at it, judging by the worry lines that sprouted and spread on Mother's face.

Bep was different from the rest of the family. She was more present than ever, begging for help on homework from her first year of school, or more often, idle and underfoot, as the colder weather made the courtyard uncomfortable and no one made time to spend with her. Shooing her away, Lena sometimes felt stirrings of guilt or moments of compassion, but she went right on shooing.

As for Lena herself, she kept busy with school, with following orders from her parents and her older sister, mostly in the kitchen, and stealing what time she could to disappear into a corner and read. Regularly, she got shouted at when her corner turned out to be next on Margriet's "to clean" list.

Books were not easy to come by, so she was reduced to rereading, but this still gave her imagination other worlds to occupy. Lately, it had been romance and adventure in Paris; a young man had fallen in love with her, and she was resisting his attentions, which grew stronger with her efforts. He wrote her letters that made her whole body turn liquid, but she would not give in. Ever!

CHAPTER THREE

"Lena!"

She looked up, startled, met Margriet's eyes and jumped to her feet to put a meal on the table, once again torn from the world in the pages of her book.

Dinnertime again.

Lena found it more and more difficult to be bothered with the tasks that were required of her. The war kept shoving itself in her way, insisting somehow that she pay attention. Putting supper on the table and keeping up in school just didn't seem to matter much. She tried to escape into her books, which she now knew almost by heart; she tried to let dinner conversation float over her; she tried to stay out of Piet's way, to avoid his latest news.

But today, the Germans had burned the port of Amsterdam, part of their retaliation for the ongoing railway strike. The Bergs had all seen the clouds of black smoke just hours before, and despite Father's insistence that Piet stay in the house, he had rushed off on foot to see the damage for himself.

Now, at the dinner table, he was so wound up he could not swallow. "Father, you should have seen it," he said, his voice high pitched, his face red. "They're destroying everything. Our whole infrastructure."

Lena stared. Infrastructure? Since when had Piet talked like that?

"The wharfs were burnt, and the water was black with oil and soot. A ship was on its side, half submerged. The cranes were twisted metal. What do they expect us to do once this war's over?" He stopped then, as if waiting for a response. "Father?"

But Father shovelled in bite after bite, his silence as solid as a wall.

Mother huffed a breath. "Eat your supper before it gets cold, Piet," she said. "You're too young to involve yourself with such things."

Lena simply refused to listen. With everyone's bowls empty, she stood to clear the table and wash the dishes, taking no pleasure in the warm water. Then she fetched her math book out of her bag. It was an ancient object, its pages yellowed and threatening to tear under the slightest touch. She sat at the kitchen table, turned the delicate pages to find her place and sank into a reverie.

Lena had never excelled at school, and math had always been her worst subject, until Sarah Cohen came along. Sarah had a head for numbers, and she remained calm even when Lena cried out in frustration.

Lena stared at her math book. Sarah hadn't been at school for a long, long time.

* * *

She and Sarah had been best friends for just over a year when the Nazis invaded the Netherlands in May 1940. They were nearing

32

the end of the first class of high school. School was cancelled for several days, and the two girls had not seen each other. When they came together again, Lena was breathless in anticipation of discussing the events of the previous days. Sarah's smile was small that day, her responses brief. After school, Lena linked her arm through her friend's, eager to enter the warm, busy hub that was Sarah's home, but Sarah disengaged herself.

"I have to go," she said. "I'll see you tomorrow." And that was all.

Lena had watched her walk away, her fear at this seeming abandonment greater than any fear she had felt at reports of German parachutists and bombers. The Nazi threat simply did not feel real to her. Sarah's behaviour did.

In time, however, things seemed to get back to normal between the two girls. Sarah invited Lena to her house again, and it was almost as nice as before. The first class ended. Amsterdam changed: more and more soldiers in the streets, not quite as much to buy in the stores, nighttime blackouts to adjust to and cope with. For Lena, the summer of 1940 was not as idyllic as the summer of 1939 had been, but she still loved her afternoons, after her chores were done, at Sarah's house or in Vondelpark. The two girls swam at a nearby pool several times a week. They cycled everywhere together, and Lena, at least, paid little attention to the war. Surely it would be over soon.

Then came the second class. The war continued, but it still felt remote to Lena. Occasionally, Sarah seemed different somehow, and she wasn't always willing to have Lena over to her house, but they still had fun together. Lena still shared all her secrets. Well, all her secrets except for one: Father. Father did not say much to her about her Jewish friend, but on several occasions, he had insisted she stay home when she planned to go out. And once he said to her, "No good will come of this friendship. That girl's family is using you, a good Christian Dutch girl." Lena had no idea what he meant, only that it was wrong and it made her sick. How did he even know that she and Sarah were still friends?

Then, one night at the dinner table early in the new year, the cold outside bitter, the snow deep, Father spoke again. "They all have to register."

Lena looked over at him.

"The Jews," he said. "Those friends of yours will have to register. And if they are here illegally, they'll be sent back to Germany, where they belong." He took another bite of chicken, not bothering to close his mouth as he chewed.

Lena saw her mother stiffen. Her look across the table was almost reproachful, as if she did not approve of her husband's attitude. Still, not a word did she speak.

Lena asked Sarah about the registration the next day, but Sarah wouldn't meet her eyes, and afterward, Lena realized that she hadn't answered, not really. Lena never knew whether the Cohens registered or not, though she thought they must have. She heard about the arrests of Jews in February and arrived at school in a terror the next day, afraid that Sarah's father and her father's cousin were among the men taken. But Sarah gave her head a sharp shake when Lena asked her about it. Mr. Cohen, it seemed, was still free, at least for the moment.

All that following summer, Lena had felt the friendship slipping away. She had hoped that the new school year would help them to renew their bond, but when they started the third class in September, Sarah still seemed distant.

One afternoon, Lena gathered her courage and suggested a walk to the park after school. Relief flooded her when Sarah agreed. Maybe now everything would be just as it was.

The day was balmy, and Sarah seemed almost cheerful. The two girls walked arm in arm, swinging along, forcing others—for the sidewalks were busy that day—to move aside. There was the park entrance ahead, visible well before they got there. The trees, towering in full leaf above the low stone wall, were just starting to turn colour. The grass was a beckoning carpet. Lena saw the white swoop of swans' necks on the lake, and she was sure that ducks would be waddling in the grass and paddling in the water. She wished she had something to feed them. Lena loved ducks and swans.

Then she noticed a small group of people near the entrance to the park. Some of the joy inside her stilled. Agitation was in the air, fear even—fear and anger. Sarah withdrew her arm and stopped, and in that moment, Lena saw two soldiers standing nearby. They looked tense, ready. Lena continued her approach. She could feel Sarah behind her and sensed her caution. The people stepped aside to let them see.

The sign was fresh; the holes in the wall and the screws were brand new, the letters crisp and black. *For Jews Forbidden.* When Lena collected herself enough to turn around, Sarah was gone.

✳ ✳ ✳

Three years had gone by since that day. So much had happened since then—much worse things, even. Lena bundled her math homework back into her bag. Without Sarah's help, she didn't understand the questions anyway.

The next morning, she and Piet walked to school together as they always did, dropping Bep off on the way, but they didn't speak to each other. Those walks had been more and more silent lately, once they left their chatty little sister behind.

They passed several groups of soldiers, one of them harassing a young couple. Lena looked the other way and mumbled the prayer that had become habit for her: "Please let this war end before the baby comes."

She had little faith in her prayers.

The school looked battered—holes in the pavement in front not mended, several of the trees in the yard reduced to stumps—but boys and girls were streaming through the big front doors as they had for decades. Lena and Piet joined the throngs and were immediately parted from each other. Lena trudged up the stairs to her first class of the day.

The bell rang just as she took her seat at the back, but several others darted in after her. At the front of the room stood the dreaded Juffrouw Westenberg.

"Now," Juffrouw said, "you are in school. It is two minutes past nine, so you three"—she pointed out three boys, one by one—"are late." And she took her attendance clipboard and marked them down.

Lena didn't know how they dared. Juffrouw Westenberg was the most frightening teacher at the school. Lena opened her book to the first lesson and tried to look like the most studious student in the room. The novel she usually snuck open in her lap awaited her attention in her pocket.

Half an hour later, a new girl showed up.

The boys stared. The girls stared too. The new girl was skinny, bony, no hint of breasts under the threadbare blouse that hung off her, no hint of hips under the straight skirt that had to be pinned in the back to stay on. But her brows arched just so, and her lips were full and almost looked as if they bore a hint of rouge. Her hair, a shining dark brown, hung in heavy waves halfway down her back. Every other head of hair in the room was blond or mousy brown, and every other girl wore her hair (usually dull, lifeless and desperately in need of a wash) cut to shoulder-length or shorter and pulled back somehow, or tucked under a bit of cloth.

"I'm Sofie Vogel," the girl announced as she strode to the back of the room, grabbed a desk and a chair from the corner and pushed them into the gap beside Lena's desk. The boy on the other side shuffled over to make space.

Sofie was a warm, bright light in a room full of mud grey moths.

Lena forgot the lesson on her desk and the novel in her pocket. Her spine straightened. She touched the fingertips of one hand to the fingertips of the other and felt something, a flicker.

"Hi, I'm Sofie."

Lena's lips twitched into a small smile. She raised her eyes and turned her head.

"And you are . . . ?"

Lena jumped. The girl was talking to her! "Me? I'm, ah . . . I'm Lena," she said.

The boy who had moved aside, Willem, leaned over and spoke in a stage whisper.

"Don't bother with her. She's some sort of halfwit," he whispered. "I'm Willem. I'm who you need to know around here."

Sofie arched a brow a little higher, but she did not turn her eyes away from Lena's.

"Is that so?" she said. "Thank you for telling me."

For a moment, Willem stayed still. Then he sat back in his chair.

"Boys and girls," Juffrouw said, "I would like you to join me in welcoming Sofie Vogel to our class. She is, I understand, quite a star at Latin."

Sofie grinned and shook her head. "Never could see the point of learning dead languages," she said lightly.

"That is not the report I have. There will be no hiding of lights under bushels in my classroom."

"Well, then, let it shine!" Sofie said, and Lena wondered if she might launch into Latin on the spot.

Juffrouw Westenberg smiled slightly. "Watch your attitude, Juffrouw Vogel," she said. "I will overlook your joking and your tardiness because it is your first day, but after this, I will accept no more of either."

Teacher and student regarded each other.

At last, Sofie laughed. "Of course, Juffrouw," she said. "Respect and punctuality. You have my word!"

The teacher scanned the classroom, raised her hand to her mouth and coughed. "See to it," she said.

Lena wasn't sure why Sofie behaved as she did, but her own habit of reading under the table ceased the moment the newcomer entered the classroom. And her delight when Sofie stuck by her at the end of the day was indescribable.

When Juffrouw Westenberg dismissed them, Lena tidied her few things into her bag slowly, hardly breathing as she waited to see what Sofie would do.

Willem paused by the door. "Hey, Sofie," he said, in that casual, gruff teenage-boy way, "want to walk with us?"

"No, thanks," Sofie said, glancing in his direction. "I'm waiting for Lena."

Lena stared at them both. Her heart soared and then plummeted, preparing itself for disappointment. What could possibly possess this new girl to choose her as a friend?

Willem shrugged. "Your loss," he said. He looked at Lena. "A big loss, actually!"

But Sofie had stopped paying attention to him. "Come on, Lena," she said. "Let's get out of here."

And there it was: the start of something new. Eager though she was, Lena hesitated a moment. After what had happened with Sarah, she wasn't sure she deserved a new friend.

* * *

Things changed between Lena and Sarah after the outing that ended in front of that terrible sign. Lena had grown less eager to reach out, less willing to go to Sarah's house. After all, she told herself, they didn't really want her there anymore. And if she and Sarah didn't go to Sarah's house, where could they go? Parks were forbidden them, as were most other public places. So she did nothing to counter Sarah's averted gaze. Then, only a month later, she went to school one day and found Sarah gone, along with all the other Jewish children.

"They'll have their own schools now," Father had said at the dinner table that night, though Lena had not asked.

She had said not one word.

"As they should," he'd added.

In the months that followed, Lena had summoned her courage twice, only twice. The first time, a few days after Sarah disappeared from school, the two girls had spent an awkward hour together at Sarah's apartment. Sarah had hardly said a word.

She doesn't want to see me, Lena had told herself. And the months had passed.

In May 1942, all the Jews were ordered to wear the yellow stars. Every time Lena saw a person with the star fixed on her dress or his jacket or her sweater, she felt a small kick low in her belly. And at last, one glorious late-June day when the third class was over, she had forced herself to pay Sarah a second visit.

It took everything she had to raise her hand and knock on Sarah's door. Moments later, the door swung open and Mevrouw Cohen stood there. Lena noticed that she didn't have to look up to meet her eyes. She must have grown; after all, she was fourteen and a half. Then she took in Mevrouw Cohen's sweater, and there was the yellow star. On her friend's mother! The kick in her belly was a jolt now. She almost recoiled. Mevrouw Cohen did smile, but there was no joy in it, just a sort of sad kindness.

Behind her, Lena sensed chaos in the house. Then Sarah was there, looking out past her mother, no kindness in her gaze, sad or otherwise. "Go away," she said sharply. "What are you doing here? Just go." And she was gone from her mother's side.

"I'm sorry, dear," Mevrouw Cohen said. "I'm afraid it's too late. We're packing up," she added. "Moving. You'd best be going."

And Lena went. She rode her bicycle past Sarah's building in August and saw strangers on the front step.

Somehow, when she got home, Piet knew where she had been. He was twelve by then, and starting to pay attention. He suggested a visit to the Jewish Quarter, where the Cohens almost certainly were housed, and she responded with shame and anger from the very deepest part of herself.

"What are you doing watching where I'm going?" she said once she had calmed down enough to speak. "Did you follow me?"

"But don't you want to see your friend?" he said, curiously focused in the face of his older sister's wrath.

"I'll see her if I want, but you . . . you just mind your own business," Lena said, horrified at herself, at the fear that snaked through her.

40

Then, there was Father behind them. "You stay away from those Jews," he said, looking at Lena and Piet hard. "They've brought this upon themselves, and I won't have my children mixed up in it."

Lena stared back at him. Could it be that she was just like her father? Was that why she was so afraid? She should go. She should. Just to prove she wasn't the same as him.

Piet looked from one to the other, made a scoffing sound in his throat and stalked off. Father rested a hand on Lena's shoulder briefly and then retreated to his study.

I will go, Lena thought. Tomorrow. I'll tell Piet tomorrow.

But tomorrow came, and she did not say a word to her brother. She did not go.

And after that, Piet did mind his own business. He shared news of the war with Lena sometimes, but he said nothing when the deportations started. The Jewish Quarter was almost empty by September, the start of the fourth class, and Lena realized that there would be no school for Sarah, segregated or otherwise. By then, the Cohens had probably been gone for some time.

Where? She didn't know.

When thoughts of Sarah bubbled up, she pushed them down as deep as she could. She just hoped she was safe. That was all.

* * *

Now, on the street outside the school, Lena quickly learned that the new girl, Sofie, lived north of her house. They could walk together. They walked slowly, lingering over the short distance, the first moments of getting to know a new friend. Lena deliberately banished Sarah from her mind. She was not quite as successful at banishing the queasy feeling of disloyalty that followed.

When they got to Lena's house, Sofie followed her inside. Lena had stopped at the sidewalk to say goodbye, but Sofie seemed so expectant that she just had to lead the way up the steps and through the big, heavy door. Her heart raced. She had been hungry moments before, but now she felt sick. They so rarely brought anyone home.

She breathed deep and turned in to the kitchen. Mother was fussing over the stove. Without looking behind her, she said, "They're saying we're almost out of potatoes here in the west. Well, I'm saying that I could live a century more and not see another potato, and it would be just fine with me."

"Mother," Lena choked out.

Her mother swung around from the stove. Sofie popped through the doorway and planted herself in front of Lena. "Hi, Mevrouw Berg. I'm Sofie Vogel. I'm in Lena's class now."

Lena's mother looked her up and down. "Well, it's been a while since Lena has brought anyone home, my dear. She knows that she has chores to do after school, and if your mother has any sense, you do as well. Perhaps you'll drop by another time." Her voice was smooth, unreal somehow, as if she just didn't know what to do with a human being who wasn't related to her.

The two girls walked back down the hallway. Sofie stopped on the top step outside and looked at Lena. Lena looked at her. She wanted to apologize, to somehow excuse her mother, but neither girl seemed to have a word in her.

Sofie managed a small smile. Forlorn, Lena thought later. That smile had been forlorn.

The next morning, when Lena stepped out her front door, there was Sofie, grinning from the sidewalk. She was keeping her distance, Lena noticed, but she was there. Lena was glad of both, really. No more family fuss, and Sofie belonged to her.

In the classroom, Sofie made faces; she made jokes; she handed in sloppy work. Then, when a particular teacher was at the breaking point, she wrote an elegant bit of prose or answered a question that stumped the rest of the class, and the teacher would pause and look at her without comment.

Sofie ignored the boys. She was polite to the girls, but Lena was the chosen one, her friend. On the way home on the second day, Lena dared to ask one of the questions that burned within her.

"Why do you come to school if you just want to play around?" she asked, tense but desperately curious.

"What else is there to do in the middle of this horrible war?" Sofie asked. "And my family is awful. It was bad before, but you know what? War brings out the worst in people."

Lena opened her mouth, and Sofie went on, "Yes, yes, I know. Or the best. I've seen that too—just not in my house. Anyway, school is fun. And I ask you, where am I supposed to meet boys if I don't come to school? I'm seventeen. I need boys!"

Lena opened her mouth again, and this time Sofie let her speak. "But . . . but you ignore them. Willem invited you to walk with them, and you said no. You barely looked at him."

"Willem? When I said boys, I didn't mean Willem! He's so short that if I danced with him, he'd have his face right in my boobs. If I had any, that is. And anyway, Lena, you don't get boys by paying attention to them."

An awful thought occurred to Lena. "Is that why . . . ?" She couldn't finish.

"Is that why what?" Sofie stared at her, at the misery on Lena's face. "Ohhh. No, you silly idiot! I'm not spending time with you just to get boys to pay attention to me. I'm ignoring them to get them to pay attention to me—if I decide I want attention from any of them, that is. I'm spending time with you because I like you. The two are not connected."

Lena's smile was small and tentative, but she found she believed the other girl. She longed to ask Sofie why she was walking home with her, Lena, when she could have chosen any girl in the class, but you just didn't ask that sort of question. You just didn't.

* * *

The fun continued for almost a month. Later it seemed amazing to Lena that a month was all it had been. The walks to and from school, the constant holding in of giggles as she watched Sofie's antics in the classroom, the way neither Mother's demands nor Father's jabs found purchase—it all seemed a permanent state. Almost immediately, Lena felt as if she and Sofie had always been friends, as if her three friendless years had never been. Then they arrived at school on a Thursday morning in the middle of October and found everyone milling around outside.

The day before, Lena, her mind elsewhere, had dumped a heap of potatoes into a pot of water, turned the knob on the stove, lit a match and stood waiting for the crackle of flames.

"Ouch!" she cried. The match's flame had reached her fingertips. She gave the match a sharp shake, paying attention at last. The stove was still out.

"What's going on in here?" Margriet said, striding into the room, the broom in one hand and a full dustpan in the other. "Cut off your finger, did you?"

"No," Lena said slowly as she opened the oven door and peered inside. "The pilot light is out."

"Well, let's get it lit again before we inhale any more fumes," Margriet said, and she reached out and flipped the light switch on the wall.

Nothing happened.

"I don't smell gas," Lena said.

And it dawned on them both together. No gas. No electricity. They ran through the house, flipping switches.

Behind them, the front door slammed. Lena expected Piet, but it was Father. "All of Amsterdam's been cut off," he said. "Except for where they need electricity for themselves." He paused. "Damned Nazis."

"The gas is off too," Margriet said.

"Yes," said Father. "We'll be getting ninety minutes each day."

"Which ninety minutes?" she asked.

"They didn't say," Father replied.

Now, Lena and Sofie joined the crowd in front of the school, only to be sent home. There could be no school without light and heat.

Lena and Sofie walked slowly, automatically, toward home. Then Sofie said, "No, wait! It's early morning. No one knows this has happened."

Lena felt something expand inside her. She looked at Sofie and waited.

"We're free," Sofie went on. "Right now, everyone thinks we're in school. We can do whatever we want! We're free!"

Five minutes later, they were tucked up against a tree in Vondelpark. The ground, thick with mouldering leaves, was damp, and they shivered a little, but the park was deserted, and for the first time since discovering the terrible sign at its entrance, Lena was glad to be there. Once again, she pushed thoughts of Sarah aside and welcomed this new opportunity with Sofie.

At first, quiet settled between them. They were angled away from each other, backs against the trunk. Lena picked up a leaf, recently fallen and perfectly intact, and began to shred it. Beside her, Sofie tipped her head back and gazed into the branches that spread above them, almost bare. Lena inhaled. The rich, rotting smell of fall with its crisp, breezy edges filled her lungs.

"I can't stand much more of this," Sofie said at last. "And now, without school . . ."

"More of what?" Lena said. "The war?"

Sofie didn't speak for a long time. Then she said, "No, but the war makes it worse, you know? At home."

Lena didn't know what to say to that. She waited.

"I always knew I'd leave the minute school was over," Sofie said. "The second it was over . . ."

Again, a long silence, this time expectant on Sofie's part, but Lena was still at a loss.

"Well," Sofie said, "now it's over."

Lena pulled away from the tree and turned toward the other girl. Panic reached the tips of her fingers. "You can't leave now!" she said.

"Why not?" Sofie replied.

"You . . . you just can't. Where would you go?"

"Lena, you know that people are leaving every day. On hunger journeys. City people are going to the country to get food."

46

Lena gave her head a shake. Yes, she knew, but she hated the thought of it. "They come back," she said, "if they can. And they don't go because they want to. They *have* to!"

"Maybe. But they brave the dangers. They don't mind the soldiers or the barricades or the flooded land."

"I expect they mind very much," Lena said. "I know I would!"

Sofie smiled. "Well, it's true that I'm not dreaming of barricades or floods. I'll think of somewhere wonderful!" She grinned, reached out and shoved Lena in the shoulder. "Want to come?"

Lena laughed, relieved, sure now that Sofie was joking. And indeed, Sofie's grin turned to a laugh, and she switched to a favourite topic. "Where would you like to go when this blasted war is over?" she said. "I think South America could be exciting. Think of the men we could meet! There's music there, you know, and dancing. Lots and lots of dancing."

Lena's imagination soared. She knew almost nothing about South America, but she imagined a warm evening on an out-door patio overlooking the sea, women in swirling dresses with bare shoulders, men in crisp grey suits, drinks in fancy glasses — cocktails, they were called, weren't they?—and one special man's hand on her waist . . .

Sofie was still talking. "Or India. The Ganges, you know. A *rajah!* Or maybe even Australia. The Outback. A cowboy! I'll take them all."

But Lena wasn't interested in sacred rivers or bleak land-scapes—or Indian princes or men on horses, for that matter. She closed her eyes. Her man was sinking to one knee and slipping a small velvet case from his jacket pocket.

Then Sofie was poking her. "Oh, Lena, has he proposed to you yet?"

Lena's eyes fluttered open.

"You're just plain dull, you know. No fun at all!" Sofie added, her smile sly.

Lena glared at the other girl. How did Sofie know what she was thinking? "I just liked the thought of South America," Lena said. "Going there. You know."

"Liar! You can't have any fun without a marriage proposal in it. Are you afraid a man might kiss you without putting a ring on your finger first?"

"No, I . . ."

"Yes! Even your fantasy man would have to propose to you before you'd think of flashing him a boob!"

Lena turned to face Sofie full on, crossing her legs in front of her. "There are rules, you know, Sofie," she said, already annoyed by her own intensity. "You can't just do whatever you want with a boy."

"See? You can't even call them men. You're almost seventeen."

"All right, a man, then. There are rules, Sofie."

"Oh, yeah. And what are those rules, exactly? And where do they get you?"

"Heaven," Lena blurted. "They get you into heaven." Now she was really annoyed with herself.

Sofie was staring at her, cheeks scrunched up toward her eyes. "Ah," she said at last. "So keeping your tongue in your mouth and your boobs tucked out of sight can get you into heaven . . . It sounds like a pretty boring place to me. I might just prefer to go someplace else."

Lena scrambled to her feet, her heart pounding. "Let's not talk about this anymore, Sofie. Just let me alone!"

Sofie guffawed. "Yeah. Me and all the salivating men out there."

"No one's salivating over me, and you know it!" Lena said. "Let's just go."

They walked out of the park then, together but not speaking. Lena hated that Sofie read her mind and then attacked her for her thoughts. She also hated that Sofie was right. It wasn't really hell she was afraid of, though—she was afraid of the feelings in her body and where she suspected they might lead, given an eager boy. Or man.

Her mother's swelling body and her father's silent rage about it scared her. Really scared her. In the new year, her mother was going to have that baby. And Lena was pretty sure that she would be expected to help with the birth. She could almost choke on the terror and revulsion that thought brought her.

Neither girl spoke until they were nearing Lena's apartment. Then Sofie said, "Let's go to my house."

"Your house? But you never . . ."

"I know what I said, but now we won't be seeing each other at school. We'll just have to go to each other's houses," Sofie said. "Unless we don't want to see each other," she added, not looking at Lena.

"We have to see each other," Lena said. "We *have* to."

"All right, then," Sofie said.

And on they walked.

* * *

Both Sofie's parents were home—her mother and a man Sofie introduced as her father, though Lena was pretty sure he was not. He looked nothing like her, but it wasn't just that. It was the reluctance with which she said the word *Father*, and the look on his face as she said it.

Her mother was young and pretty, but tired looking.

49

Meneer Vogel greeted Sofie a little too fondly, both hands in her hair as he kissed one cheek and then the other. She yanked herself out of his grasp just as he finished the second kiss. He looked hurt, and her mother looked sad.

Lena held out her hand to seal the introduction. Was that what Sofie hated so much, an overly affectionate stepfather? Or was there more?

"Would you like some tea?" Mevrouw Vogel said when she had ushered them into the kitchen. Lena shivered in the frigid room and looked at the stove, cold and black.

"No, thank you, Mevrouw Vogel," she said. "I must be getting home."

"No, Lena," Sofie said in the same moment that her mother said, "All right, dear," and ran a hand over her forehead, brushing back wisps of hair.

She had deep black shadows under her eyes.

"No, really. Mother will be expecting me," Lena said.

Sofie followed her out into the street, but she didn't seem to have anything to say once they got there.

Again they walked in silence. Lena was surprised that Sofie came along, but she felt unable to comment.

"They're not the greatest family," Sofie said once Lena's building was in sight.

"Your mother seems nice," Lena said.

"Sure, if you don't know her."

Lena started at the venom in Sofie's voice. Once again, silence fell.

Then, just as they were turning up Lena's walk, Sofie said, "My real father's dead," her voice flat now and her feet carrying her right up to Lena's door, where they could no longer converse in private.

Strange, Lena thought, as she followed her friend inside.

Moments later, they were standing in Lena's kitchen doorway just as they had some weeks earlier and not again since. This time, Mother was standing at the far side of the table, facing them, her belly keeping her at a bit of a distance from the wooden surface. She held a filthy, misshapen object in her hands. She was worn and grubby, her hair—greyer than Lena remembered—pulled out of its bun, a smear of dirt on one cheek. She looked just as tired as Mevrouw Vogel, but much, much older.

Far too old for having babies, Lena thought, and she wondered in that moment why the young Mevrouw Vogel had only the one child.

Mother looked up at the two girls but hardly seemed to register their presence.

"Hello, Mevrouw Berg," Sofie said brightly.

Lena stared at her. How could she speak so nicely to that miserable, numb-looking woman, and how could she be so cheerful after her announcement on the front step?

"What's that?" Sofie added.

As Lena's mother answered, she turned the thing over in her hands. Lena was transfixed by the dirty fingers, the torn nails. "It's a sugar beet," said Mevrouw Berg.

"A sugar beet?" Sofie said. "You mean to make sugar?"

Now, Mother's voice took on an edge. She looked at her daughter. "You're late, you know," she said. "I've been expecting you."

The woman paused and Lena squirmed.

At last she spoke again. "Not that it matters. I don't know what we're going to eat. No potatoes now. No butter. No gas in the middle of the day. Unless you would like a bite of this raw . . ."

And she thrust the beet toward Sofie, who actually stepped back. "I'm afraid I've got nothing to offer either of you. And . . . well, normal people make sugar out of sugar beets. We, though, are going to eat them. Lena has her work cut out for her."

"I'll go, mevrouw," Sofie said quickly, backing away a step as she spoke. "But—"

Lena broke in. "School's ended," she said. Her mother's gaze swung around to her. "No electricity," Lena went on. "No gas. They can't—"

"Yes, yes, I know. Bep's home already. In there." She nodded her head vaguely toward the hall. "No sign of Piet. Not that I'd expect it." She paused and looked at them. "I've been waiting for you, young lady, for well over an hour. I thought I was going to have to peel the beets all by myself." But she didn't seem to care. Not really. And she didn't seem to mind that Lena had brought Sofie home. She agreed readily to Sofie's return after some chores had been done and a meal, such as it might be, had been eaten.

Half an hour later, as she paused in her peeling to suck a bleeding knuckle, Lena wondered what the coming winter held in store. Surely Sofie wasn't serious when she talked about leaving; the world was at war, the Netherlands was occupied, and the Nazis were squeezing, squeezing, driving them all to the brink of starvation.

Besides, with a new baby coming, Lena would be needed at home.

CHAPTER FOUR

As October passed, Lena seemed to see less and less of her brother. More and more, it was Sofie she wanted to spend time with, not Piet.

One morning, Piet seemed distracted when they were gathering wood together. Lena was the lookout. He was removing a wooden tie from between the tram tracks. The trams couldn't run anymore anyway, so the ties had recently become fair game, though you didn't want to be seen taking them.

He dragged the tie to where she stood and dropped it. "Twenty-nine men were shot yesterday," he said, "in retaliation." His voice dropped to a whisper. "I saw the bodies."

Lena turned away. She reached down and hoisted the piece of wood. "Let's go home," she said.

"Don't you care?" he said, his voice too loud now.

Lena stopped. "Hush," she said. "You can't just talk about these things in public. It's dangerous."

Piet stepped up to her and talked into her face, his voice quiet but fierce, his breath stinking, as everyone's did, from hunger and bad food. "Dangerous? You think talking's dangerous? What about all the work the Dutch Resistance is doing? For us." He glared at her and repeated himself: "For us. I saw the bodies. They laid them out all in a row by the side of the street. Because one German officer was killed. *One.* Twenty-nine in retaliation for one. And they burned a building too. They don't even care if their victims are in the Resistance. They can be anybody."

"Stop it, Piet. Stop it." She didn't want to know. She really didn't.

"You could help, you know."

"No," she said. "I couldn't."

"Why not? Why are you so afraid?" He paused. "And you actually called that girl your friend. For years. If they hauled Sofie off, would you turn your back on her too?"

"They're not going to—"

"No, they're not. Because she's not Jewish. But remember the girl you never speak of? Remember the girl you wouldn't visit? She's probably dead right now. Just like the men by the road. And you don't even care."

Lena barely heard his last words because she was running by then, leaving the wood for him to lug home somehow. She did care. She did. But Piet needed to shut his mouth. She didn't want to know about dead bodies at the side of the road. And she didn't want to think about . . . about . . .

Those were the thoughts flying around her head when she pelted through her own front door. Safely home, she actually rebuffed Mother and took an ancient novel, one of her favourites, into the freezing courtyard.

But the courtyard was the wrong place to go. The magnolia stood over her sternly, bare of leaves now, fat buds tight against the cold. The book stayed unopened on the bench by her side. On this same bench, her brother had given her the worst news of her life.

54

Once Sarah was gone, the Jewish Quarter deserted, Lena had constructed a story for herself: the Cohens were in Germany working in a factory somewhere, or in some kind of a camp, maybe even seeing grandparents and other family again. She had imagined barracks like those where soldiers stayed.

Lena had seen a camp once before the war, when she and Bep and Mother had taken the train to the coast to bring Margriet home. Back then, she was jealous of her big sister. She had wanted to go to camp too.

It was awful to think that the Cohens had been taken somewhere against their will, but she imagined Mevrouw Cohen making do, putting together delicious meals with whatever was available. Somehow, Lena managed to make the imagined camp a warm and welcoming place, thanks to its warm and welcoming inhabitants.

Or she had, until that summer afternoon when Piet came home, his face grey.

Lena was in the courtyard reading, in exactly the spot where she was now sitting. Piet came out through the door from the kitchen, closed it behind him and sat down beside her.

He gave her no chance, not one, to stop the terrible words from leaving his mouth. "They pack them onto trains, into cattle cars, and take them to places far away," he said. "They kill them, Lena. They kill them."

"What are you talking about? They kill who?" She heard the hysterical note in her voice, as if she were a third person listening from far away, wishing that she would just shut up, that he would shut up, that this conversation had never begun.

"The Jews," he said. "Your friend. Her parents and sisters. All the people who are gone."

"I don't believe it," Lena said. "They haven't killed all of them." Even as she said it, she could hear how awful and pathetic that sounded.

"All. Some. I don't know, Lena. But I heard it today. That's what the Nazis do. They want to kill all the Jews. They want the world to be *Judenrein,* Jew-free." He fell silent.

Brother and sister sat there in the courtyard under the magnolia tree, the sun, high in the sky, casting dappled shadows down upon them, and tried to think of people killing other people because they were Jewish. Tried to and then tried not to. Sarah came into Lena's mind then, and a spike of pain pierced the back of her head. She reached up and tugged at her hair. No. She could not think about Sarah. The happy camp of her imagination was in ruins, but she had no idea how to construct a new one, a real one.

Where was Sarah right at that moment? Was she hungry? Was she in pain? Was she . . . dead?

"I have to help in the kitchen," Lena said. She picked up her book and walked inside, leaving the door open behind her. Moments later, Piet came in and closed the door. He did not linger, though.

At the dinner table a few days later, Father announced that Jew-lovers were spreading lies about terrible concentration camps. "They'll stop at nothing," he said, his words soaked in distaste.

Piet's fork had barely clattered to a stop on the table when the front door closed behind him. Lena sank down in her chair and concentrated on her food, willing her father to drop the subject.

"That boy is nothing but trouble," he said, but that was all. She breathed her relief and took another bite of her supper.

* * *

Now, Lena shivered under the magnolia and thought about the layers of horror presented to her by her brother. First the concentration camps. Now all those men murdered, their bodies lined up along the road. She found it hard not to be very, very angry with her brother.

Numb from cold, bad news and dreadful memories, Lena picked up her book and went inside. Surely there was a sugar beet that needed peeling and grating; her knuckles had almost healed from the last one.

* * *

For two weeks after school stopped, Lena did not manage to see Sofie as much as she would have liked. Most of the time Mother would not let Sofie in, and she would not let Lena out. Lena's fingers grew stained and raw from peeling and grating the sugar beets, which had to be boiled and boiled again to be edible.

But with gas a rare event, boiling required wood. Lena soon discovered this was her salvation. Wood. After running away from Piet that day, she went alone several times, most often to abandoned buildings that could be combed over, but the lonely journeys frightened her.

Then one day, Sofie showed up just as she was on her way, and nothing could have been more natural than for the two of them to go together.

They went straight to the park, which Lena had been avoiding on her own, and spent a glorious morning there, dismal though the place was since desperate foragers had reduced many more of the trees to stumps, including the tree they had leaned against so recently. When they parted outside Lena's door, each had a respectable supply of wood secreted about her person.

After that, Lena looked forward to her hour or two out of doors. Sofie showed up like clockwork every morning at ten, hovering on the street until Lena joined her. They had to get wood every day, but so did the rest of the city, with everyone looking harder and harder as the precious stuff grew scarcer. They broke up furniture they found in abandoned homes, pulled boards off walls. The Germans still objected, so they hid the wood in bags or under coats, but they did not consider going out during curfew. Lena had not done that again since she and Piet were almost chased down back in September.

Sometimes in those days, when she was out with Sofie, Lena felt happy, truly happy—a rumbling belly, bleeding fingers and a world at war notwithstanding.

* * *

November arrived, cold and damp, and with the first of November came the last of the bread. Father decided that it was time for a hunger journey, and Margriet and Lena must be the ones to go. They had had no bread in over a week. The girls were to travel outside of Amsterdam to the country to beg for food.

In the last few weeks, more and more Amsterdammers had set off for the country in search of food for their starving families. Lena had seen some of her neighbours return, bicycles or carts laden. She had seen others arrive home on foot and empty-handed, bicycles gone to the Germans. One had not returned at all.

No one had dreamed that the food supply could shrink down to so little, but in response to the ongoing railway strike, the Germans had placed an ever-tightening stranglehold on the western Netherlands. They took food out, but they would not let it come in. Lena had thought she knew what hunger was. It turned out she had not. Not until now.

Her belly ached. She could not get warm, no matter what she did. And where before she had sat reading books whenever she could because it was what she loved to do, now she sat with a book idle in her lap because she could not summon the energy to decode words on a page. She could almost feel her brain in her head, heavy and sticky, weighing her down.

And now Father wanted her to go on a hunger journey. He wouldn't go. He could be taken to Germany as slave labour, or so he said. Piet couldn't go for the same reason, even though he was really too young to be taken. You never knew what could happen. Of course Mother wouldn't go. Of the family's bicycles, only two remained, hidden away in the back of the shed. The rest had been confiscated at one time or another, until Father insisted they hide the two that were left against an emergency. Here it was: the emergency. They had two days to prepare.

Lena told Sofie about it the minute they were outside the next morning, in search of wood. And Sofie's reaction stunned her.

"They're making me go on a hunger journey," Lena said, near tears.

"Oh, Lena, I'll come. It will be such an adventure!" Sofie turned and walked backwards in front of her friend, her excitement palpable. "I'd give anything to get out of this city, even for a day."

Hope surged in Lena's chest. With Sofie there, it might be all right. She was so strong and brave. Lena could just step into her shadow and go along for the ride.

Margriet, grown up and bossy though she was, was no leader. She cast only a sliver of a shadow, nowhere near enough for the protection of a sixteen-year-old girl.

But the hope went as fast as it came. Sofie had no bicycle, and Father would never consent to her going in Margriet's place. No, Lena and Margriet would be off to the country on their own the next day.

Sofie saw the refusal in Lena's face and fell back into step beside her.

"I'm getting out of this city one way or another," she mumbled, eyes on the ground.

Lena was surprised by the speed with which she gave in, and by the abrupt shift in her mood. Sofie usually fought for what she wanted. They didn't have much to say to each other on the rest of that morning's foraging expedition.

* * *

In bed on the night before their departure, Lena lay wide awake next to her sleeping sister and wished with all her heart that Margriet could go alone to the country. Weaknesses aside, Margriet was grown up, after all. Nineteen. Lena's sister shifted in the bed and let out a low moan. Margriet might be asleep, Lena thought ruefully, but she was not having peaceful dreams.

Their bicycles were ready for their departure, already laden. Mother had gone through the linen closet, pulled out every sheet, every pillowcase, every tablecloth and napkin they owned and stacked them on the dining table. "You need things to trade," she told them. "You're not asking for something for nothing. Do you understand?"

And Margriet and Lena nodded as they packed the heavy linens into canvas bags and readied themselves to leave before dawn. It was not going to be fun riding such a long distance with wooden sections fitted around the bicycle rims in place of their long-ago worn-out tires.

Lena must have drifted off eventually, because Margriet shook her awake when the clock struck five. They hoped to arrive at the Hembrug, the only bridge over the Noordzeekanaal, close to seven o'clock, when curfew was lifted. That would give them the longest day possible in the country on the other side of the canal. They wheeled their bicycles onto the street in the pitch dark. The streets were silent. The darkness was deep, damp and cold, and dawn seemed far away.

Lena mounted her bicycle and followed Margriet north in the dark. The roads were treacherous places in broad daylight, and in the dark a wheel could get caught much more easily in one of the many potholes or snag on one of the hundreds of loose cobblestones, sending the rider toppling to the ground or straight into a canal. Lena rode slowly, hoping for the best. She heard Margriet some distance ahead of her, wooden tires loud on the stones, and pedalled a little faster to catch up. She shuddered at the thought of being alone on the streets at this hour, or even worse, being discovered. They rode straight north as far as they could on the Hoofdweg and then veered northwest. Eventually the sky began to lighten, but the bridge loomed into view before the sun did.

The two girls stopped and wheeled their bicycles into a narrow alley. The sun in the sky would signal the end of curfew, and they had to wait longer still or the Germans would know they had broken the rules. Lena looked over her shoulder as she stepped into the building's shadow. She could make out the concrete barrier, the dark blots of German soldiers and the larger blot of a tank. Fear made her gag, her slight breakfast trying to push itself back up her throat.

"We left too early," she whispered a moment later.

Margriet just shrugged her shoulders. Lena stared at her. She could actually see her shaking.

The longer they waited, the harder it got to step back out into the road, into full view of the soldiers. Margriet's teeth started to chatter, and Lena thought it was from terror rather than the frosty morning.

She pushed her own terror deep down inside herself. She knew that the Germans might take the bicycles and send the girls packing. The Germans had been confiscating bicycles for years now, taking them for their own use. And they could also deny passage out of the city if they wished. It all depended on the whims of the men ahead of them on that bridge.

At last, in full daylight, Lena mounted her bicycle. Show no fear, she thought. Smile at them and show no fear.

"We have to go," she said, and Margriet nodded and pedalled off ahead of her. When they reached the foot of the bridge, Lena put her foot down on the brake and watched Margriet approach the soldiers. Margriet had stopped just ahead, so she had to push her heavy bicycle up the incline while the men watched. Lena had to push hers even farther. Tension built in Lena as she waited for someone, anyone, to speak.

Then came "Where are you going?" in German.

Father had coached Lena and Margriet on their response, but Margriet seemed frozen, lips pressed together, as Lena came up beside her. When the pause had gone on far too long, Lena choked out, "We go for food," in German as instructed, and Margriet managed to pull their papers from her pocket and hand them over.

The man took the papers and laughed. "I do not understand you," he said.

"We go for food," Margriet said this time, her voice loud and clear but shaking.

The men nudged each other and spoke German in low voices. All Dutch children learned German in high school, and Lena was getting good at it after more than four years, but she could not make out what they were saying to each other. One looked over and she felt his eyes on her body, even in her loose jacket and long skirt. She resisted the urge to pull her jacket further around herself. Two others were looking at Margriet even more brazenly.

Then the German who had already spoken to them said, "Go," papers held out to them, the word followed by a guffaw. Margriet grasped the papers and gave Lena a small push. "Go!" she hissed, terror in her voice, and the man roared with laughter.

They were off, toiling to push the heavy bicycles with their wooden wheels and linen baggage up the rise of the bridge. Lena was aware of weakness in her muscles and lack of fuel in her body as bile made its way up her throat. She retched and stood up to pedal harder. The Germans laughed and shouted behind them. Lena retched again. Then they were over the rise, and they could coast.

They left the main roads as quickly as they could, and soon they were riding through countryside. The sun was hidden behind clouds. The fields were brown, farms tumbled; they rode around enormous craters from bombs. Why here? Of course: the railway passed nearby. Dutch railway workers remained on strike, all of them in hiding or under arrest, but the Germans had seized control of the trains. Now the trains in the Netherlands served only the enemy; they had become British targets.

The fields were mostly empty, but Lena did see a skinny cow in the distance, halfway out of sight behind a small, uncared-for farmhouse. No chickens, though. She had been searching for chickens, she realized, and dreaming of eggs, but chickenfeed was good for humans too, so Dutch chickens had gone early into the soup pot. They would be taking no eggs home that day.

The two girls rode on, seeking a more prosperous-looking establishment. It started to rain. Margriet had been riding in front, but her pace was slowing. Lena pulled up alongside her. "Stop a minute," Margriet said. Lena put her foot down, bringing her bicycle to a halt. Her hair was soaked, and strands had pulled out of her pigtails and were plastered to her face. She stared at her handlebars.

"That farm with the cow seems like the best one so far," Margriet said at last.

Lena raised her eyes to her sister's. Margriet's expression was grim.

"I don't want to do it," Margriet said. "It's begging. Look at us. We're pathetic, coming to the country to grovel for scraps. And who knows what we might find on these farms?"

Lena said nothing. She wheeled her bicycle around and started off back the way they had come, rainwater running down her neck and into her eyes, her mind whirling. How could Father make them do this? Her sister was terrified and humiliated, and she herself felt as if she might throw up at any moment.

It took a long time to get back to the farm with the skinny cow. And once they were there, no one answered the front door, no matter how hard and long Margriet pounded.

"Let's try the back," Lena whispered when Margriet had stopped pounding and leaned her forehead against the door. She would much rather flee. But where to?

The two girls set off around the house to the attached barn, where the back door had to be. As they turned the corner, they could see the door standing open, steam billowing out over the muddy ground. Margriet picked her way up to the doorway and looked in. Lena, right behind her, peered over her shoulder. A bony woman was doing laundry, turning the crank on a mangle over a washtub, some sort of grey fabric squeezing out between the rollers. Two small children played nearby.

Margriet's voice was tentative at first, and the woman did not look up. The small boy stopped what he was doing, stared and poked his sister so she too stared, but they did not speak.

Margriet cleared her throat. "Mevrouw," she said. Lena flinched at the sound of her sister's shrill, frightened voice competing with the grinding of the mangle. It worked, though. The mangle stopped. The woman looked. She looked and she was upon them.

"I know who you are," she said as she strode across the room, the children attaching themselves to her thighs as she passed. "City girls after food. Never done a moment's work in your life, either of you—bones nicely tucked away inside your flesh—and you come to me for food."

Margriet stumbled backwards a step, throwing Lena off balance, but when the woman paused for breath, she jumped in, "Mevrouw, we—"

But the woman had no intention of letting her speak. "My men are gone," she said, "taken a year ago and more, husband and son. They're in a German labour camp. Or they're dead. I've heard not a word. Not one word. They promised to leave one

65

man at home on the farms. But not here; not for me. I'm left with the infants and the farm."

Margriet tried again. "But, mevrouw, we aren't asking for a handout. We have things to trade."

The woman's grin was ugly, revealing rotting teeth, gaps where the teeth had fallen out altogether and not a trace of happiness. "And those things you have, can I eat them? Can I feed them to my children? Do cows like them? I have no need of things, girl. Like you, like all of us in this Godforsaken land, it's food I'm after. My cow is too hungry to give milk. My body is too hungry to work for more than an hour at a time. And where is the end to it? I think you know as well as I do where the end is." She looked down to ensure that her children's eyes were not upon her face, raised her right hand and drew her finger across her throat.

Margriet was already backing away, Lena matching her stride for stride. "Thank you, mevrouw. I wish you well," she said, and the two girls turned and ran.

Margriet's shoulders heaved as they pulled their bicycles off the fence where they had leaned them and wheeled back onto the road. Lena could tell that her sister was struggling with tears, but she herself felt dry inside. Yes, her belly ached, but she had never turned to tears as easily as her sister did.

She mounted her bicycle and pedalled in pursuit of her sister, who seemed to have got herself under control. They rode in silence for a long time, hungrier and thirstier with every moment that passed. They were not alone on the roads. Now and again, they came upon local people journeying here or there, and more often, others like themselves. City girls and city women. And once in a while, a city boy or a city man.

They passed several farms with people already lined up in the yards, waiting for handouts. No wonder the woman had been so frustrated. Lena and Margriet probably hadn't even been the first of the day. She was alone and desperate, and one after another, people arrived to take from her, but no one arrived to give. The ache travelled up Lena's body and settled deep behind her eyes. Still, though, no tears.

They rode a long way down a narrow road with a canal on the right. At last, on the other side of the canal, Lena saw a farmhouse that looked promising, smoke pouring enticingly from its chimney and no journeyers gathering outside. "Margriet," she called, "let's go there." And she pointed.

At the next crossroads they turned and crossed the canal on a narrow wooden bridge. They had not seen any cityfolk for a time, just one old man on foot pulling a cart and a girl on a distant road riding a bicycle. The rain had turned to drizzle a while ago, and now it had stopped, although the sky remained grey. Lena did not know what time it was, but the day was wearing on. They would not make it back to Amsterdam by nightfall. And if they did not get something to eat and drink soon, they would not be able to continue at all. She fought off surges of anger at her father, who had told Mother not to pack them food for the trip.

"They're going to the country to *get* food," he had stated. "They don't need to take food away with them."

The two girls rode down a long avenue lined by trees. The trees were tall and leafless, waving in the strong wind, majestic. Those trees were exactly the same as they would be without a war on. Lena wanted to stop and hug one, to ask its secrets. She tilted her head far back as she rode and almost came to grief in a big pothole. Then they were in the yard, which was bare but tidy. They leaned their bicycles against a fence and, this time, went straight round to the back of the house. Front doors, it turned out, were just for show in the country.

The back door of this house was closed, as was the huge barn door nearby. They saw no chickens or cows or any other livestock. Margriet knocked, putting effort into it. And they waited. Silence stretched on, and then they heard footsteps and the door creaked open. A woman stood in front of them.

The woman looked at them. "Ah," she said. "For some reason, I don't see many of you here. They're calling them hunger journeys, aren't they? This, what you're doing."

Lena listened to the words, the kindness in them, and felt tears spring into her eyes. I will not cry, she willed, and felt a tear spill over.

"Yes, mevrouw," Margriet said, "and we have linen to trade for food . . . if you have any to spare, that is. We know it's hard in the country too."

"Oh, not so hard as all that," the woman said. "Come in, girls. Come in. I'm Vrouw Hoorn. Not mevrouw. No need for those city titles here. You come from Amsterdam, I think. Did you leave this morning?"

Peering out from behind her sister, Lena nodded and another tear spilled from her eye.

"You have come far," the woman said.

They passed through the spacious entryway, the area that joined house to barn, where Lena glimpsed signs of laundry, just as she had at the other farm, and into an enormous kitchen. It was warm in that room, and the warmth and the smell of food brought more tears to Lena's eyes. A real fire burned in a big black stove. A lamp cast golden light over a round table set for a meal. And beyond the table, near the stove, an elderly man sat in a wingback chair. He looked across at them and smiled, but he did not rise.

"Meneer," Lena said respectfully.

His smile broadened. "Visitors," he said. "Welcome!"

"That's my father," the woman said, "Boer Bruin." She hurried to set out two more bowls and mugs, two spoons. "It is simple food," she said, "but nourishing. We have a bit of meat and some potatoes."

Lena sat, and the next hour passed in a blur. They talked and ate and ate and talked until sleep crept among them. Margriet fell silent. Lena put down her spoon. Voices slowed almost to gibberish, and food ceased to matter at all.

Their hosts bundled them away into a big bed beneath a thick comforter, warm bricks at their feet, and they slept.

* * *

They woke up to sunlight streaming into the room and the woman's voice urging them to rise. "If you plan to arrive home today, you must go soon."

Breakfast was porridge with milk and a teaspoon of honey, washed down with big mugs of weak, milky tea. Tea!

"I've looked at your bicycles, and although I don't want to take your things, I believe I must if we're to fit much food in those bags of yours," Vrouw Hoorn said as they scraped their bowls clean. "Your mother filled them right up."

An hour later, they were on their way. Deep inside, along with the sips of tea and the taste of porridge with creamy milk and honey, Lena tucked away that lovely feeling of human warmth.

They rode back the way they had come, but in the sunshine now and with full bellies. Margriet rode alongside Lena and chattered at her. Lena wanted to cherish what had happened, not blather on about it. Also, she had something particular on her mind.

There was that cow again. Lena had been watching for her. She pushed down on the brake with her foot. "Stop, Margriet. We're back at the other farm. I just need to do something."

"What are you talking about?" Margriet said. "We've got nothing to—Hey!"

Lena had pulled a bulky parcel from the top of one of the bags strung across the back of her bicycle.

"You're not going to give them food!"

"I am. I spoke to Vrouw Hoorn about it, and she put this parcel together for them." Lena looked at Margriet's outraged face. "Oh, come on, Margriet. They're hungrier than we are."

Margriet fell silent at that, but she stayed by her bicycle. Lena found the back door closed this time. She paused to summon her courage. It took only a moment for the woman to answer her knock. And there were the two children, attached to her thighs again.

"You," she said. "How dare you—"

"No, mevrouw. No. I brought you this." Lena held out the parcel. "Some beef. And potatoes. And a jar of milk."

The woman's brow furrowed. She held out her hand.

The larger of the two children stepped forward and spoke. "Is it food? Is it really food?"

The woman pushed him away. She let the door open wider, holding the parcel in her hands.

At last she looked up and met Lena's eyes. "Well," she said, "I . . ."

"I am only the delivery person," Lena said. "I thought perhaps you could make use of it."

"Yes," the woman said. "You . . . you . . . you better go."

Lena smiled as best she could and turned and walked away. She did not really understand the woman's response, but she felt better than she had in a long time. Margriet was pacing by the bicycles. As soon as she set eyes on Lena, she mounted hers and pedalled off. "What would Father say?" she called over her shoulder as Lena rushed to catch up.

"Who cares?" Lena shouted back with a rush of fierce joy. Not me, she thought, and pedalled a little faster.

* * *

Curfew was approaching by the time they reached the Hembrug once again and faced a new set of German soldiers. The man who stepped forward smiled warmly and took their papers politely, or so it seemed. But then he passed the papers to one of his companions and strolled behind the two girls and their bicycles. Lena turned her head, struggling to hold her position. Casually, he flipped up a canvas flap and pulled out a parcel wrapped in cloth.

"What have we here?" he asked.

Did he want an answer?

Before Lena could decide, words spilled out of Margriet's mouth in stilted German. "Our mother is sick. This is for her, to help her—"

A raised hand silenced her. "Bicycles were to be turned in, and trips out of the city "—he paused—"for any purpose are forbidden." He paused again, meeting the other men's eyes with a slow grin. "Even sick mothers."

"But, Officer—" Lena started.

Again the raised hand. "You will leave this bicycle with us, its various parcels too." He put his hands on the handlebars, right up against Lena's, and she snatched her fingers free. "You may go," he said. "And you may take the other bicycle. Just be

71

sure you turn it in once you're home. We have made a note of it."
At that, the man who held the girls' papers jotted something in a
notebook and handed the papers back.

Teeth gritted, tears barely in check, Lena mounted Margriet's bicycle behind her sister, and they coasted down the
remaining stretch of bridge with her on the seat and Margriet
standing on the pedals. She reminded herself that they still had
the food Margriet carried and they still had one bicycle, but the
tears seeped out from under her lids just the same.

Father was angry when they arrived home on one bicycle,
and Mother was silent. Bep danced around in the kitchen calling
out the items one by one as Mother unpacked the panniers. But
Father soon sent her out of the room, and Lena settled down to
peeling once again: at least she was peeling potatoes this time,
and there would be meat for supper.

At the dinner table, Father insisted on an extra portion for
himself from the meal made with the food they had brought.
He was the biggest and a man. "I need my strength," he said.
And Mother thinned her lips and slopped an extra spoonful
into his bowl.

Father had not even asked about their journey.

Still, they all went to bed that night with full bellies and
the comfort of enough leftovers for another good meal, along
with knowledge of the small sack of potatoes and carrots in the
root cellar and the bag of good flour and jar of fresh butter that
would last at least for a few days. Margriet fell asleep instantly,
exhausted, but Lena lay awake, best and worst images running
over and over again through her mind.

Even with the theft of their bicycle and Father's greed, the
journey had been a success. Father had said that they would
not turn in the remaining bicycle, but there would be no more

hunger journeys for two—not unless they were prepared to walk.

If there werc to be more journeys, Margriet would just have to go on her own. That was all.

Taking care not to wake her sister, Lena turned over in bed and allowed herself to drift off to sleep.

CHAPTER FIVE

Lena twirled, her skirt flying out in a circle around her knees, her hair flying out in a circle around her head, the ball flying in a torrent of colour up, up, up to the wall and bouncing back to land in her raised hands just as she came around. Her hands snapped around the shining rubber, drew back and let the ball fly once again. Another spin and another. Dizzy and breathless, eight-year-old Lena caught the ball for a last time and collapsed on the big stone bench. She stroked the ball's red and orange streaks as she caught her breath.

Tap, tap, tap. Knuckles sounded on glass.

Lena's head jerked up. Margriet glared at her through the kitchen window, her arm raised in a familiar gesture. Get in here, that arm said, clear as shouted words.

Lena sighed. She had been shivering in the courtyard, door to the shed open, peering into the dim interior. What was she doing? That ball must be long deflated, caked in grime. And she was not eight but seventeen, long grown, such childhood games now closed to her. Anyway, it was far too cold to be outside. She closed the shed door, met Margriet's eyes and nodded.

Minutes later, she was settled at the kitchen table, slicing away at sugar beets, trying to create thin shreds from the dirty, misshapen objects. Three weeks had passed since her journey with her sister: the potatoes were long gone, and so was all the rest of the food.

That day, years ago, when Lena had spun in the back garden bathed in the heady scent from the magnolia tree, she had been free in ways that she could never be now. Nowadays, even when she was out gathering wood with Sofie, she still felt diminished by the misery of war. Her body insisted on lengthening and filling out, despite the hunger that now spread from her belly into her limbs, and her clothes grew shorter, tighter and more threadbare with each week that passed. December bore down on Amsterdam. The city had grown cold.

"Lena! We're lucky to have food at all, and look what you're doing to it!"

Lena looked up at her sister. Margriet looked angry, yes. But worse than that, she had lines in her forehead that Lena had not noticed before. Her cheekbones stood out on her face, and brown spots marked one cheek and her chin. Do I look like that too? Lena wondered.

"Yes, Lena. Listen to your sister," Father said as he passed by the kitchen.

Margriet glanced up at him and turned back to Lena. "Well, if you can't slice the beets properly," she said, "at least you could get the water ready. You could cut some kindling. Don't just sit there staring at me."

The quaking girl of their hunger journey was gone, and the

tyrant who was happy to take up giving orders where Mother and Father left off had returned.

Lena was slicing a small piece of cabbage for the soup pot when Mother came into the kitchen, one hand on her waist. Her dress hung off her bones, with no hint of flesh beneath it except where her hand held the fabric against her body, and where her belly, grotesque to Lena, pushed the fabric out into a mound. Her thin fingers sank into the deep hollow at the top of that belly. Lena stared. Her mother seemed to be getting thinner faster than her belly was getting rounder. Could there really be a baby in there?

Her whole family was changing. Well, except for Father, Lena thought. She felt her lip curl and bent her attention firmly to the cabbage. Father was strong—tall and muscular—and he did not let food shortages threaten his physique. A wave of anger washed over her. Sometimes it had seemed as if the food they brought back from their journey was his own personal supply, as if he drew his strength straight from the flesh of his family.

"We have no meat or fat for the soup," Mother said.

"We will make do," Father said, his large body filling the doorway. "And tomorrow Margriet will go to the country again for food."

Margriet looked up fast, her whole body rigid.

Mother swung around. "It's too dangerous. The Germans are searching people."

"Margriet knows the risks," Father said, "but she's a brave girl. Aren't you, Margriet? Your mother needs to eat. Look at her!"

Lena gritted her teeth and chopped.

* * *

Margriet left before dawn the next morning, and curfew fell that night with no sign of her. Lena rolled over and over in bed all night, watching and waiting instead of sleeping. The next morning, even Father's eyes looked bloodshot. The second day— rain drumming on the windows, the apartment dank and dim and very cold—was longer than Lena had thought a day could be. Sofie knocked on the door in mid-afternoon, soaking wet in her threadbare coat but still there, smiling at the door. Lena looked at her and shook her head. She couldn't imagine going out, and she knew that Sofie would not be welcome in the midst of their waiting.

In the early evening, they ate a bit of leftover soup and set themselves to wait some more, but at ten o'clock Mother sent all the children to bed, her voice permitting no argument. The second night passed, as silent as the first.

At first light, Lena stood in the frigid kitchen preparing the tiny kindling that would allow her to heat water in the make-shift tin-can stove they now used to save on fuel. Rain poured down in the courtyard, battering the magnolia's bare branches and turning the heaps of fallen leaves to mush. She was trying not to think about how much colder her sister must be without shelter in the winter rain that refused to let up. She could hear Mother and Father and Bep in the next room. Soon all four were gathered in the kitchen, and Piet joined them moments later, everyone accepting mugs of warm, bland liquid.

An hour passed. And another. It seemed impossible that Margriet could be gone for so long and still be safe.

Then, "She's coming! She's coming!" Bep flung open the door and ran down the street into her sister's arms.

Lena made it outside in time to see Margriet, still astride her bicycle in the pouring rain, trying to hug Bep back without falling over. Piet was there too in a moment, and Lena stood with her parents and watched as Bep pushed the heavy bicycle toward them while Margriet walked, leaning on her brother.

Margriet was soaked to the skin. She was shivering uncontrollably. She was shaking with fear as well as cold. She was weeping, and her teeth were chattering so hard that she could not speak.

Mother took her from Piet when they reached the door, put one arm around the sodden body and led her inside. In the kitchen, Mother took her eldest daughter's shoulders in her hands and looked into her face. Then she let go with one hand and used it to push a thick strand of wet hair off Margriet's forehead. She let the back of her hand rest there for a long moment. Checking for fever.

Off to the side, Lena stared. Was Mother's chin wobbling? No. Mother dropped her arms to her sides.

"Lena," she said, her voice brisk as always, "get your sister into some dry clothes. Wrap her in her blanket and bring her to the kitchen. I'll go see if she has brought anything that we can use to nourish her back to her senses."

Margriet stood in their bedroom, offering no assistance as Lena peeled her out of her clothes. Lena looked at her sister's skinny, goosebumpy body. Had she been hurt in some way? Lena could see no sign. She wrapped a blanket around her sister and rubbed and rubbed. She towelled her hair as dry as she could. Then she dressed her in dry clothes, which was difficult because the clothes were too small and so threadbare that they tore under pressure. When Lena shoved Margriet's hand right through the elbow of a long-sleeved blouse, Margriet found enough of herself to assist with the rest of the dressing.

"What happened?" Lena asked.

"It was horrible, every second of it," Margriet said. "The soldiers were cruel, going and coming. One grabbed me. He—" and she gave a sob.

"He what? Did he . . . ?"

"No. No. It was just so awful, so humiliating. He laughed and he . . . said things. And he wouldn't let go, and the others laughed too. And then they let me go and sang a song in German as I was riding away. A filthy song. I felt like the skin would crawl right off my back. I wanted to find the farm with the nice woman who gave us all the food, but I couldn't. I don't know why. There were so many people out on the roads, and I got farther and farther away." She leaned down and pulled on a sock and stayed bent over for a few moments, her head on her knee, before she continued. "A farmer did feed me and let me stay with his family that first night, after I asked at six houses. One woman yelled at me. A man gave me scraps. Another man let me do an hour's work and then gave me a slice of bread. The rest just said they had nothing to give."

She had stopped shivering now—warmed, it seemed, by her own unhappy memories.

"Then I found the man who helped me. His wife had died and he was quite old, there with three small children. I cooked their supper. I was afraid for what the man might ask in exchange for a bed and food, or for what might happen in the night, but nothing did. And I left early yesterday, but the distance was just too great. I got closer and closer, but never close enough. And the closer to the city, the less people will help, and the more others are begging too." She had all her clothes on now, except for shoes, and sat crosslegged on the bed, wrapped in a blanket and continuing her story. It was one, Lena knew, that she would not want to share in all its detail with Mother and Father.

"I slept in a shed last night, just the other side of the Hembrug. I got there long after curfew, so I could come no closer. I slept in straw. And it was wet and it was cold and it stank. Then this morning, I woke up and there was a man there. He was opening up one of the bags on my bicycle. I don't know what I was thinking. I yelled at him. And he looked at me and roared. I swear that he roared. I think he was so hungry that it just came out of him. And I roared back. Or I screamed. Anyway, I told him that he had to go away, that he couldn't have one bit of my food. And he looked at me. And then he went. He just went. That was when I started to cry and shake. I was crying and shaking when I got to the bridge. The soldiers thought that was really funny. They were the same ones we saw two weeks ago. They remembered me. They remembered that I was supposed to turn in my bicycle. They said that they were going to take it, and I just stood there and cried. I just cried. And in the end, they let me go."

Margriet had been looking at her lap as she spoke. Now she looked up at Lena. "I think I just need to sleep," she said. "Can you get me something warm to drink and something to eat and bring it to me here? Tell them I just need to sleep."

Margriet slept all day, refusing to stir even when Lena came to tell her that supper was ready. She shifted and groaned quietly when Lena crawled into bed at nine o'clock, but she slept on. Lena lay awake for a long time, turning her sister's story over and over again in her mind, its edges blurring and its shape changing as her own dreams mixed in.

CHAPTER SIX

Neither Margriet's struggle on that journey nor the family's long, agonizing wait deterred Father. Soon he was sending Margriet in search of food almost weekly. She had to vary her route, leaving the city to the south or the west sometimes, so as not to encounter the same soldiers over and over again.

Father never suggested that Lena go in her place. She was two years younger, after all. And Lena never offered.

Each time Margriet left before dawn on her bicycle, Lena lay in bed battling a mixture of guilt and relief. Next time I'll offer to go in her place, she would think. But "next time" came and came again and she did not.

She and Sofie talked about it more than once.

"If I could get my hands on a bicycle, we could go together," Sofie said early one morning as they worked together to pry up one of the few tramway ties left to be found. "I'm dying to get out of this city."

Lena sat back on her haunches. "You think you are, Sofie, but you have no idea."

"No idea?" she said, pulling on the piece of wood. "Don't just sit there. Help me with this."

Soon they were headed for Sofie's house, slush freezing their toes through the holes in their shoes, on the alert for soldiers who might confiscate their prize.

"You come to my house and see what it's like. My stepfather is afraid to set foot outside. If the Germans have another round-up, he might dive—you know, go into hiding—or get taken, and my mother . . . well, she's scared, Lena. She's hungry and she's scared. She's . . . she's never been good on her own."

Lena stumbled on something hidden in the snow, and Sofie crashed into her from behind. They stopped to juggle their load.

"If I could get out to the country like you did, maybe I could bring her some food," Sofie said. "I'm afraid that Father will go, and that something will happen."

Lena noticed the word *Father*. She also noticed the tiniest hesitation before the word left Sofie's lips.

* * *

That conversation had happened in late November. After that, Lena began to feel guilty about eating the food that Margriet brought home. Bep dragged around, weak, weepy and cranky with fatigue. Both Bep and Mother had developed leaky boils on their bodies that refused to heal. And the skin on Mother's face and the backs of her hands was translucent. It looked like it would slip right off if you pinched and tugged. Mother looked like an old woman. And the older and sicker she looked, the more her belly seemed like some sort of malignant growth rather than a source of new life. As much as she could, Lena tried not to look at her.

December 6 should have brought Saint Nicholas: treats in wooden shoes, joking poems all round, a delicious meal, fun for everyone. In 1944, it brought nothing. And they were all too tired and sick and busy to notice, at least in the Berg household. Even Bep, the one among them who might still believe in Saint Nick, did not seem to be aware of any special significance to the day. Innocent childhood was done, Lena supposed.

Then Mother went into the bedroom and returned with new mittens for all. Lena recognized Bep's old green sweater; too small now and full of holes, it had been sacrificed for the mittens. The Berg family would boast matching hands through the winter. After Mother had distributed the gifts, she still held something in her hands: a tiny sweater. Newborn-sized. As she gazed at it, Lena mumbled one of her prayers to herself.

Perhaps Saint Nicholas had stopped in after all.

Sofie came to pick Lena up for their daily wood-collection rounds. The rainy weather of November had given way to crisp, cold days. The canals boasted a thin film of dirty ice. Lena enjoyed the clear sky and her warm green hands. Sofie reached out and tucked a twist of paper into Lena's palm.

"Well, it is Saint Nicholas Day!" she said, not meeting Lena's eyes.

Lena pulled off one ridiculous mitten and unscrewed the bit of paper. It was a poem, but it was not the traditional joking kind usually exchanged on this special day:

> *I know that you're a special girl.*
> *Let's give a hunger trip a whirl!*
> *We'll send some food, a bit of wheat,*
> *And beat their hunger with some meat.*
> *No bicycle? I shall not grieve!*
> *With two train tickets, we will leave.*

Lena finished reading and looked up into Sofie's face. Surely the girl was not serious! But a glance told her that she was.

"Train tickets? The Nazis run the trains!" Lena said. "We're not allowed on them. And where would you get train tickets?"

"Leave that to me," Sofie said, smiling slyly now.

"Thanks for the poem, Sofie," Lena said, speaking through a stir of panic, "but we can't go. It's too dangerous. It's crazy."

"Leave it to me!" Sofie said again.

"No, Sofie. No. We just can't! I can't. I can't leave Mother!" Lena said.

"Does your mother need you, or does she need something to eat? People send packages. My neighbour got one all the way from Friesland."

"I just can't, Sofie," Lena said, guilt mixing in with her insistence now.

Well, even if Sofie could get tickets—was that possible?—she couldn't force Lena to get on a train. She was staying put.

But she did wish that Sofie hadn't mentioned those packages. It seemed impossible that parcels of food could make it from the country to the city, but Lena didn't need to hear Sofie's story to know otherwise. Mother had complained of it more than once: a neighbour with a son in the north receiving parcels and hoarding the contents. As if she could be expected to do anything else!

They collected wood in silence. Sofie seemed to have figured out that she should keep her plans to herself for the time being.

* * *

Two weeks later, Piet caught up to Lena one afternoon as she was heading down the block.

86

"They're going to try to bribe us," Piet said. "We have to stop them."

Lena was bewildered and annoyed. "Who? What are you talking about?" she said as she tried to sidle past her brother. She was due at Sofie's in a few minutes, and she was eager to get away for a bit.

"The Germans," Piet said, annoyance in his voice as well. "Who do you think? They're going to call up all the men again, but this time they're promising to help their families. They know how desperate everyone is."

"But you're not in the age range, Piet. Right? And neither is Father."

"Is that all you think about? Your own family? They're calling up all men between sixteen and forty!"

Lena felt a stirring of guilt. How could her brother care so much and she so little? She also felt anger. Why was everyone always putting their stuff onto her? It wasn't fair. Didn't she do enough at home already? That was what her war effort amounted to: peeling and cooking sugar beets!

Some of the determination was gone from Piet's voice when he next spoke. Still, speak he did. "They're going to poster the city right before Christmas, ordering men up and offering food for their families and exemptions for those who need them. We're going to be right there after them with our own posters. We're going to cover theirs up. Tell people the truth."

"We?" Lena echoed.

"Yes, we," Piet said. "And 'we' could include you. There's a lot of work to be done, Lena. We're all needed."

Lena shivered. Not far from where they stood, a woman and a boy were rooting through a heap of garbage, hoping for something useful or, even better, edible. The one street sign that she could see was in German, not in Dutch. Stumps stood where trees had been. Barbed wire coiled where there had been gardens. And the canals were frozen solid, but Lena didn't think she had seen a single person skating. Not one.

Lena took it all in. Then she tried to imagine sneaking around the city with her brother, posters in hand. The very things that made action so necessary also made it deadly. "Piet, I . . . I have to go," she said, shoving past him and taking off down the street.

* * *

December turned to January with little more than a bone-chilling midnight mass to mark Christmas and nothing whatsoever to mark the new year, except the fact that now it was 1945. The war had entered the second half of the decade. Darkness had tightened like a noose around the days and showed no signs of loosening its grip, despite the fact that the days were growing longer instead of shorter. The cold sank deeper and deeper into everyone's bones. Food grew scarcer still. Margriet's journeys grew longer, and she came back with lighter and lighter loads.

Lena had seen the posters Piet warned her of, the coaxing, bribing posters. And she had seen the response, the posters warning men not to go and advising wives to keep their men at home, not to be seduced by lies. She avoided her brother as much as she could; she could not bear the judgment that spilled over her or the guilt that bloomed inside her when the two encountered each other.

Then, one morning when Margriet was away—wasn't Margriet *always* away?—Father knocked on Lena's door. "Your mother needs you," he said, his voice sharper, higher pitched than usual.

Behind him, from the bedroom down the hall, Lena heard her mother cry out.

She scrambled from her bed and into her clothes, oblivious to the frost that had formed on the blanket or the clouds that her breath made in the frigid room.

"I'm going for the doctor," Father said, and he was gone.

Lena emerged into the hallway to find Piet standing outside Mother's door, tears pouring down his face. Bep was at his side, her shoulders heaving. In the bedroom, Mother wailed again.

Lena looked at the closed door and thought of the weak, broken woman on the other side. She straightened.

"Piet, boil water," she said. "Bep, Piet needs your help." She waited until they had disappeared into the kitchen, reached out her hand and opened that door.

Mother looked as if she was trying to crawl backwards up the wall at the head of the bed. The blankets and sheet had fallen from her; her hands were behind her on the wall, her feet pushing at the mattress. Her eyes were squeezed shut, but tears nonetheless found their way out and snaked down her face.

"Mother," Lena said, "I'm here."

The pain seemed to end for the moment. Mother sank back down onto the bed, her nightgown riding up her thighs as she did so. Her eyes opened, and she looked at her daughter. "I'm not strong enough for this," she said.

"Yes, you are," Lena said, glad that the right answer was clear to her, though not at all sure that it was true. She reached out and pulled the hem of the nightgown down, pulled the sheet and blankets up. "It's freezing in here. Let's cover you up!"

She heard her voice, cheery almost. Where did that come from?

The doctor did not arrive for three hours. Lena managed to keep her prayers silent, but she sent off a steady stream. "Please let the doctor arrive before the baby comes. Please let the doctor arrive before the baby comes." On and on she prayed, as she let her mother grip her hand when the pains came, settling her back down under the blankets when they were over. She got warm water and a cloth from Piet and wiped her mother's forehead and neck. She made soothing noises. She countered her mother's despairing words with pat assurances. And she prayed and prayed and prayed.

The pains seemed to get worse. Mother seemed to grow more desperate. Once, when her mother screamed, Lena bit her own lip so hard that she tasted blood. "Please let the doctor arrive before the baby comes. Please!"

And at last, he did. She saw him look her mother over. She saw the worry in his eyes. And she saw him push aside that worry and decide to get down to work.

"You've done a good job, young lady," he said. "Now out with you."

Lena waited in the kitchen with Bep and Piet. Father paced the hallway. Any blame he might have felt toward his wife for allowing herself to get pregnant seemed to be washed away now with fear.

Lena's prayer changed. "Please let Mother and the baby live. Please let them live."

They had to put up the blackout paper again before Mother's cries stopped.

Soon after, silence fell, the door creaked open and Father was ushered into the room. Lena waited for what seemed like forever, then tapped on the door herself. The doctor opened it. "Come on in, all of you," he whispered.

Lena saw blood first. A lantern had been lit in the room, and it illuminated the bloody sheet heaped on the floor at the foot of the bed. She saw bloody stains on the bed itself as well. A blanket had been pulled up over Mother's chest, and she was half sitting, leaning against the wall, holding a small bundle. Father stood over her, looking down at the face that the small swaddling exposed.

The baby was tiny, wrinkly and badly in need of a bath, with scant black hair stuck down on its head.

"Nynke," Father said. "You have another sister, and her name is Nynke."

Mother was silent; her face, even in the lantern's glow, was grey.

"The doctor said she might not have enough milk," Father went on. "He said your mother is starving. The baby came too early and your mother is starving."

CHAPTER SEVEN

Lena stood in the dimly lit bedroom looking down at her sleeping mother and the tiny baby, now a few days old, tucked up beside her in the big bed. That tiny, hungry baby. It had consumed Mother from the inside for almost nine months, and now it was trying to consume her from the outside. But Mother had little to give. Lena didn't know which one of them to worry about most.

She reached down and lifted the baby bundle away from her mother's side. Mother shifted, but she did not open her eyes. Lena tiptoed out of the room and into the slightly warmer kitchen. She sat down on the chair between the stove and the window, where the weak January light could reveal her new sister's face.

She pulled the ancient baby blanket back, just a bit. And she gazed.

Nynke's eyes were tightly shut, kind of crinkly. Her nose was the tiniest nub, like a new growth, and her mouth was . . . her mouth was perfect. Lena didn't know if Nynke looked like her or anyone else in the family, but she certainly looked like her very own small self.

A quiet voice, a wondering voice, spoke next to her ear. Lena almost started, but she managed to hold still. It was Bep. Only Bep.

"You've got her," Bep breathed, and the words floated into the room, dusted with wonder.

Lena turned her head slightly and smiled, almost overwhelmed with love.

Margriet had returned from her journey the day before, and there was food in all their bellies and milk in Mother's breasts, at least for the moment. But the warm feeling inside Lena was caused not by food, though food made it much easier to feel it, but by a person, a brand-new special person.

Best remember this, she thought, as Bep tilted her head to the side so it rested on Lena's shoulder. Together, they looked at their new sister.

Then the front door slammed, and Lena did start; in fact, she jumped enough to wake the baby. And Bep sprang away from her as if they were doing something wrong.

Angry wails filled Lena's lap and spread to greet Father as he practically stormed into the kitchen. "What's going on in here?" he demanded. "What's that baby doing away from her mother?"

"I was just—" Lena started, but the creak of a door interrupted her. She was on her feet by then, and she stepped into the hall just in time to see Mother in her thin nightgown, leaning against the wall for support.

The baby's cries grew louder, if that was possible, and Father bore down on Mother and swept her into his arms. She sank against him.

"You're supposed to stay in bed," Father said, speaking into Mother's hair as he steered her back into their room. Lena followed, cooing in Nynke's ear in a desperate attempt to quiet her, while wondering at the tenderness she was witnessing between her parents.

Moments later, Mother was settled in bed, Bep was taking Nynke from Lena's arms and placing her beside her mother, and Father was striding from the room.

"Time to start on dinner, Lena," he said in passing. He paused. "And no more sneaking around with the baby. Your mother could have been hurt, coming out of bed like that."

Tears of frustration shot into the back of Lena's throat.

"Well," Father said, "what do you have to say for yourself?"

Lena had followed him into the hall. It took her two tries to get the words out. "Yes, Father," she said at last. "I'm sorry, Father."

He gave a single nod and went on into his study.

Lena walked into the kitchen and stopped, her hands in tight fists at her sides. A gasping sob escaped her. Just one. She cast around the room, saw the paperback she had been reading earlier, grasped it and sent it flying. It settled in a corner, its weak spine snapped at last. Then Lena yanked open the root cellar and wrested the last sugar beet, the ugliest yet, from its depths.

When she stood, Bep was there in the doorway.

"Can I help?" she said in her soft voice.

"No, you can't," Lena said.

Bep stayed where she was, shoulders slack, lower lip trembling.

"Oh, leave me alone, can't you?" Lena said, her voice a little softer now. Soft enough that Bep dared to enter the room and lean up against the table near her sister.

Dinner preparation was under way.

CHAPTER EIGHT

"Almelo," Sofie said. "We'll go to Almelo!"

Lena stared at her.

"Well, you said you want to leave, so let's go!"

"I didn't mean . . ."

"Of course you did. Your family's starving. So is mine, but you've got six people to think of. Plus yourself. That little baby could die, Lena. She could die!"

Lena thought about reaching out and slapping Sofie. She imagined the smacking sound, the satisfying feel of her hand making contact, the shock on Sofie's face.

"We'll go somewhere where there's lots to eat, too far away for the hunger journeyers from the cities to reach. Almelo is far away. It's almost in Germany. And I know people there . . . family."

Lena put her hand in her pocket and her violent impulses out of her head. "How would we get there?" She was just humouring Sofie, really. "You said something about train tickets?"

"Yes," Sofie said, jumping up from the stone step where they were huddled in the late January cold. "Train tickets to Almelo. I know exactly how to get there. I've been there. My mother . . ."

She paused.

Sofie's expression, eyes downcast all of a sudden, puzzled Lena. She did not seem fully committed to her crazy idea.

"If we're going to go somewhere," Lena said, "why don't we go to Maastricht instead, or leave the Netherlands altogether? Let's go somewhere that's already liberated!"

Sofie laughed. "Yes. We'll swim across the Rhine while Germans shoot at us with machine guns. It will be an adventure!"

Lena smiled at her. "So you acknowledge how impossible *that* is. Well, we can't just go and buy train tickets, Sofie, even if we had money. They're not letting Dutch civilians on the trains."

"We won't *be* Dutch, Lena. We'll be German. I'll get tickets to Rheine. That's not far across the border. We'll say we've been living here for the whole war. We're sisters."

Lena looked at Sofie. She couldn't imagine two girls looking less like sisters.

"And our mother has just died, and our father is sending us to our grandparents in Rheine."

"You can say all that in German?" Lena asked.

"Hey, I'm good at languages, remember? And Juffrouw Westenberg said that I have an excellent German accent!"

Lena changed tack. "You don't know what they're like, the German soldiers. I dealt with them when I went to the country with Margriet, and what she goes through when she goes alone . . ."

Sofie shrugged, and Lena fought down a wave of annoyance. "My German is much better than yours, and I'll bet it's better than Margriet's too. The soldiers will see lovely young German women when they look at us. We'll be fine."

Lena was silent for a long moment, struggling with herself. She could feel herself getting sucked into Sofie's plan, even though she knew it was dangerous. Terribly dangerous. Still, if she didn't give in, Sofie would just keep at her.

"How about the tickets?" Lena asked. "How will you get those?"

At this point, the excitement leaked out of Sofie's face and a little bit of fear showed in her eyes.

They had left the land of fantasy.

She knew a man, she said, a Dutch railway worker who had not gone into hiding when the strike started. Or rather, her stepfather knew him. That man would help them. He could get them tickets and escort them right onto the train. He could also help them get false papers. Sofie would need to take Lena's identity card, to use the photograph on a new one, a German one.

Lena had never in her life thought of doing anything even remotely like this. It was a terrifying plan, filled with flaws. But it would mean that she could try to get food back to her family. She would find a way. And even if she failed, even if packages failed to arrive, hers would be one less mouth to feed. They would have her ration card and could use her rations for themselves.

From her pocket, she withdrew the hand that had ached to slap Sofie's face and held out her identity card to her friend.

Sofie beamed. "We're going," she said. "We're actually going!"

* * *

Two more weeks passed before Sofie had the tickets and the identity cards. During those weeks, Lena stayed home as much as she could, and went in terror on her wood-gathering missions, knowing that at any moment a German soldier could ask to see her card.

Each day, Lena worked in the kitchen, helped with the baby, sat at the dinner table, all while her secret grew and grew.

Once she had the new card in her hand, her terror deepened. Now she was German. Her name was Aubrey Schulze. She imagined looking up at a German soldier and convincing him that she was the girl on the card. She could not. But there was no going back. She would never have a legitimate identity card again.

In the end, it was actually hard to leave, even putting aside her fear. When she held Nynke in her arms for the last time and felt the weight of her and the life in her; when she hugged Bep and remembered the little girl's head on her shoulder, felt her loneliness and longing; when she looked at her brother, so full of purpose; and even when she thought about her bossy big sister, her greedy father and her pale and fading mother—she felt love. Some of that love surprised her.

On Monday, February 5, 1945, Lena ate her last meagre lunch at home. Piet stood by the window stroking a velvety leaf of the African violet, calm and silent. Lena's heart twisted in her chest. He was going to think she was running away.

Well, it would be as it would be. She busied herself tidying up the kitchen and awaited her moment. Her old battered suitcase was already packed, hidden under the bed. In her pocket were her ration cards, along with a short note for her family. At last, Piet went out, as she knew he would. Margriet had gone to line up for this week's sugar beets. Father was in his study, and Bep was in the bedroom with Mother and baby Nynke.

Lena dried her hands, took off her apron and hung it over the back of a chair. Then she went into her bedroom, took the folded papers from her pocket and put them in the middle of the bed, where they could not be missed. She hoped that Bep and Piet wouldn't worry about her too much. She had done her best, writing that she was with Sofie, that they would be safe, that she was leaving her ration cards so everyone could have more to eat. She adjusted the note on top of the cards, put on her wool coat, her favourite hat and her funny green mittens, pulled her suitcase from under the bed and walked briskly down the hall and out the front door.

* * *

She and Sofie met at Sofie's house, since their journey was not a secret from Sofie's parents. And they walked to the station, exhausted long before they reached it from the combination of fear and exertion.

The plan went well at first, though—or seemed to. Sofie led the way into the red brick station, down the incline at the back, and marched up to a man at the bottom of the steps to the first platform. Lena knew he must be Sofie's contact, but he gave no indication of ever having seen her before. He glanced at their identity cards, smiled politely—a little deferentially, Lena thought—took their tickets, nodded and returned them. Then he took a suitcase in each hand and walked ahead of them up the stairs.

Lena had not been in a train station in years, and in many ways, nothing had changed in all that time. The train loomed in front of them, and the sounds and sights of the station poured over them, promising (if you ignored the men in uniform) a journey, new places, new experiences. Lena felt a longing almost past bearing for the days when trains actually fulfilled that promise.

Well, she thought, there would be a journey, wherever it led.

The man led the girls onto the first car, waited while they settled side by side on a red leather bench, lifted their bags up to the rack, mumbled "Pleasant journey" in German and departed. Moments later, the train creaked and groaned and they were off, travelling into the dark, early in the evening.

The train had to be dark. No lights to alert British planes. That meant blackout on the windows and little light inside the car. Lena's heart pounded as the train pulled out of the station. Her eyes strained to see in the dim light, her ears strained to hear the other passengers, few though they were. She could not get the gist of any conversations. She had felt eyes on them as they walked down the aisle, but no one spoke to them, and with no seats facing them, they were guaranteed a small measure of privacy.

Beside her, even though their bodies were not touching, she could feel Sofie's excitement. "We did it," Sofie hissed in her ear when they had been travelling for a few minutes. "We did it!"

"Shhh!" was all Lena had to say in reply. She gripped the armrest. The train had come to an abrupt halt. She broke her own vow of silence. "What's going on?" she whispered.

"Something on the track?" Sofie said back, her voice not quite a whisper.

And Lena remembered that trains had to move at a snail's pace, with a lookout on the front, watching for sabotage. Derailment and British guns threatened every train at every moment. Lena would have been glad of those threats to the enemy at any other time. Now she prayed for safety.

Then, in front of them, a light glimmered in the aisle. A lantern.

It stopped at the first set of seats, and Lena heard German voices. An officer—as he came closer, Lena could see his cap and the glint of medals on this chest—was working his way down the aisle, checking tickets and identity cards. Sofie saw him too and gripped Lena's arm. Hard.

"Let go," Lena hissed. "That hurts!" In the same moment, she realized that Sofie, the great German speaker, should be sitting on the aisle. It was too late to change places without attracting notice. And once Sofie had let go of Lena's arm, she seemed to have huddled herself over by the window. Lena poked her.

"Remember, you have to do the talking," she whispered, her voice sounding like a shout in her own ears in the dark.

Sofie straightened up a little bit.

At last the officer reached them, the metal on his uniform gleaming, his eyes in shadow. He hung the lantern from a hook on the luggage rack. "Tickets and identity cards, please," he said, but Lena was already holding them out, doing her best to paste a smile on her face. He stood, holding the papers in his hand, and looked down at them.

"Where are you going, two girls on your own?" he asked.

There was a pause in which Lena pinched Sofie's thigh under her coat. Sofie sat up straighter still and leaned across Lena just a bit, but she seemed to choke on her words when she spoke, and to Lena, her German accent sounded decidedly Dutch. "Uh, Rheine," she said. "To our *Oma* and *Opa*." At least the German and Dutch for *grandpa* and *grandma* were the same.

"Rheine," he repeated slowly, thoughtfully.

Lena's stomach churned. She was glad that it had been a long time since she ate.

He turned to the papers in his hand. First the tickets. They seemed to pass inspection. And they should. After all, they were real. Then the identity cards. Lena had been worried about those cards from the first. She had never seen a real

German identity card, but the forgeries just didn't look right to her. She could see where the photo had been attached, where the stamp had been copied over the edges. Maybe in the lantern light, though . . .

No. He opened the cards, gazed at them for a moment and smiled. "You girls will wait here," he said then. "I will return." And he unhooked the lantern and walked on to check the tickets of the next passengers. Ten minutes later, he was back, taking the seat on the other side of the aisle. "You'll be coming with me in Utrecht," he said.

Utrecht. That was where they were supposed to change trains, not much more than thirty kilometres south and a little east of Amsterdam.

Sofie put her head against the blacked-out window and started to cry.

Two hours later, the train came to a full stop, and the officer gestured them to their feet. Lena pulled the two bags down, handed one to Sofie and put her hand under Sofie's elbow, pulling her up. "Stop it, Sofie," she hissed fiercely. "What are we going to do?"

For the whole journey, Lena had been trying to think, but in all that time, not one useful thought had come to her. And her worry about her friend, as Sofie sobbed on and on, had turned to annoyance well over an hour ago. Now, as she walked down the dark aisle, sheer terror took over.

"They're going to kill us," Sofie said, crying all the harder. "I just know they are."

Lena's knees turned liquid for a moment. She actually swayed on her feet. What if Sofie was right? They probably wouldn't kill them exactly, at least not on the spot, but they could ship them off on another train, first to a camp in the Netherlands and then on to Germany. They might never come back. Lena swallowed hard. The officer was looking over his shoulder, and anger had overtaken his face. Weak knees or not, she had no choice but to take one step and then another, Sofie stumbling along behind.

When they reached the train exit, Lena paused and sensed more than saw the huge open space of the Utrecht station, almost entirely unlit. The voices of other passengers echoed eerily off the faraway walls and ceiling. She remembered coming here to visit cousins during a heatwave the summer she was twelve. How different life had been then!

The man marched them across the platform and knocked smartly on a wooden door with a small window in it. Moments later, the door opened and words were exchanged. Then he stepped back and gave Lena a small shove through the door. Lena felt Sofie's arm pull free from her hand. She looked back. The officer had pulled Sofie close to him. He took her chin in his fingers, and he was looking into her face and grinning. Sofie tried to pull away, but he laughed and leaned down and kissed her on the mouth. Then he said something in German that Lena didn't understand and sent Sofie stumbling into the room. He walked past them, knocked on a door at the far end of the room and disappeared through it.

Lena stared at Sofie. She had been kissed by the enemy. Sofie dropped her suitcase, grasped Lena's right arm in both of her hands and huddled halfway behind her.

"I'm going to be sick," she murmured.

This should not be happening, Lena thought, and for a moment she wanted nothing more than to slap the other girl, to slap her as hard as she could. It occurred to her that this was not the first time she had longed to slap her friend. This time, though, she had more reason. Instead, she ignored Sofie altogether, kept her head low and looked around as best she could.

The room was large, and it buzzed with activity. Many men and several women sat at half a dozen oversized wooden desks speaking on telephones, barking instructions, again all in German, and typing loudly. No one paid any attention to the two girls.

Sofie tugged at Lena's arm. Lena raised her head slightly and took a deep breath. "Please," she said in German, "my friend needs a toilet." The loud voices and the typing carried on just as before.

The door at the far end of the room opened and three men entered, one of them the smiling officer who had kissed Sofie moments before. Phones clattered onto receivers. Typing ceased. People froze.

"Well, well, well, what have we here?" said the largest of the men. His uniform showed his high rank, but even without it, he would have commanded attention. The other two men stood on either side and a little behind him, smirking. Lena's own stomach clutched at itself. Was she going to be sick too?

"We are going to Rheine, sir," she said, willing her voice to cross the expanse of the room.

"Ahh! They are going to Rheine," the man said, looking to each side as he spoke, informing the room. Everyone laughed obligingly. He turned back to Lena and Sofie. "First, that is a lie. You are not trying to take a train to Germany. Second, your papers are false. Do you think you can trump up false papers and just walk onto one of our trains?"

And Lena saw that he held their papers in his hand.

"I . . . No, sir," Lena said.

"Where are you really going?"

She looked at the ground. "Almelo," she whispered.

"Lena," Sofie said urgently in Dutch, "I'm going to be sick."

"Almelo," the man echoed. "Well, you don't have much to say for yourself, do you?" He thought for a moment. "But then you are young. You have much to learn."

Lena looked up and met his eyes. She didn't know why she looked at him, but she did. He looked back; his eyes locked with hers. There was something very scary in his face. Lena knew it. She could see it clear as day. This was a man who had done terrible things and would not hesitate to do more terrible things.

"You are a pretty little thing, aren't you?" he said. "And you got all dressed up to come see us today. Such a lovely little hat!"

Lena's hand flew to her head, and the man laughed. She had loved that hat, and now it was ruined. He might as well have trampled it into the mud.

"Bring them into my office," he said. And he turned and disappeared through the door.

The other two men stepped forward and grabbed an arm each. They shoved Lena and Sofie ahead of them. Lena looked around frantically as she stumbled forward, her arm twisted behind her. Was there no one here who would help them? But no one was looking anymore. Everyone had returned to work. Or, no, there was one man, way in the back, staring at her. She couldn't read his look, but it didn't scare her like the look the officer had given her.

"Ah," the big man said, looking up from a desk in the next room that would have dwarfed the desks outside. "Now we have a little privacy." Lena and Sofie stood side by side a metre or so in front of the desk. The two other officers stood behind them, one on either side of the door. Slowly, the man rose, walked around the desk and leaned against it, close to them. "I am willing to help you," he said, smiling. Lena looked up at him. She had never seen anyone look less helpful. "A train leaves the station early tomorrow. It will take you to Almelo." His voice was oily, nasty. Lena blinked. It was as if he was licking her with his voice. She took a tiny step back.

Something about what he had said seemed wrong. Everyone knew that the trains now travelled only in the dark. Surely a train would not depart first thing in the morning. It didn't make sense.

"You don't trust me, do you?" he said. "Here I am trying to help you, and you act as if I am hurting you." He closed his fingers around her wrist and tugged her close again. "Well, you are right that I am not offering you something for nothing. These gentlemen and I have rooms down the street. And you have many hours to pass before your train leaves. You will come with us, you two; you will come with us to our rooms to while away the time until morning. There," he said, releasing her, "is that too much to ask: a little company in exchange for a train trip all the way across the country?"

Lena's stomach heaved. He wanted them to sleep with him and the other men. On her arms and her back, Lena's skin tightened. Her thoughts tore around in her head, but she could find no escape, just deeper and deeper fear.

"Please," Sofie said, loudly now, no longer whispering in Lena's ear. "I'm sick." And she bent over and retched.

"Sir," Lena said, "is there a toilet? My friend is sick."

"A silly trick," he said. "There is a toilet back at our rooms. You can wait."

And Sofie vomited, her hands on her knees, her hair swinging into her face. They had had nothing to eat since their departure, so she was throwing up thin, clear liquid, but it splashed off the stone floor and onto the cuffs of the officer's pants.

"You little bitch!" the man shouted and raised his arm. Lena wrapped her arms around Sofie and pulled her backwards, out of his reach.

"She's really sick," she said. "She was throwing up before too. Please, can't you let us go?"

He lowered his arm, pulled a handkerchief from his pocket and wiped at his pants. "Get someone in here to clean that up," he said sharply, and instantly the room was abuzz with activity. The man who had taken the girls off the train opened the door and shouted into the other room. A woman appeared with a bucket of soapy water and knelt before the big man, sponging away at his shoes and the cuffs of his pants. Someone else came in with another bucket and began cleaning the whole floor. The phone rang, and the officer took the call, barking into the receiver and listening for a long moment. He put his hand over the mouthpiece. "All right, everyone out," he shouted.

Lena didn't need to hear anything more. Determination took her over. "Take your bag," she whispered, grabbing her own small case with one hand and Sofie's wrist with the other, and slipping out the door. Her back crawled. Any second a shout was going to stop her like a hook in a fish. But no shout came. Keeping herself straight and tall, she walked through the huge outer office and headed for the door that led back onto the platform. Dimly, she was aware that someone was walking with them, not far behind. She let go of Sofie's hand and reached for the doorknob. What if it was locked? But it was not. The man came through the door just behind them. It was the man who had looked at her so oddly (was it kindly?) from the far side of the room. On they walked, down the stairs, through the long tunnel under the tracks and straight out of the station. Footsteps followed them. A bench loomed. Lena dropped the bags, pushed Sofie into a sitting position and turned to face their new companion.

Darkness had settled in long ago, but there was a moon, and she could see enough to tell that he was a small man, short and slender, clean-shaven, though not within the last day or so, with dark hair that curled around his ears. He needs a trim, Lena thought, but then many German soldiers were looking a bit scruffy these days. His uniform was neat enough, but it had been mended here and there and was a bit stained. His jacket showed his low rank. An ordinary soldier, more or less, as expected from one so young. He didn't look more than twenty to Lena, but he was probably older. He shivered.

"Ladies," he said, "might I offer you my assistance?" He spoke in German and his teeth chattered violently, but Lena found that she could understand. She looked at him in sympathy. He had followed them outdoors in his shirtsleeves and his jacket. "Where were you going on the train?" he asked.

"Almelo," Lena said without thought.

Sofie glared up at her, but Lena found that she did not regret her honesty. Anyway, she had already announced their destination inside.

"Come with me," the man said.

Lena was slowly feeling the cold herself. At their feet, where it had been cleared of snow, the ground was covered in a thick layer of ice. Tree stumps cast squat shadows in the garden area behind them. As far as Lena could see, the street was deserted, except for one man who wandered by, looking more like a bundle of rags than a respectable citizen. And she was sure that the ghostly stores and restaurants that lined the other side of the street were abandoned. Nothing to sell; nothing to serve. Just like Amsterdam.

Occasional flakes of snow floated down out of the dark.

The young man looked at Lena for permission as he bent and picked up their bags. "Please," he said, "follow me."

There was nowhere else to go, nothing else to do.

Lena met Sofie's gaze but found no help there. Sofie was not crying anymore, but her eyes pleaded for rescue and she was shaking hard. Lena turned inward and was surprised at what she discovered. Her stomach, which had churned with fear just moments ago, had now settled down. She felt calm. Maybe this was a man they could trust.

Huddled together, Lena and Sofie shuffled after the German stranger, who carried their lives along with all their possessions. He led them right back into the station.

Lena pulled Sofie to a stop as they approached the entrance, and their leader stepped back to their side. "You're going to Almelo," he said. "The train leaves soon. If you are to be on it, you must board now. I can find you a place to hide. You must board now. I will be on the train as well. I go home to Germany. I will protect you."

"He's lying," Sofie whispered, but not so quietly that he wouldn't hear. "I know he is."

Lena shrugged off her words and kept her focus on him.

"Why would you protect us?" she asked, her voice as quiet and calm as she could make it. Two men pushed by the small group. At any moment someone might accost them. "We don't know you," she added, but desperation made her step forward anyway. They had to keep going. They couldn't just stand there. And even as she said the words to him, she knew somehow that he would not lie to them. He would help them and protect them if he could. It was right there in the way he looked at her.

Lena had no time to reflect on exactly what the look meant, what he might want in exchange for his assistance, why she felt calm before him when she squirmed before boys her own age. No time to reflect on anything but the need to get to a safe place. "That officer said the train to Almelo leaves in the morning," she went on, but of course the big man had lied. Once she and Sofie had set foot in his rooms, they would have been trapped there until the men tired of them, and after that, she could only guess at their fate.

Lena had to gather all her strength to walk back through the enormous doorway into the station. And Sofie seemed to have no strength at all. She clung to Lena with both hands.

Ordinarily, it would not have been difficult to feel anonymous and invisible in the huge echoing space of a train station, but she knew that she and Sofie were the only civilians, and they were certainly the only two young women. Even in the dark, she shrank against Sofie and took step after step, matching her pace to the young man's, keeping close. He led them back under the tracks to the far side of the station, where they climbed a different flight of stairs and emerged on a platform beside a massive train looming in the dim light. They were looking at a passenger car, its dark windows covered with blackout paper on the inside. The man turned right and led them past another passenger car and two freight cars before he slowed down beside a big wooden carriage.

"This is a cattle car," he said, reaching up and using all his strength to pull back the heavy door just far enough to admit a small body. "Here, let me help you up."

And Lena and Sofie submitted to being lifted bodily and shoved into the car. Something scratchy enveloped Lena, and she felt a surge of panic. "What is it? It's full. The car is full!"

"It's straw," he said. "Just straw. It will keep you warm and hidden." And the next thing she knew, he was in the car with them, burrowing into the straw. "You must take your things and crawl in deep. I will bring you food and blankets. I will make sure that no one hurts you. You will be safe, I promise."

"Why are you helping us?" Sofie said out of the darkness, speaking to the man for the first time. Her voice sounded thin and small. "Why would you help us?"

It was pitch dark in the car. And silent for a moment.

"I want you to be safe," he said at last. "I . . . I can't explain to you now. It is too difficult. But I want you to be safe."

For a moment, panic flooded Lena again. Please let his reason not have to do with sex, she said to herself—or to God. Another prayer: this one rather strange.

It would be bad enough to be noticed by a boy, any boy, but to be noticed by a German man? He might seem calm and kind, but even putting sex aside (which Lena was eager to do), that did not change what it meant for a Dutch girl to be noticed by a German in the real true world of occupied Holland. Dutch girls were not supposed to be noticed by Germans. Not in that place, at that time. It only led to trouble.

She sighed as she heard the man's feet hit the ground as he jumped from the car. "My name is Albert," he said, and the big door clanged shut.

And Sofie came to life. "What are we doing?" she whispered, her voice harsh. "He will have us killed. He will send men to rape us. He will rape us himself. He will abandon us." She reached out and felt around until she found Lena's arm. Then she grasped on tight.

"Hey," Lena said, "let go of me! Whose idea was it to take off on a train? And who kept us safe back there in the station when those men wanted to take us away? I wasn't the one moaning and puking."

"It was my puking that saved us," Sofie spat back. She was no longer whispering. "Without me, we'd be back in their rooms right now, and innocent though you pretend to be, you know what they would be doing with us."

Lena shuddered. "All right," she said, hoping that Sofie could hear the appeasement in her voice. "Throwing up wasn't such a dreadful thing. But after that, what would we have done without Albert's help?"

"Found a way to go home?" Sofie said. And she started, once again, to cry. Her hand had fallen from Lena's arm.

Home, Lena thought. Over and over Sofie had said that her home was a terrible place, that she wanted to get away, that she longed for adventure. Yet now she was snivelling for it. Doubt threatened. Lena thought of Bep and Piet and baby Nynke, and a knot of grief made it halfway up her throat before she managed to thrust it back down to her belly where it belonged.

She reached out and found Sofie's body huddled in the dark. Not sure about it, she put a hand on Sofie's back and let it rest there. Sofie was surprising her again and again. At home, she had always seemed so brave, so quick to laugh no matter how awful the circumstances. But in Amsterdam, the danger had never been real. Or real, but not immediate. Maybe Sofie hadn't known how bad it could be.

And I didn't know either, Lena thought. I would never have come if I'd known. She thought back to those sickening moments on the Hembrug, with the soldiers laughing at her and Margriet and taking their bicycle. She had thought that she was frightened then. Now she suspected that she had a great deal more to learn about fear.

Round and round went the thoughts inside her head,

but they didn't change the facts: she was shut up with a terror-stricken girl in a frigid, dark cattle car, part of a train run by the enemy, soon to head east into unknown territory.

Her head snapped up. She had got one part wrong.

"We're not locked in here," she said. "We can climb out and hide and . . . and find our way out of Utrecht. We'll walk home. Why not? You should see the trips Margriet takes!"

Sofie's sniffles stopped. She sat perfectly still. Well, Lena thought, she had put it out there. Let Sofie choose.

In that moment, the train platform came alive with German voices and stomping boots. The two girls clutched at each other. The area had been deserted when they came up.

"Have you checked the cars?" said a voice, almost right beside Lena's and Sofie's heads.

"Schultz and Biermann started at the other end. I'll do these three. Here, jump up with me," a deeper voice replied.

A grunt of frustration. "Can't get this door open. Hey, help me, will you?"

Lena gripped Sofie's neck and leaned to speak into her ear. "They're searching the cars. We've got to find our bags and dig right to the back." She felt Sofie nod just as the door to the next car opened with a loud creak.

"You take the far end, Rauch, and dig deep. I'll start here. Any hideaways in here, we'll flush them out like rats."

Lena's body went rigid. They know we're here, she thought. Of course they do.

The two girls were sitting almost on top of their bags, so only a moment passed before they were digging frantically in the straw, the noise masked by the men in the next car, who seemed to be enjoying their work. They laughed and joked with each other as they speared the hay over and over again, hoping to encounter flesh. At least, that was what Lena imagined from the sounds she heard.

"You two in there," a voice shouted. "You think this is a game? Put your bayonets to work and get on to the next car. We're due to leave. You hear me?"

It took Lena and Sofie a long moment to take in the word *bayonets* in German, but soon enough the meaning penetrated. They both stopped digging for a moment, only to start again, more frenzied than before. Lena had guessed pitchforks. Bayonets were worse.

The men were loudly bemoaning the lack of bodies in the straw when Lena and Sofie heard the door to their own car creak open. The men heard it too.

"Hey, we're taking care of it," one of them shouted, his feet hitting the platform as he spoke. "What do you think you're doing?"

"Come here. I want to tell you something," a smaller voice said. A familiar voice.

Another pair of boots hit the ground.

Lena and Sofie were at the back of the car now, backs against the cold wood, awaiting their fate. They couldn't hear the whispered conversation. They would never know exactly what deal was struck, but they did hear the heavy boots move on to the car on their other side, and they heard a body pull itself into their car.

Moments later, they leaned back, looking up into the face of the man who had come for them.

It was Albert. Together, Lena and Sofie let out their breath.

"I brought you two blankets and some food and water," Albert said. "And those men will leave you alone. Stay out of sight, though," he added, his voice a whisper now. "They don't know you're the girls from the station. I'll come when I can."

Lena's jaw didn't want to move, to speak, to seal the bargain, but she forced it, and her words squeaked when they came. "Thank you, sir," she said.

"It's Albert," he said. "And I don't know your name."

Lena stared into the dark. "I can't tell you that," she said. "You've been good to us, but you're a stranger. You're a man. And you're, you're . . . Well, even though you're helping us, you're . . ."

"I know," he said. "I'm the enemy." He was silent for a moment. "At least call me Albert," he said. "This train trip will last for two nights or more. You have to call me something."

"Albert," Lena said.

"Yes," he replied, "that sounds much better. Now what am I going to call you?"

But he was gone before she could make up her mind how to reply.

Lena took the bundle that Albert had left them and crawled through the straw to where Sofie huddled at the back of the car.

"It's all right," Lena said. "He brought us food and blankets. And water," she added. Sofie grabbed the bundle from her, and soon they were both wrapped in blankets and gnawing on the first food they had had since breakfast, and the first bread they had had in months.

They were still chewing when the train rumbled to life. With a small lurch, a screech of metal on metal and the strong smell of burning oil, they were on their way.

"To Almelo," Lena said.

"To Almelo," Sofie replied.

CHAPTER NINE

The sound of rapid fire woke them both. Lena and Sofie were wrapped around each other, inside coats inside blankets. Their teeth had chattered as they lay there trying to sleep. Lena was tired—more tired, she thought, than she had ever been. But how could she sleep on a train going to a place she had never been, to people she had never met, with men poised to kill her in front and behind?

After lying awake in the cold for what felt like hours, she had just been drifting off when the most terrible question occurred to her: What if that man was on the train? *They don't know you're the girls from the station,* Albert had said. What had he meant, exactly?

But men must always search the trains. It couldn't all be because of Lena and Sofie. After all, the officer hadn't sent anyone after them when they walked out of the station. A bit of vomit on his pant cuffs and he had lost interest. Hadn't he?

But he could be on the train. Why wouldn't he be?

Lena twisted away from Sofie and sat up, leaning against the wooden wall, her blanket tight around her. The train creaked and jolted and roared, and the dark seemed darker even than home, though Lena knew that could not be. She shook from cold and swayed with the motion of the train and thought and thought and thought.

She must have slept, though, because then came the guns. The sound brought her up from where she was lying again with Sofie. The two girls reared up together, blankets falling from their shoulders. The train had stopped, but it shook as if it had turned into a gun itself and was firing. It *was* firing, Lena realized. Anti-aircraft guns. The Tommies were shooting at them, and they were shooting back. The sounds and sensations tangled with each other as if the earth were shattering around them, and light brighter than day sliced through the gaps in the walls behind them, lit the girls and their surroundings for an instant and was gone, only to come again minutes later. The first time, Lena ducked instinctively. Then she realized that the lights were flares dropped by the planes, and that the pilots could not see inside the cars, gaps or no gaps.

They sat, silent, in the mayhem. It went on for hours or a moment. And it stopped. Darkness returned, and silence and stillness settled on the night. Sofie and Lena sat for long minutes tensed for the next flash of light, the next explosion, until without further words they settled back into the straw and into sleep. They hardly noticed when the train rumbled to life once again and began to creep forward through the night.

* * *

"Sleep is good, but food is better," said a voice.

Lena knocked her head on Sofie's elbow as she sat up abruptly.

"Hey, now! It's only me. Me and breakfast, that is!" Albert

had cleared the straw from around them without waking them, and he knelt, holding out a canvas sack.

Sofie was sitting up and rubbing her elbow. Lena stared at Albert. He had opened the door, entered the car, created a path to them, shoving aside mountains of straw, and they had slept on, oblivious. Through the gaps in the wooden walls, daylight striped the heaps of straw, turning it gold. The train was still. Her heart beating fast, Lena stood and put her eye against a knothole in the wood. She gasped at what she saw. It was something out of stories and years gone by: a snow-covered wood, trees growing close to the track, leafless branches glittering icy white in the sun. Beneath the trees was a world of wonder—no undergrowth, just white, unblemished snow and grey shadows dancing among the tree trunks. A few rows of rabbit or deer tracks added to the perfection.

She turned and looked at Albert and Sofie. Sofie was wolfing down a piece of bread, but Albert was watching Lena. "It's a field of stubble on the other side," he said. "We're stopped here until dark. Can't move in the day or the Brits will see us and shoot."

"They saw us in the dark," Sofie said through the bread in her mouth.

"In the day, we make a better target," Albert said. "Believe me." He tore off a piece of the loaf he held in his hand and held it out to Lena. "I have a bit of cheese too," he said.

Birds and fairylands forgotten, Lena dropped to her knees and reached for the bread. Albert handed her the cheese, and she took a bite of bread and cheese together.

She looked at Sofie and grinned. "Train travel is looking up," she said, taking care not to waste her mouthful by spraying food.

Sofie grinned back. "It's a feast," she said.

Albert looked back and forth between them. "You are an unusual pair, aren't you?" he said.

Sofie's eyes glittered.

Albert reached into his sack. "If bread and cheese has you in hysterics, what will an apple do?" he said, all innocence. "Or what will you do for an apple," he added, as if he had only just thought of it.

"A kiss," Sofie cried. "I'll give you a kiss for an apple." And she crawled forward on her knees, took Albert's face in her hands and kissed him right on the lips. She shuffled backwards, apple in hand.

Breathless, Albert turned his gaze on Lena. She saw that he held a second apple. "And you, nameless one? What will you give me for an apple?"

Lena fell back on her haunches, stunned by what had just happened. Why did Sofie have to behave like that? What had happened to the snivelling girl of the night before? And why did he let her kiss him? Even encourage it? It wasn't Sofie he gazed at . . .

"I can't kiss you, Albert. Keep your apple if you must," Lena said, her voice loud in the cold, straw-filled space. She took her last bite of bread and cheese, willing her mouth to produce enough moisture to choke it down.

"Oh, why are you so stuck up? Kiss him! He deserves it. You know he does. And you're the one he wants, not me!" Sofie said in Dutch, munching her apple while she spoke.

"I'm not kissing anyone, Sofie. And I don't know why you—" Lena couldn't speak anymore because she was fighting back tears, her back turned to them both, furious with herself, with her friend and with that man. She heard mumbling but didn't take in any words. Then she heard the door creak open. Boots hit the ground, and the door creak closed again. She kept her back turned, reached behind herself for her blanket, curled up and thought of sleep.

"He left the apple for you," Sofie said, her voice subdued.

Lena ignored her.

* * *

For a long time she lay there, awake but drifting. Nynke came to her, snug in her arms in the kitchen; Bep, her head resting on Lena's shoulder as they gazed at the baby together; Piet, trying to save the world; and Mother; Father too, and Margriet. Were they growing hungrier? Did any of them give a thought to Lena? Less than twenty-four hours had passed since her departure, but it seemed like so much longer. She thought about Sofie's impulsive gesture and told herself that it meant nothing. Why did it matter anyway? Could she be jealous? That seemed ridiculous. Frightened?

Sofie was brazen one moment and sick and whimpering the next. She couldn't be counted upon, not even to stay out of things. And men. Lena did not understand Sofie and men. It was as if Sofie knew something she didn't. But not just that. Try as she might, Lena could not solve the puzzle that was her friend.

Last, she thought about what scared her most. If that officer was on this train and he found them . . . they would not escape so easily again. She must talk with Sofie, tell her of the danger.

The thought of talking to Sofie brought that kiss back to mind. Disgust and fury held a brief battle inside Lena's heart.

Sofie's warning would have to wait. Lena pulled the blanket tighter, tucked her head down and willed herself to sleep.

It must have worked, because she became gradually aware of light and laughing voices. She opened her eyes and poked her head out to nothing but heaps of yellow straw. She listened. And dread flooded through her.

Sofie was speaking nearby in stilted German. Her voice loud and full. "You come from Worms? Do not people laugh when you tell them you are from Worms?"

"*Ja*, and what about some of your towns? All countries have towns with strange names." The responding voice was young, younger than Albert's, and at ease with itself.

"Not like that," Sofie said.

"Albert will have to answer to the captain for bringing a girl on board!" This voice was older, filled with authority, but humour too. It didn't sound as if the price Albert would have to pay would be too great. Laughing, the man added, "If the rest of us had known, we would have brought girls for ourselves as well."

"Have you forgotten why we're here?" said another voice, this one stern. "We are fighting a war. And your *girl* is the enemy."

Lena sat up in her nest of straw. This was what Albert had been protecting them from: all these men knowing there were girls on the train. In her mind she saw the officer again, heard his oily voice.

"I'm not Albert's girl. He's just helping us," Sofie said. She paused and silence fell. "I mean me," she finished lamely.

"What are you hiding in that car?" the last man, the stern one, said. "Move aside." And Lena heard the creaks and thuds of a heavy man swinging himself into the car. Moments later she crouched, her back against the wall, staring up into a broad, frowning face. "You'll come with me," he said. "Both of you." He leaned down and clamped rough fingers around her wrist, yanking her to her feet. The straw fell aside and Lena saw Sofie sitting in the doorway, dangling her legs, but looking back with her face caught in such a distorted expression—guilt and fear all mixed together—that Lena might have laughed . . . if she hadn't been afraid for their lives.

Albert fell in with them as they walked in the train's shadow, trying to keep up with the angry man. "What's going on here, Hans?" he said, with barely enough breath to get out the words. Wherever he had come from, he had come fast.

Hans neither turned his head nor spoke. And Albert did not fall back to walk with Lena and Sofie. Lena had no chance to ask him where Hans was taking them, and what might happen once they got there. She looked across the barren fields to her right and saw not a single dwelling, no church spire in the distance, not even a clutch of trees that could hide two frightened girls. She kept walking.

At last they reached the rear of the train. Lena, Sofie and Albert stood outside while Hans stepped up into the car. Lena looked sideways at Albert. Should she lean over and whisper her question? His feet shuffled in the dirt and his body was rigid.

She looked up. A row of windows overlooked them, no blackout in sight. Anyone could be watching. She straightened and turned her gaze to the ground.

"I'm sorry, Lena. I—" Sofie muttered.

"Shhh," Lena hissed back. "I think they're watching."

Lena heard, rather than saw, the door open and booted feet descend the steps. Did a pair of those feet belong to the officer? She waited until she could see the two sets of black boots lined up in front of them. Then she raised her head.

A man she had never seen before in her life looked back at her.

She started visibly, and the man's lip twitched in what looked like disgust. He was seeing the fear in her, not the relief.

He turned his attention to Albert.

Albert's face was white, and he could not keep the tremor out of his voice. "I . . . I saw them in Utrecht, sir. They're just Dutch girls. They . . . they're going to an aunt in Almelo. They're not traitors or . . . or Jews, sir."

On the last word he stopped, and his chin snapped up and he met the man's eyes for the first time.

He's afraid for his life, Lena thought, her own fear creeping back into her belly and down her arms and her legs. If we were Jews, they might well take him down into the fields and shoot him on the spot. Us too. Will they believe that we are not?

The door to the car the sergeant-major had come from stood open, and he seemed to have trouble keeping his eyes on the three young people in front of him. His face was drawn and his fingers would not stay still. At last he turned his gaze on the stern man, who stood at attention off to one side.

"I have more pressing concerns than how my men entertain themselves," he said. Now he looked at Albert and glanced at Lena and Sofie in turn. "I simply don't care about young men's urges." He looked more intently at Albert and the stern man. "I care about getting my train, cargo and all, back to my country, whether or not that country is in ruins. Now, all of you, get the hell out of here."

"Yes, sir," the stern man said smartly. Lena tried to hear anger and resentment in his voice, but all she heard was obedience. Perhaps he's saving his resentment for people who will give him more satisfaction, she thought. Like me, she added to herself and shivered.

He marched off, leaving Albert to escort his charges back to their makeshift home. As they were walking away, the sergeant-major said, loudly enough for all to hear, "We're going to hell anyway, girls or no girls." Lena looked back over her shoulder in time to see him shrug and step back up into the car.

Albert hustled them along, his usual warmth gone for the moment. "How did they find you?" he said. "Did they come into the car? Did they hurt you?"

"It was me," Sofie said quickly. "I heard them outside, and I slid the door open a crack and peeked." She paused. "I guess they saw me."

A young man lingered outside their car. Albert stopped two cars short. "You guess they saw you?"

"How could you do that?" Lena said. "You could have got us killed."

"Or worse," Albert said, as if to himself.

The young man was striding toward them, his arms swinging. He grinned at Albert. "Don't you think you're being a bit selfish, man?" he said.

"Selfish, Ulrich?"

"There's only one of you. Why do you need two of them, when the rest of us have none?"

A chill settled in Lena's gut. Did all men talk about women in this way?

* * *

Hours had passed since their journey to the end of the train. Albert had brought food to eat and warm water to drink. Then he had left them.

Now it was early afternoon, and Lena was in the car alone. She had arranged the straw so it made a cozy nest but let in stripes of light through two wide gaps in the wood. She was huddled, coat buttoned to her neck, hat pulled down over her forehead, sunshine on her face, trying to warm herself, and trying not to think about what Sofie had done. Sofie had gone off with that young man, Ulrich. And good riddance, Lena thought.

She heard a scrabbling outside and turned to see Albert hoist himself into view with one hand, his other hand behind his back. She stared at him. He came into the car and stood looking down at her for a moment. Then he gave a small smile and sank onto one knee. Lena shifted backwards, more deeply into the straw, and found herself contemplating a trio of tiny white flowers that hung gleaming from their stalks. He held them out to her as if they were jewels.

It seemed impossible. Flowers here. Now.

"Flowers? In February?" she breathed. "There's snow on the ground!"

"Snowdrops," he said.

She took them from him, holding them gently between her thumb and forefinger.

"They are so delicate," she breathed.

"Come," Albert said. "The woods are beautiful today. Let us go for a walk."

* * *

Lena knew she should not go for a walk in the woods. She should not spend time with Albert alone.

But when he asked her, in the midst of her joy over the

128

flowers, their shared experience of something so beautiful, she said, simply, "Yes."

The stubbly field stretched into the distance on the north side of the train, but the two of them slipped between two cars to the southern side, where the sun hit full on, using the leafless trees to cast delicate patterns on the snow, their branches perfectly still on the windless day. It was exquisite. Lena shivered despite the sun, and Albert went to wrap an arm around her. She flinched.

"No, Albert! Don't you understand? You mustn't touch me. It isn't right."

He slipped his heavy coat from his own shoulders and draped it over Lena's. It was as if he had passed his body's warmth to her. Her hands pulled the front of the coat together, tighter around her. If anyone saw, what would they think? No need to ask that question. The coat was a part of the man. His heat was on her. Was this a small taste of what it was like to be held by a man, to lie with his arms around her? Lena walked forward, her eyes half closed. To feel the whole length of his body . . . Her foot cracked through the icy surface of the snow, and she stumbled. What was she doing imagining such things in this man's coat and him right behind her, watching her?

Lena shrugged the coat off and held it out in her arms. "Thank you, Albert. I'm quite warm now," she said.

His teeth were chattering violently, and he took the coat without argument. "Come," he said. "The snow is less under the trees. I think there's a path. Walk with me."

They walked in silence for a while, picking their way. More than once, Albert put out a hand and grasped Lena's elbow to help her over a rough patch. Each time, she felt a small surge of flame lick through her body. Each time, she hoped that he did not notice the lengthening interval between when his fingers touched her and when she pulled away. In the back of her mind, she was reminding herself that it didn't matter what he saw. God saw all.

But the little flame was new, new and special. What could be wrong in a kind man's fingers on a girl's arm? And Lena let Albert's fingers lie on her for one beat of her heart, then two, then three, but no more.

The last time, he used his fingers to stop her in the snow. "Let us stand here a moment," he said. "It's such a pretty spot."

And it was. Lena looked up to see that they had come right through the wood. Snow-covered fields dotted with farmhouses stretched away from them. Lena gazed in wonder, looking from left to right and back again. A pair of birds, she didn't know what kind, flew high overhead. "There is no sign of war," she said. "No sign at all. The only sign of war here is"—and she paused—"you." She wished she had left that last thought unspoken. Somehow, the words sounded even more accusing in her stilted German.

The muscles in his cheeks tightened and damp rose up in his eyes, but he righted himself. "I am a sign of war, I suppose," he said, "but not in my real life. Not at home, where I belong. Do you know what I do when I am at home? I stick flowery patterns and stripes and curlicues on people's bedroom and living-room walls. I am a wallpaperer. Not a soldier. Just a man. I am twenty-nine years old, and I am alone. I have been away from home since I was twenty-four. I have no woman. No wife. No fiancée. I am not playing with you." He stopped and smiled. "I look at you, and I . . ."

And he stopped. His eyes were still damp and his face still taut. Lena could see that he meant each of his words, and she understood every one, German or no. She imagined him decorating a lady's bedroom with creamy wallpaper covered in sprays of yellow roses.

Albert's hand slipped into the pocket of the jacket under his coat and came out holding a small object. "Please accept this gift from me," he said, "even if I am the enemy."

He placed the object in Lena's palm. She had to give it back to him so she could pull off her embarrassing green mittens. Then he held them for her while she worked the little bag open and reached two fingers inside. She pulled out a tiny crystal bottle with a cork stopper. It held a few drops of golden liquid.

"It is a small thing," he said.

"Where did you get it?" Lena said as she slid the cork from the bottle and held it to her nose. Her nostrils flared. The scent was acidic close up, but she pulled back a bit and got a whiff of roses. She put the mouth of the bottle tight against the inside of her wrist and turned it on its side for a moment. Then she waved her arm in the air, to release the scent. "It is so beautiful. And the scent is lovely."

He hesitated, watching her. "Oh, I traded something for it," he said. "I wanted to have a gift for you."

Lena smiled up at him. *He looks at me, and he—He what? What did he see when he looked at her?* She found that she wanted to know. Desperately.

I will always remember this scent, she thought, holding her wrist to her nose again. She shivered, and her teeth chattered briefly. *Well, the setting was perfect, aside from the cold.*

"We must go back," Albert said. "You are shivering."

"Yes," Lena said. Then she looked right into his eyes. "Lena," she added. "My name is Lena."

* * *

Lena's beautiful wool coat with the velvet collar seemed thin and worn as she trudged through the snow at Albert's side. Her mittens were back on her hands, but her fingers would not grow warm, and she held her body tense in an effort to keep whatever warmth there was inside. It wouldn't work, she knew. And Albert might want to be a gentleman, but under his heavy coat was only a thin army shirt and jacket—no protection at all in a winter like this. Lena thought about the cattle car with its straw. Straw could hold heat in, but it could not create heat, not unless you lit it on fire.

Fire. Could they build a fire? Could they heat water? She imagined plunging her hands into hot water. She imagined gulping it, feeling a column of heat bury itself in her body. Surely in the daytime, they could build a little fire.

She turned to ask Albert, only to see him stopped, staring up at the sky.

And his hand was on her arm. "We must run," he shouted. "Planes." Not yet understanding what he meant—there were always planes—Lena broke into a run, looking up as she did so. And she saw planes. Planes heading straight for the train, straight for them.

She tore through the snow, stumbling as she tried to keep up. The last time she ran this fast, she had sprinted at her brother's side, clutching a few sticks of wood while a German voice shouted "Halt!" and German boots sounded on the pavement in pursuit. Now a German soldier held her arm and the planes they feared came from the west, not the east.

Here was the train. They crouched and darted between the cars. Albert lifted her and bundled her into the cattle car. "Make sure your friend is here. Close the door and stay inside, in case we must move suddenly," he said, his breath coming quickly, his mind already on his next task. "I must go. We must man the guns."

As he turned to go, Sofie emerged from the straw. "There you are," Albert said, relief in his voice. "Stay in the car, both of you. And close the door," he shouted as he ran.

Lena could hear many feet running on the strip of earth beside the track.

She knew that the train was armed, had felt the bedlam of shooting and being shot at the night before. Anti-aircraft guns— guns that could shoot at planes. Now she could hear the planes too. Sofie was blubbering again.

Moments ago I was cold, Lena thought. I wanted fire, hot water. And moments before that, I was transported by a bit of glass and a sweet scent. Terror does not mix with cold. Or with romance, come to that.

Then all such thoughts left her as terror took a deeper hold.

The plane was shooting at them. It was broad daylight, a sunny day, and the plane was shooting at them. They were in a train. A great big train that sat still along a stretch of track. And the plane was shooting at them. The sound was worse than it had been the night before. It tore through Lena's skull; it wrapped itself around her heart, it squeezed her lungs.

"You're hurting me," gasped Sofie through her snotty tears. And Lena looked down to find her hand digging into Sofie's arm so deeply that the first segment of her fingers was all but invisible. She released her hold.

And as she did so, she heard a different sound, deeper, a sound that entered the body through the flesh. The train shook violently, and both girls screamed. They had been hit. Metal tore, wood splintered—at least that was what it sounded like to Lena. She reared her head, but it wasn't their car. Not yet.

It would be their car next. Why not? She could feel the anti-aircraft guns on the train shooting back, the tremor each time a gun was fired, but the answering shots kept coming. Lena's hands were on the door and she was wrenching it open.

"Well, are you coming, or are you going to stay here to get blown up?"

"But Albert said . . ."

"I don't care what he said. We could be struck at any moment." And she bent her knees and jumped. It was a long way down with no platform, and the ground was frozen solid, hard as concrete. She landed on her hip instead of her feet, and rolled over several times before she could stop herself. Above her, Sofie crouched in the doorway. Farther up, Lena saw the grey underside of the low-flying plane; she even saw the gun aiming out the bottom at the front. Sofie jumped, and together they dashed through the rotting stubble to a row of low brush lining the field. Together they dove into the brush, wiggled forward and lay there, faces to the ground, long after the plane had stopped shooting, its whining roar fading to nothing and birdsong taking its place.

The sun was low in the sky when they crept from the field, shivering. Cold had retreated in the face of death, but now, as night came on, it loomed as the worse enemy. Lena and Sofie stood looking up at the door to their car. It was open, as they had left it, but it was far above them. "I'll boost you," Lena said, "and then you can pull me up."

"I . . . I don't know if I can," Sofie said. "I'm so tired, so cold and so hungry. We just spent the afternoon hiding from the good guys," she added.

"I know," Lena said. "It's weird."

"What are you doing?" Albert's voice came from behind them. "I told you to stay in the car."

"We could have been blown up," Lena said. "It was safer out."

Albert was silent. Then he said, "Listen, it's unlikely more planes will come now. We're going to make a fire while it's still light. We'll heat some water and some food. Warm ourselves."

Soon there were groups of soldiers all the way along the train, bunched around tiny fires, heating pots of water and soup. The fires could be out in a moment, dowsed if need be. And Lena had never been gladder of a bit of warmth in her life. Since Sofie had revealed their presence earlier, there was no need to hide now, and Sofie was at her chatty best. The other young man, Uli, joined them, and he and Sofie flirted with each other as if they would never have another chance. As the light grew dim, they slipped away from the fire and spread a blanket on the ground away from everyone. Albert and Lena gazed after them.

"She is not worried about kissing the enemy," Albert said.

"No," Lena said. "What could she be thinking?"

"Maybe she just wants a bit of joy in a hard day, a bit of fun."

"That kind of fun costs a lot," Lena said, but her eyes locked with Albert's, and her mind snapped back to Sofie's lips on his. What had that felt like? she wondered, holding her wrist up to her mouth, feeling her own warm pulse with her lips and catching the faint scent of roses.

CHAPTER TEN

"I will help you find the people you are seeking," Albert said later on, as the day wound down and soldiers began to douse their fires and slip away into the cars.

Lena knew they had passed through cities: Amersfoort, Apeldoorn, Deventer. All were between Utrecht and Almelo, and all were on the route straight east to Germany. The train travelled only at night and trundled slowly through country and city alike, stopping only to fix damage to the track. By morning they would reach Almelo, and there the train would stop.

"You have to stay with the train," Lena said.

"We will spend two days in Almelo. Maybe more. We will take on cattle and other supplies that will travel east with us."

"Oh," Lena said, thinking of the people starving in the west while good Dutch food moved east.

Albert must have been thinking too, for he said nothing more.

Their fire had burned down to ash. Albert poured the remains of his tea over the ashes and poked at them with a stick. Lena rose to her feet and waited. She looked to where Sofie and Uli twined around each other on their blanket, but she could see little more than shadows. Albert looked too and gave a small smile.

What if she went and got a blanket of her own and invited Albert with her into the dark? He would not hesitate, she knew. The notion warmed her more than tea or fire could. She thought back to Albert's coat around her body. It was a towering sin to imagine Albert's body in place of that coat. Yet she did. She was, right that second. She imagined his hands on her bare skin. The imagining was almost past bearing, as if her skin would rise up in response.

Albert's hand on her arm made her jump and let out a small scream. His touch prickled all the way up her arms, all over her body.

"Lost in your thoughts?" he said, smiling.

She shook her head fiercely and forced herself to smile back.

Together they walked to the car. Lena was silent as Albert boosted her up and followed her inside. She cleared a path to the back, then turned and spoke again at last, bringing the topic back to their imminent arrival in Almelo. "Well, we will be all right on our own. We can find the way."

"I would like to help you," Albert said, the muscles in his neck tightening under his collar.

Lena knelt and began arranging her blankets for sleep. She reached out a pair of fingers and touched the snowdrops where they lay on top of her bag, wilted but shining white in the dark. How wonderful it would be to accept Albert's help. She gritted her teeth. If it weren't for this—she pushed the word *damned* out of her mind—terrible war . . .

"I know, Albert. You are kind," Lena said, gazing up at him over her shoulder. "I . . . I need to sleep."

His hand came out of the dark and brushed a strand of

hair from her forehead. She remained still while he stood for a moment, waiting until he turned and left the car. At last, Lena pulled the blankets around herself, curled up in the straw and gradually drifted off.

* * *

It was cold in the straw. Lena spun up out of a light sleep, shivering. She turned and twisted, shoving straw and a blanket under her legs and her back. She had ended up right on the icy floor. She thought for a moment about her warm bed, with Margriet's warm length—or Bep's short one—next to her. Her teeth clanked together involuntarily.

The straw near the door rustled. She sat up.

"Lena. Are you there?" It was Albert. What was he doing in the car? Was he coming to her? If he did, what would she do? Lena felt a rush of excitement blended with dread. Behind her, she heard more rustling and a small moan.

"Sofie?" she whispered. "Sofie?"

"It's all right, Lena." That was Albert, closer now.

She heard Uli's voice, a murmur. And Sofie's giggle.

A hand touched her shoulder and she started. "Ah, here you are," Albert's voice said. "Are you all right? I brought you an extra blanket."

Lena widened her eyes into the pitch black, but she saw nothing. A bundle of thick, rough wool was thrust into her hands. She gulped but held her silence.

"I won't go far," he said. "I want to keep an eye . . ."

Even though she didn't want to think about it, Lena knew what he meant, *who* he meant. He wanted to make sure that Uli didn't . . . that he didn't . . . For a moment, Lena let herself imagine what Sofie was doing with that man, then she pushed the thought away. It was not possible they would be together like that. Not all night! Not right next to her!

She jumped as Albert's hand touched her arm, alarmed at the heat it sent right through her.

"There you are!" he said again. "I'll be nearby. You sleep now."

And despite the proximity of Sofie's and Uli's entwined bodies, despite her own desire for the man watching over her from so near, Lena eventually did sleep. She awoke several times more in the darkness, but the train was creeping along again, with all its familiar sound and motion, and it lulled her back to sleep, wrapped in the extra blanket. She heard no more moans or giggles. No guns shot at them that night. Aside from the cold, nothing disturbed her slumber, not even dreams—which she had feared—until the train rattled and banged to a stop, long, long before it should.

* * *

The train had stopped many times during its two-night journey. Men rode on the front of it, checking for damage to the rails. By the fires the previous afternoon, Uli had gone on and on about the Dutch Resistance and what a mess they made of the tracks. He hadn't been blaming them exactly, but he hadn't been honouring them either. Lena had had to bite her tongue to keep from blurting out, "Well, you *are* the enemy, aren't you? And *your* trains are filled with *our* food."

This time, though, they were so close. And this time, the damage was very bad, as Albert and Uli reported when they returned from investigating. It would take the rest of the night to mend, and they could not travel by day.

A part of Lena felt elated at the offer of another day with the train, another day before they had to face whatever awaited them in Almelo, another day with Albert. The two men went off to help with the daunting task of mending the rails, and Sofie and Lena curled up together, bundled against the cold. As they lay there—whispering one minute, silent the next—Sofie's breathing deepened and lengthened into sleep, and Lena found herself reliving each moment she and Albert had spent together. She held her wrist to her nose and inhaled, only the faintest hint of roses now. She imagined herself a German wallpaperer's wife. It did not feel like so dreadful a fate: a nice little house in a small town; children—two girls, she thought, and a boy . . .

Someone was grabbing her, shaking her. "What?" Lena shouted. "Leave me alone!" She rose to her knees and fought free of the hands that held her arms.

"Hey! Watch it!" Sofie shouted right back. "It's just me, you idiot. You're sleeping the day away. And you're going to miss breakfast."

Lena had to apologize after that, and listen to a good bit of teasing. What dream had she been so keen on that she would fight to stay asleep?

Albert and Uli smiled as they passed out cups of something hot, along with old bread and hunks of cheese. The four were gathered around a small fire, just as they had been the night before, though the countryside had changed. The fields of stubble were gone, and the landscape was more heavily treed and not nearly so flat.

Lena sipped her watery drink and gazed at the others. Clearly they were happy about the delay. The tracks were mended already; the train would leave again as soon as night fell. She watched Albert as he talked and laughed with Uli and Sofie.

She looked at his face, the bones that structured his rounded and stubbled jaw, his broad forehead. She wanted to reach out and smooth his unruly hair back behind his ears. He looked at her and she snatched her eyes away, cheeks burning.

It was a long day.

"Will you walk with me again?" Albert said, the moment she put down her empty cup. "A stroll in the forest?"

Sofie and Uli were already gone, only they knew where. Lena had the feeling that if she walked with Albert, if she went with him anywhere, there would be no resisting him. "No," she said. "No, I want to be alone."

Hurt wrinkled his brow, and he lowered his eyes to the ground.

"I'm sorry, Albert," she said. "I'm not like Sofie. I can't."

He looked up, brow cleared, hope shining from his eyes. "I'm not asking you to be like Sofie," he said. "Just walk with me."

"No," she said again. "I can't."

"All right," he said at last, and walked away.

Lena sat hunched over by the fire, shivering. She lowered her head to her knees, smelling smoke and listening to the voices of the men gathered around their own nearby fires, the squeak of their boots in the snow. She heard birds too, and tree branches brushing each other in the wind.

Eventually, an idea came to her. Salvation of a sort. In the bottom of her small suitcase, the first act of her packing, were two tattered paperbacks. It was quick work fetching them both, though first she had to ask a soldier for a boost up. She had to move the tiny flowers to get into her bag, so she placed them, thoroughly wilted now, between the pages of one of the books. She wrapped a blanket around herself and jumped back down onto the snow.

Lena climbed the bank back up to the fires and made for a large tree at the edge of the wood. Looking back, she saw Albert standing two cars away, watching her. She hunkered down and swept away the snow at the foot of the tree, clearing a spot for herself. There, she would wait. She would wait and read.

She knew both books by heart, and it was a good thing, because few words found purchase that day. She turned the pages regularly and resisted too many visits to the flowers pressed in the back. And in this way, the hours passed. Sofie brought her food at one point, but Lena barely spoke to her, though she did eat the food—wolfed it down, in fact. Lena was conscious of morning turning to afternoon, of the shadows lengthening. It may be that she dozed at one point later on, because she didn't see Albert approach.

He knelt beside her and held out his hand. "Come," he said. "We will eat and then we will go."

Blinking, she allowed him to grasp her hand in his. He rose and pulled her gently to her feet. But he did not lead her toward the train. Instead, he stood over her, his body shielding her from others' view. With his free hand he held her chin softly, so softly, and tilted her face upward. She saw him bend toward her, and instinct made her close her eyes and soften her lips.

It was the briefest of kisses, just his lips against hers—against her upper lip, really—a gentle pressure, which she returned, her own lips kissing his lower one. And then it was done. The warmth receded. She opened her eyes, and he was smiling down at her.

"You kissed me back," he said.

And Lena could not deny it. She nodded, smiling.

The gathering together, the warmth of another fire, the food, the talk—all of it happened in a blur for Lena. Albert sat close to her, but he didn't try to put his arm around her. He hardly spoke through the meal.

As soon as they were done eating, Sofie and Uli disappeared into the car. Apparently they weren't going to be bothered with the great outdoors this evening. Lena watched them go and then met Albert's eyes.

"I know," he said under his breath. "You're not going to do that. But the train is going to leave soon, and we have to get inside." He rose and got to work putting out the fire.

Lena got up and gathered her blanket and her books. She let Albert boost her into the car, ignoring Sofie and Uli's rustlings. Perhaps a goodnight kiss would be all right, she thought. Just one. Just one on her last night.

At the back of the car, she knelt to put the books into her bag. If she was going to kiss him, she had to make sure it stopped there. Gathering her inner strength, she leaned her forehead against the wall for a moment and let her weight fall back onto her haunches. She was about to turn back to Albert when her gaze fell on a patch of wood right at eye level. Even in the dim light, she could see that something was written there. She bent closer.

Letters and numbers were carved into the wood. Lena reached out and touched them with her fingers. They spelled out a name: *Rachel.* And a life: *June 12–Sept 17, 1943. RIP.*

Something let go inside Lena as what she was seeing sank in. Nausea swept up her throat. The trains had been used for a terrible purpose. She knew that, or at least she had heard. But on this journey, she had not given it a moment's thought. Not for one second had it occurred to her that what was for her an adventure was for thousands of others a death march, that this very car might have held such passengers. Now she knew. Right here, where she knelt contemplating a kiss, a baby had died. And her mother had scratched her short life into the wall.

"Lena," Albert said from behind her, "what are you doing?"

She turned, fierce all of sudden, protective of a dead baby she had never met. "Look," she said. "Look at that."

Albert knelt beside her and looked. He looked for a long, long time.

"I'm sorry," he breathed. If his mouth had not been next to her ear, she would not have heard. His next words were even quieter. "I worked on those trains." He paused. "This train."

She thought she must have heard wrong. Or she tried to think so.

For many moments, both of them stayed where they were and said nothing. Then Lena pushed into the straw beside her and emerged holding the three snowdrops that Albert had given her, flattened by their hours between pages. She did not look at him as she placed them on the floor beneath Rachel's epitaph.

The man and the girl knelt side by side some more. He put his hand on her arm at one point, but she drew back. He took his hand away.

The light faded entirely. At last, Albert spoke. "I must tell you a story," he said. "I have no right to, but I think I must."

Lena remained as she was, head bowed.

"I had to force people into the cars," he said.

Lena flinched.

"No, I'm not going to tell . . . I'm not . . ." He paused. "And one time, a man stopped in front of me. Others flowed around him, but he stopped. He was old. He wore a grey wool cap, and he was clean-shaven. His skin hung loose on his face. He was too close to me for the rifle butt to be of any use. I would have had to use my hands or my voice to get him moving. I did neither. I couldn't. I found myself staring straight into his eyes.

"'What you are doing is wrong,' the man said. 'You are a person. I am too. And so are they.' He gestured with his arm, all around to the hundreds of men, women and children already on the train and still on the ground. 'Every one.' And he touched my arm. Then he turned away and disappeared into the car. I never saw him after that.

"And that was the last train."

Silence.

In her imagination, Lena stood next to Albert, a crowd in front of them, a crowd of desperate people, and in the midst of that crowd, she saw Sarah. Sarah was looking right at her, reaching for her. And Lena did nothing, nothing at all.

She started, eyes wide open in the dark. Albert was finished, she realized. His story was over. She had heard it, and she would think about it. Right now, though, the man next to her had turned into the enemy. And she was her own enemy too.

"Please, Albert, leave me," she said. She still didn't look at him. She did not want to see his face, even its pale shape in the dark, nor did she want to feel the tears on her own. Once he was gone, she reached down and felt along the ground until she found the tiny flowers. She pulled them toward her, stood, bent over and positioned them carefully. Then she spent long moments grinding them under her heel.

* * *

Sometime later, the train creaked and groaned and roared into motion. Later still, Sofie giggled and Lena started back into her-

146

self. She listened to whispers, words she could not hear, rustling in the straw. Had Uli also sent people to their deaths?

Almost bodily, Lena shoved Albert's story out of her mind and the feelings it stirred in her out of her heart. She had practical things to think about now.

She and Sofie could not arrive in this unknown town seeking the assistance of strangers with two German soldiers as escorts. It was easy to predict their reception. And what she had seen and heard meant she could no longer have anything to do with Albert anyway. These men had done bad things. They were part of something evil.

Now Albert's sweet words to her, his lips pressed against hers, seemed more sinister than romantic. She had received her first kiss from a murderer. Received it and thrilled to it. No, Albert could not be part of her future. And she could not be part of his.

Sofie's voice rose, loud and desperate in the quiet. "I will miss you so, Uli," she cried. "How long will you stay, do you think?"

"Just two days," Uli said. "But we must make the most of them!"

Sofie had had no trouble at all with her German accent or vocabulary since she met Uli. The language flowed from her as if it were her birthright. Lena's bruised heart sank. "Sofie, you can't see each other in Almelo," she said in Dutch, sending her voice crashing through the car, breaking into their conversation. "What will your relatives think? You know what they'll say. 'Lover of Germans,' they'll call you. 'Mof lover.' They'll run us out of town."

Sofie scrambled out of the straw, brushing up against Lena. She heard Uli breathing behind Sofie in the darkness. "Well, I

147

don't exactly have relatives there. Just this family, these friends of my uncle's—at least I think that was it. We were passing through once, and they said we should let them know if we were ever back this way."

Lena sank back against the wall. She never should have placed all her faith in Sofie's vague assertions, in Sofie's shoddy fake papers, in Sofie's on-again, off-again courage—or in a German soldier, come to that. But why hadn't she pressed her friend for details? Sofie would have told her the truth long ago if she had just asked.

"I suppose the last time you saw them was before the war," Lena said.

"The only time. Well, yes. Not much, though. Maybe in '38."

"Seven years and a war. Five years, almost, of occupation. And you think these people will welcome us with open arms?"

"Well, it's better than what we left behind," Sofie said fiercely. "Even on this train, even in the freezing cold, with our own Allies firing at us, I've been happier and better fed than at home with my nearest and dearest and soup made from potato peels and sugar beets. And so have you."

Lena knew that her glare was lost on Sofie in the dark, but she had no words. And Uli moved in then, because next thing, Sofie was gone from the conversation and giggling once again in his arms.

Soon, Sofie and Uli retreated into the straw. The muffled sounds they made grated on Lena. She tensed at each moan and rustle, pulling a blanket tight around herself. She cringed when longing washed through her body, battling with her pain, her annoyance and her new knowledge. It made her feel ill, all of it.

She reached her hand out and placed it against the cold wooden wall, trying to imagine a mother crouched right there

148

and cradling a dead baby. She tried to imagine Albert outside the car brandishing a rifle. She imagined the gun sinking to his side as he watched that brave man climb aboard the train that would carry him to his death. She imagined Sarah, huddled with the rest of her family, or worse, without them, in that same car. Tears of frustration and anger squeezed from her eyes. She couldn't understand any of it. Not one bit. She could not change Albert into the man who had done what he had done. But he *was* that man. By forcing them onto the trains, he had helped kill innocent people—hundreds and hundreds of them, probably.

And she could not free herself of her own guilt. She had abandoned Sarah to the very fate that Piet and Albert had described to her.

She could not grasp Albert's guilt, but she could feel sick at the memory of her longing for his touch, and of the touch itself. She wished that she had a basin of water, scalding hot, so she could scrub her skin raw. Tomorrow she would take the tiny bottle of cologne and throw it far, far away. She would cleanse herself.

* * *

It took longer than ever to fall asleep that night. And when the train rattled to a stop long before daylight, Lena could almost have wept. Without looking outside, she knew they had not reached their destination.

"The damage is quite bad," Albert said to all of them minutes later when he swung himself into the car. "It will take some time to fix—maybe an hour, maybe more. And we are right outside Almelo. Less than an hour's walk. Perhaps this is the time to go. We can slip away in the dark. Uli and I can rejoin the train as it arrives in the station, departure and arrival unnoticed. What do you think?"

Lena was glad that in the darkness she did not have to meet his eyes.

She did not want to walk off into the dark with two German soldiers, but she could not bear the thought of waiting one more hour, of being stuck in that car for another minute, and she could not imagine herself and Sofie striking out through the countryside in almost pitch dark all on their own. Besides, they couldn't exactly beat the men off with sticks.

"Perhaps," she said.

Albert's relief was obvious in his voice. "I have been meaning to give you these," he said. "Where's your hand?"

Lena reached toward him and felt him place two stiff pieces of paper into her palm. "Our identity cards," she said, the shock like ice in her belly. "How did you get them?"

"It was not too difficult," he said. "They were just sitting on the corner of his desk."

Lena grasped the cards, imagining his bravery in stealing them for her and Sofie. Before he even knew them. The ice melted.

"I knew you might need them," he added.

Lena lifted the top card to her face and peered at it. Aubrey Schulze. It was hard to imagine that it would be any use. It could well turn out to be dangerous. Still, she tucked it away. "Thank you, Albert," she said. She would give Sofie hers at the first opportunity.

It was time to prepare to leave the train.

It was not going to be easy walking through open country in cracked shoes full of holes, but they would have to manage. At least Lena's shoes fitted her feet—her father had come up with shoes for all of them the previous winter, from one of his mysterious sources—but the soles were almost worn through, and the toe on the right shoe had peeled back. Long walks on the streets of Amsterdam had been difficult enough, but here the snow presented a far greater challenge.

Albert and Uli spoke together quietly when Uli and Sofie emerged blinking and dishevelled from the straw. Lena did not want to meet Sofie's eyes, but Sofie came right to her and pulled her away from the men. "I love him, Lena, and he loves me," she said. Even in the dark, her eyes peered out, large and red.

"You hardly know him," Lena said. "And he—"

Sofie broke in. "I *do* know him. Just as you know Albert, even though you won't let him touch you." She paused. "There's a lot of comfort in letting a man touch you, Lena. A man who cares about you."

"You don't know these men, Sofie," Lena whispered, shocked at how harsh her voice was. "They . . . they are not good. You don't know what they've done."

A small voice in Lena's mind tried to remind her how unaware she herself had been before she saw the engraving on the wall and heard Albert's story, but she silenced it. Sofie should know better. That was all.

"They *are* good men, Lena. You know they are. They just happen to be on the wrong side. They can't help it!"

Lena opened her mouth to tell her, but she could not form the words. She could not share Rachel's death or Albert's story about the brave man, nor did she wish to bring Sarah back into her mind's eye. Instead, she said, "You were raised as I was. How can you play with your fate like that? Ignore everything that you were taught?"

"Oh, Lena, just for one minute think about who was doing the teaching. Are you so eager to follow your father's rules? I'm not playing with my fate. I am trying to survive, to snatch a little bit of hope, of warmth, right here in hell. We don't need to wait for hell, Lena. It is all around us. And if I can find a bit of love here . . . well, then, I'm going to grab hold and not let go."

"Ladies." It was Uli. "Are you arguing? Don't be angry with her, Lena. She needs you. Now, Albert and I have talked, and we are going to walk you to the town. It is a good distance and it is dark, and there may be men about. We will walk with you and protect you, and when we come to town, you will go on without us."

The sun was not quite up in the east and only a bit of light had managed to dribble over the horizon when they closed the cattle-car door for the last time. Lena hoped and prayed that the next occupants would not be prisoners, that no more words would need to be scratched into the wood, no more misery contained by the wooden walls. No. Surely the next occupants would be cattle. She drew a breath of relief. Of course they would. Uli and Albert were to help load the train with cattle right here in Almelo.

With her hand above her on the wooden door, she said a few silent words of prayer for Rachel and her mother. She breathed deep and added a prayer for Sarah.

She gave Albert a curt nod, and they set off. Nothing had changed, she told herself. She was letting the men guide them because she had no choice, but it did not mean that she accepted what they had done. She thought of the snowdrops ground under her heel and wished that Albert had seen them. Then he would know.

The two girls had managed to bundle the blankets into their satchels along with their few clothes. Albert carried Lena's, and Uli carried Sofie's. They slipped between the cars to walk on the side of the train away from the doors. The sergeant might not care about the two stowaways skulking off into town, but he would not take kindly to two of his men accompanying them.

The train had stopped amid fields and farmhouses, which were dreary in the early light and the harsh cold. They walked alongside the train until they were close to the front, and then they veered off across a field. The track joined another one just ahead and curved to the right, so they could rejoin it almost immediately and be out of sight of the train.

Crossing the open space was exhausting; Lena broke through the icy surface with every step and had to bite her lip to keep from crying out in frustration. After a short distance, Albert noticed and adapted his stride so she could use his footprints. But that was awkward: snow found its way inside her shoes, and accepting Albert's assistance galled her at every step. Sofie whined, even though Uli was practically carrying her. They were going to a town where they knew no one, except maybe a certain friend of an uncle. And their only protection was from enemy soldiers whose company would soon become a curse rather than a blessing.

Baby Nynke swam into Lena's mind, gazing up at her from a bundle of blankets in her arms. Bep joined the baby, looking at her with big, hungry, accusing eyes. Could it only be three days since Lena had slid her suitcase out from under the bed and slipped out the door? Three days since the soldier had asked to see their identity cards on the train? The journey might have been short in time, but it was long in every other way. Lena tried to imagine a package of food making its way back along the route they had come. Such a thing could not be possible.

Had she left her family to starve?

"Are you stuck?"

She looked up. Albert was standing just ahead, on the other side of the long heap of snow that lined the train track. She looked down at her feet. She must have stopped walking, she supposed.

"No," she called. "I'm all right." And she scrambled onward and accepted Albert's hand to pull her over that last bit of snow. It was a relief to feel a wooden tie, solid beneath her feet. She would worry about packages of food later; for now, she let her hungry family slide from her thoughts.

The open track stretched straight before them. At first, they saw no sign of human occupation except for the track itself and a few farmhouses far off on both sides. Uli kept his arm around Sofie, and she leaned into him, even as she took the awkward steps that the spacing of the railway ties required.

Lena stayed a few paces behind, her back stiff. Albert matched his steps to hers, but at least he made no attempt to touch her.

"It might be nice to walk like that," he said once, his eyes on the couple in front of them.

Lena had no answer for him.

He fell silent again. After about ten minutes, Lena made out a church spire and a few buildings. Was that Almelo? It didn't look big enough.

No, Albert informed her without her having to ask the question, that was Wierden. But Almelo was not far beyond.

"Well, we can't walk right through the centre of town with two soldiers," Lena said, aware of her bitter tone.

"We're not leaving you here," Uli said, turning his head to look back at her. "It's still a long way. Look, we can skirt the town."

Paces ahead, a country road crossed the tracks at an angle. If they took the road off to the right, it would bypass Wierden, and then Almelo would be straight ahead, Uli assured them. "And it's early yet," he went on. "No one's about."

No guarantee of that, Lena knew, but Sofie clung to Uli so tightly and both Albert and Uli seemed so determined that Lena found herself bending to their will.

They turned onto the road.

It was a relief to be off the track. The road had been used often enough since the last snowfall that walking was easy, and any farmhouses were set well back, so Lena felt reasonably confident that no one would see them in the early morning light.

After fifteen minutes on that road, though, they reached a crossroads. They would turn left and follow a wider road, which Lena could see immediately would just barely skirt Wierden on its way to the much larger Almelo, still out of sight in the distance.

The time had come to take their bags and part.

Uli and Sofie had stopped, and Uli was speaking urgently when Lena and Albert came up to them.

"It is a bar where the German officers go," he was saying. "One of the men told me that we could meet you there. You can come tonight. It will be easy for you to come in unseen. We will be together one more time!"

Sofie swung around and looked at Lena. "You hear what he says? One more time. They have done so much for us."

Lena stared back. She didn't know what expression her face wore, only that she felt a weight on her belly of anger and fear. It had been over, this strange and unsettling association between two Dutch girls and two German men. The men were about to take their own path to rejoin the train. Sofie would put her bad behaviour behind her. She and Lena would walk forward together. And now, these men had connived another way to get at them, to bring them danger, to keep Sofie hooked on her German soldier.

"We don't even know where we're going to sleep tonight. How can we . . . ?"

"Let us say that we will try, Lena. Please!"

"That is all you can do, either of you. Do say that you will try." That was Albert, his voice pleading.

Uli squeezed Sofie's waist. "Think what it would be to sit around a table instead of crouching in a cattle car or by the tracks, to sip Schnaps or beer instead of stale water. It will be a real date!" He grinned down into Sofie's face.

Albert put his hand on Lena's wrist and pulled her aside. "I know what you are thinking," he said. "I saw the flowers, crushed. I thought of that baby, Rachel, all night. How many babies did I send to their deaths? I cannot know. I was following orders—"

Lena wrested her arm free.

"I know I am responsible still. I feel responsible. That is why I told you the story of that man. You are the first I've told."

Lena looked and looked into his eyes. No matter how deep her gaze, how steady his, she could not know his heart. Then a thought occurred to her. He had not been forced to tell her the story. He could have pretended never to have been party to any transports, any killing. She would never have known.

She looked from his eyes to Sofie's and back.

Her heart softened, just a little.

"Thank you for helping us," she whispered, and she saw Albert's heart leap into his eyes. "We will try to meet you tonight," she said then, to all of them. "Now give us our bags. We must go. We must find people who will take us in."

Sofie grasped Uli's neck, and he swung her right off the ground. Part of Lena wanted to smile indulgently at their joy in such a small thing as a promised hour. The other part of her knew that it was no small thing at all.

"We will try," she said again, this time directly to Albert, "but we may fail. We will not come if the risk seems too great."

"We wish no risk for you, my love," he said. "You must come only if it is safe."

Lena started at the word *love*, hating the tremor it sent through her. "Give me my bag," she said sharply. "And I will pry my friend away from her man." As her fingers grasped the satchel's handle, Albert's fingers slid over top of them. Lena willed herself to pull her hand away, but instead she found herself standing perfectly still as he caressed her hand. She did not acknowledge it, but she felt it. Enemy or not, all the way through her body she felt it.

"Sofie, get down and pick up your bag. We must be in the town before the day begins."

"Why?" Sofie said. "What difference does it make?"

"We don't want them to know how we got here," Lena said, her voice sharper still. "It might make a very big difference indeed."

The parting was hurried: a noisy kiss between Uli and Sofie, a small smile from Albert and a cool gaze from Lena. When she noticed that she had set her bag down and was running the fingers of her left hand over the fingers of her right where he had touched them, she snatched her hand away.

CHAPTER ELEVEN

The road was rough and icy; tank treads had torn up the earth. But trees grew along the way, their branches bare now, but not sacrificed to feed fires. They passed by Wierden quickly, houses on their left, fields on their right. It seemed a pretty town, still and silent in the dawn.

"The people here must be better off," Lena said. "I can feel it."

Sofie didn't answer her. She was far away, no doubt constructing a future for herself as a German housewife. What a fate that would be, Lena thought, and she felt no longing in that moment for a similar fate for herself.

The sunlight that came to them was thin and cold. Perhaps there would be food in Almelo, but winter and the German army held it in as firm a grip as the rest of the Netherlands. The soldiers who had kept them safe for the last two days would be filling their train with food for their own people that day. She and Sofie had better stay out of sight, Lena thought. Imagine a German soldier from the train greeting them in the town centre!

The distance between the farmhouses decreased, and the road passed over a broad canal. A farmer walked his fields in the far distance. Lena could not tell if he saw them or not.

On they walked.

They passed a cemetery on their right, and then, all of a sudden, they were in town. Lena marvelled at the long, straight row of mansions and the beautiful, broad tree-lined street. She could see the signs of five years of war, but they were nothing like in Amsterdam. The houses and gardens looked a little worn, the snowy street a little torn up, but that was all. And some of these houses, she suspected, had been commandeered by Germans. They always took the best ones.

Sofie stopped and gazed around in wonder. "The people in Almelo are very rich," she said.

Lena laughed. "You mean the people on this street are rich," she said. "I'm sure that Almelo has poor people, like everywhere else." She reached for Sofie's arm and quickened her pace. It would not do to be caught in the street by the enemy with curfew barely over and them obviously from elsewhere.

"What is the name of the family that you know?" Lena asked quietly.

"Wijman," Sofie said shortly. She paused. "I think."

Lena's stomach lurched. No. She would not respond to those last two words. They would find the Wijman family and ask for shelter and food in exchange for work.

Both girls stopped abruptly then, frozen in place by the sight of a man opening his front gate right beside them. He wore a heavy winter coat, leather gloves and a grey cap; he looked well-to-do, a match for the imposing house behind him, though when Lena looked closer, she could see that his coat was worn and his gloves had been mended.

"Hello," he said, his voice friendly. "I saw you coming from the upstairs window. Where did you spring from?"

Lena had no idea why she told him the truth. Or part of it.

"Amsterdam," she said. "We came from Amsterdam."

He looked from one to the other and back. "How have you done that?" he asked. "Two young girls?"

"We walked some of the way and we begged rides," Lena said. Then quickly, before he could ask more questions, she added, "Do you know the Wijman family?"

"Wijman . . . Wijman. Why, yes, I think so. At least I know of one Wijman family. A butcher shop right in the centre of town bears that name. Or did, before the war. Just keep on going, my dear, and keep on asking, and you will find it." He paused, looking at them thoughtfully. "But have you been walking all night? Why don't you come in for a bite and something hot to drink. It must have been a while since you had a proper meal."

Gratitude swept over Lena, almost overwhelming her, and with it came hunger. They had had hardly a bite that morning, and she had not liked to guess when they might eat again. Sofie grabbed Lena's hand and squeezed hard.

And Sofie had the presence of mind to answer him. "Oh, thank you, Meneer. We are hungry. You are so kind!" She babbled their thanks as he led them up a long path through the front garden and to the left of the house to the back door.

Lena followed in silence, almost as grateful for Sofie's chatter as she was for the prospect of breakfast.

"We live in just a few rooms now," the man said over his shoulder as he opened the door.

They entered through a mudroom, where all three removed their shoes and coats and hats, and walked on into the kitchen, which was steamy with heat from the stove and steam from the bread that must have just come from the oven. Lena inhaled the scent and wondered if she might swoon from pleasure.

"Janneke," the man called. "I've got guests." A tall woman in a much-mended apron came through from another part of the house. A few words from her husband, and she hustled Lena and Sofie onto two chairs at the large table and reached for the bread knife.

"This is my wife, Mevrouw Klaassen. She will take care of you," the man, who must have been Meneer Klaassen, said to them, and he left the kitchen through another door.

Moments later, Lena and Sofie were sinking their teeth into bread spread with real butter, mugs of milk to hand. The bread was coarse and the milk thin, but to eat fresh bread and drink milk at all was untold luxury.

"We've found paradise," Sofie said through a mouthful. "How can there be such plenty here?"

Mevrouw Klaassen's face tightened. "We do not have plenty like we did before, but we are not starving. Even with the Germans commandeering all the livestock, including the milk from the cows, we manage to collect enough for ourselves. But what we used to send west is now taken east, so the cities see none of it. We scrape by. They starve." All the warmth and generosity in her expression was gone.

Lena had stuffed half the bread down her throat before she remembered the need to eat slowly. "Sofie, slow down," she said quickly. "We'll be sick. Our bodies aren't used to this." She chewed what was in her mouth and took a small sip of milk.

Mevrouw Klaassen left the room for a few minutes, and they heard her talking in the hall but could not make out the words. When she came back, she sat down at the table with them. "You came from Amsterdam, you say?"

"Yes," Sofie said.

"And you know a family here?"

"Yes," again.

"Well, I expect that the Wijmans will help you, but even though things are better here than in your part of the country, we are all of us struggling, and they perhaps a little more than my husband and me. They may not be able to support two of you."

She paused and looked at them.

"Our sons are gone," she said, "both of them. The elder worked for the railway. When the call came for the strike, he went into hiding. We have heard nothing of him since. The younger was taken right in the street—rounded up like sheep with other young men. They took him away to Germany, more than a year ago now. We have had one note. One."

Lena saw the anger once again. Here was a woman who knew exactly who her enemy was. Here was a woman in pain. Lena didn't know what to say. She opened her mouth to say something, anything at all, but Mevrouw Klaassen spoke first. "We would be happy to take in one of you. You seem like good girls. And you look strong and willing. We could use some help with the boys gone."

These were not the people they had been seeking, but what the woman said seemed right. Who could take in two extra mouths in these cold months of war? The Wijmans could take Sofie. After all, they knew her. And Lena would stay here. She felt a warmth around her heart to go with the warmth in her belly. Angry or not, here were people who really wanted her. She smiled and looked up just as Sofie spoke.

"I'll stay with you," she said brightly.

Lena stared. "But, Sofie, what about the Wijmans?"

"Oh, it doesn't make any difference which of us stays with them. It's not like they're going to really remember me."

"What do you mean they won't remember you?" Lena said, keeping her eyes averted from their host. "Then why would they take in either of us?" She could hear the anger in her voice, but she didn't care.

Mevrouw Klaassen put a hand on Lena's wrist.

Sofie looked at Lena for a moment, her eyes wide and round. Lena itched to slap that pretend innocence off her face. She clenched her fist, and then felt her fingers loosen. There was something behind those round eyes. Fear. That was what it was. Sofie was afraid to stay at the Wijmans'. Alone. She was afraid to stay there alone. When there were two of them, it had been just fine. Thoughts tumbled in Lena's head, but she felt her anger lessen just a bit. Even though now *she* had to stay there alone. And Sofie didn't seem to give a moment's thought to that.

"I only mean," Sofie continued, "that they'll be just as happy to have you as me. Don't you think?" On the last words, she turned her gaze on their hostess.

"Well, we'll just have to see, won't we?" Mevrouw Klaassen said. "My husband will take you, Lena. And, Sofie, why don't you go along just for the introductions? As I said, we are willing to take in one."

Lena pinched her tongue between her teeth. She wished that she knew what Sofie was afraid of. And that Sofie had voiced those fears *before* they travelled all the way across the country. Lena bit down hard.

"Meneer," Mevrouw Klaassen called then, "we have news!"

And he was there again, grinning. When he heard which girl was to stay, he reached out, grasped Sofie's hand and shook it vigorously. Lena's chest tightened as she watched Sofie enter the fold.

"Come," he said. They bundled up again, though Lena hated putting her warm feet back in those cold, wet shoes. He hefted her bag, leaving Sofie's where it was.

Outside, Meneer Klaassen set a brisk pace, striding over the packed snow on the sidewalk. Lena and Sofie had to scurry to keep up. They passed a few people in the street, and he nodded briskly at each but made no move to stop. All returned his greeting respectfully and stared at the two young girls who followed him. Lena watched Sofie preen a little under their gaze.

Annoyance flooded her, and she jabbed Sofie with an elbow. "What is wrong with you?" she hissed. "You think everyone's an admirer. We are strangers. We're in tatters. Of course they stare."

Sofie's small smile froze on her face. She turned a sharp gaze on Lena and fixed her eyes on the ground, preening done.

The broad street and the beautiful trees and houses went on and on.

Some minutes later, Lena looked ahead and came to a stop. Her fingers slid insistently around Sofie's forearm. She pulled her sometime friend close and spoke right into her ear. "The train station. We are going to walk right past the train station. And look, there's the train. It's arrived already!"

They both looked then, almost tripping over their feet and falling rapidly behind their guide. The station was on their left, not fifty paces from where they stood. The track crossed right in front of them. And in plain view, not far away at all, was the train. It had to be their train, not another one. Lena could hear the shouts of men on the other side of the engine, the station side. The repairs to the track must have gone more quickly than expected. Or perhaps they had really taken as long as that.

Meneer Klaassen stopped and turned right in the middle of the track. He put down Lena's bag and stood, staring back at them, as they stared at the train.

"Girls, what are you doing?" he called back to them.

Lena smiled broadly and raised her hand in a sort of wave. "Nothing!" she called. "We're coming." She jerked Sofie's elbow, and they were on their way.

Meneer Klaassen looked at them oddly when they came up to him, and it was he who followed them as they almost ran across the tracks, heads turned slightly away, determinedly not looking in the direction of all those men.

Moments later, the station buildings shielded them. Lena took a deep breath. "I guess that's one of the trains that take all the food," she said. She did not have to pretend the edge to her voice. She had only to think of her mother's bony body, her sister's dangerous hunger journeys. It seemed odd, almost impossible, that only several hours before, she and Sofie had been asleep on that very train.

"Yes," Meneer Klaassen said, his suspicions apparently at rest. "But don't you girls worry. You'll neither one starve here in Almelo. None's starved yet." And he smiled reassuringly.

Lena pinched Sofie's arm hard, and Sofie twitched herself out of her reverie. "We so appreciate your generosity, Meneer Klaassen," she said, but her voice was flat, and her eyes left the ground for only a moment. She had Uli in that head of hers, Lena knew. How much it must have cost her to look the other way as they crossed those tracks!

Their guide paused again and looked at Sofie thoughtfully. Lena watched him, worried, but he turned away and started walking again without saying a word.

Freestanding houses had given way to row-housing on the

east side of the tracks, but the street still had a nobility about it. In the distance, Lena saw, it opened out into what could only be the market square.

Soon they walked right out into that long, open space. On their left, almost behind them, Lena saw a large cluster of masts. A canal must end there, she thought, getting goods to market. Across from them, the long east side of the square was lined with buildings—a bit battered, yes, but not dominated by German signs and barbed wire like so many were in Amsterdam. Evidence of war was here too, though. She saw a tank off to her right, and three German soldiers stood talking some distance away.

Still, Lena had not set foot in a small town since she was a young girl before the war. Family holidays flooded her senses. Almelo was just about as far from the seaside as you could get and still be in the Netherlands, but she almost felt that if she sniffed, she would smell salt and fish. If she listened, she would hear gulls. If she looked, the signs of winter and war would fall away and she would have her bathing costume on under her clothes.

But no, she was in a small town almost on the border of Germany in the middle of a terrible war. Still, it was nice to be away from the starvation and misery of Amsterdam, and the more private misery of her own family.

The girls followed Meneer Klaassen straight ahead, into a narrower open space that led out of the square. That quickly came to an end, and they turned left onto what was obviously Almelo's main business street. "Grotestraat," Meneer Klaassen said over his shoulder.

Moments later, he veered to his right and stepped up to the door to what appeared to be a small shop, although it bore no sign. Its display windows were empty, like most of the others, and its plain white curtains were drawn.

Meneer Klaassen reached out his hand, but the handle on the shop door would not turn. He looked at Lena and Sofie and shrugged. "You never know for sure that a shop won't be open," he said. "Though they almost never are." He moved over to the left, to another door with a small window sporting a crisp white lace curtain. Lena had seen nothing that white in years.

The man raised his hand and knocked smartly. You could see the holes where a knocker had been in years gone by, but it must have been a casualty of war. They must have been ordered to turn in their metal here, just as they were in Amsterdam, Lena thought. Not so different.

After a short wait, the door swung inward, revealing a girl, her hair almost hiding her face. "Who are you?" she said, looking right past Meneer Klaassen to Lena and Sofie behind him.

Lena looked at Sofie. Surely she should be the one to speak first. But Sofie stood still, eyes fixed on the doorframe or something above their heads. Lena gave her a small push. Had she turned into some sort of puppet? What had happened to her here, and if it was so bad, why had she wanted to return?

Sofie hesitated for what seemed like forever. Then she stepped forward. "I know you," she said to the girl. "You were . . . hmmm, I think you were nine when I was here that summer. With my family. Do you remember?"

She's the same age as Piet, Lena thought, and homesickness coursed through her. She wrapped her arms around herself and blinked back tears.

"No," the girl said. Her voice was flat, her head bent forward a little, but her eyes, when flashes of them showed, were fierce.

A voice came down the hall behind her. "Who's there, Annie?"

168

The girl, Annie, said nothing. She turned and marched down the hall, to be replaced a moment later by a large woman wrapped in a white apron with damp patches all down the front. Sofie saw determination in her gait and fierceness in her expression. A toddler came running down the hall behind her, as fast as his short, chubby legs would carry him. He caught up and grasped her skirt, peering out at them, all smiles. He liked visitors, it seemed. His mother did not. Lena took a tiny step back.

The woman ignored the two girls and looked, almost glared, at their guide. "Meneer Klaassen, I believe," she said, bowing her head briskly.

"It's me, Mevrouw Wijman," Sofie said, stepping in front of him. "Sofie Vogel."

The woman's expression hardened. She knew who Sofie was, clearly, but she did not acknowledge the relationship.

"Vrouw Wijman will do fine for me," she said glancing at Meneer Klaassen as she spoke. "I'm a butcher's wife, after all. You'll find we don't put on airs so far from the big city. We don't get above ourselves."

Vrouw, Lena thought, remembering Vrouw Hoorn, the kind woman who had fed her and Margriet so well on their hunger journey. She was not in the big city anymore. It seemed so old-fashioned to say *vrouw* to a butcher's wife and *mevrouw* to a woman in a huge house on an elegant tree-lined street. She had the sense that Vrouw Wijman did not like her title one bit. Was there any chance that this angry woman would take her in? The notion of staying there was terrifying, but the notion of being turned away was worse.

Perhaps Meneer Klaassen would take pity on her too.

At last Vrouw Wijman lowered her eyes to Sofie's face. "Sofie Vogel," she said slowly. "Why, yes, I do remember you. You were just a girl, weren't you? Ten or eleven?" She looked past her. "Where is your mother? And what are you doing travelling now?" The toddler released her skirt, stepped around her and stood gazing up at the visitors.

Meneer Klaassen entered the conversation then, and there were further introductions and explanations, including the information that the small boy's name was Bennie, but there were not too many questions. In times like these, people left you with a little privacy. Or was there something more to the silence?

The oddest moment in the conversation came when Meneer Klaassen said that he and his wife would be happy to take one of the girls and asked if the Wijmans would take the other.

"Well, I just don't know," Vrouw Wijman said. "Food is short for us." Was there an emphasis on the word *us*? Lena thought back to the Klaassens' large house and comfortable kitchen. "And now," she went on, "with the baby, space . . ."

Somehow, Sofie knew to jump in at that moment. "The Klaassens have invited me to stay with them," she said. "We were wondering if Lena—"

Lena had read in books about people's brows clearing, but she had never seen it for herself. When Sofie said that the Klaassens had invited her to stay with them, Vrouw Wijman's brow did just that. She didn't grow friendly, exactly, but she grew a little less rigid. And in the face of Meneer Klaassen's obvious expectation that she would do her duty, the matter was soon settled.

Then Vrouw Wijman changed in another way. "It's a chilly morning," she said, smiling down at Sofie and then, perhaps a touch more intently, at the gentleman behind her. "Would you like a cup of tea before your walk back?"

"You are very kind," Meneer Klaassen said, "but my wife is expecting me."

Vrouw Wijman puffed up just a little more, broadened her smile and gestured through the door. "Come now, meneer. Your wife wouldn't want you to make that long journey unrefreshed! And my husband, Marten, will be home soon. He would be honoured!"

Obsequious, Lena thought. The woman was being obsequious.

"I'm sorry, ma'am, but I must go," Meneer Klaassen said then, his voice almost brusque. "Come, Sofie. Goodbye, Lena. Ma'am." And he turned on his heel.

Sofie darted up into the doorway, clutched Lena's elbow and gestured down the road with her chin. "The train station," she whispered, "ten o'clock." And she was gone, smiling and waving over her shoulder as she scampered up the road a few steps behind her new chaperon.

Thus Meneer Klaassen and Sofie set off for the beautiful house on the straight, wide street, and Lena lifted her satchel and followed Vrouw Wijman, who pulled her wool shawl a little more tightly around herself as she walked, down the long hall, herding the toddler before her. "How rude!" she mumbled to herself. "We'll have no beef for him once this blasted war is over."

Lena noted that Vrouw Wijman expected the attentions due her, and perhaps an extra measure. That was useful information.

The living room, tucked in behind the butcher shop, was cramped and cold. "We spend most of our time in the kitchen," the older woman said, and she and Bennie led the way through another door that took them deeper into the house.

The kitchen was even smaller than the living room, but it was warm and boasted a bit of natural light through a window over the sink. A fire burned in the woodstove in the far corner, and a pot of water boiled away on top of it. Lena marvelled at the luxury, stepping close to the stove and holding out her hands.

"Marten has a nasty job to do today," Vrouw Wijman said, seating herself at the small table and brushing Bennie away when he tried to crawl up on her lap. "He will accept my decision to take you in, but you understand that we take you in for service. Help is hard to come by nowadays. Your place is with me and the baby in the kitchen."

She stopped and Lena nodded, since some response seemed to be called for.

Vrouw Wijman was winding herself up. "Marten works with the cows and for what? So he can be called out before dawn to provide cattle for the Third Reich. It is not to be borne. And I am stuck at home with a sullen girl who's gone half the time and hardly lifts a finger when she's here." She stopped and glared at Annie, who sat opposite her, a tattered book clutched in her hands. Annie did not look up. "And a child in diapers." She paused. "You will have enough to eat here, though not as high in quality as your friend will be getting, I'm sure. And you'll have a bed, but don't be expecting a room of your own upstairs. I will expect you to work hard, to earn that food and that bed, and to stay out of my husband's way." Again she paused. And again Lena nodded, foreboding growing inside her.

"You can start by brewing some tea," Vrouw Wijman said. "Then you can put your things in the alcove behind that curtain. There is a cot there. We'll find you some bedding before the day is done."

Lena followed directions and made tea. She glanced periodically at the curtain in the corner. Another piece of white lace, this one lined so no one could see through.

The day was long. More than help with cooking, more than cleaning, it turned out that Vrouw Wijman wanted that child off her hip and out from under her feet. Annie was no help. For a long time she sat, sullen and silent, reading at the kitchen table, and then, without a word, she was gone, not to return until just before the noon meal.

At one point, Lena stopped by the table and turned Annie's book over to read the title. Her breath caught in her throat at the sight of a book she had never read. Perhaps one day Annie would lend it to her. It was too bad that the girl seemed so prickly.

"Stop that," Vrouw Wijman barked at her. "I won't have another one in my house turning to books instead of chores."

So Lena left the book and got down on her knees on the kitchen floor. Bennie gazed at her with big blue eyes obscured just a little by blond curls. "My name is Lena," she said, working hard to keep Bep and Nynke out of her mind and tears out of her eyes. "And I'm going to be living here for a while."

Bennie smiled, picked up a crudely shaped block from the floor and shoved it at her. Lena took the block and turned it over and over in her hands. "It's beautiful!" she said. She looked to where eight or ten other blocks were scattered under the table. "Shall we build something together?" Bennie went from smiling to beaming, and Lena put the special block into his hands and reached for one of her own.

Vrouw Wijman used the table to heave herself up. "Remember, your job is to keep him out from under my feet!" she said as she took a large cast-iron pot from its hook on the wall.

Lena shifted herself, Bennie and the blocks toward the wall.

I will see Nynke again before she even knows what a block is, she swore to herself, and Bep will forgive me for leaving. She will.

She looked up to see Vrouw Wijman with several carrots and a potato in her hands. How soon could she bring up the subject of sending food to Amsterdam? she wondered.

For the rest of the morning, Lena played with Bennie, chopped vegetables and stirred the stew. She was relieved not to be asked to cook the entire meal. Specific tasks, she could handle. She had chopped enough potatoes in her time. Still, Vrouw Wijman frowned when she saw the bits of potato heaped on the chopping board. They were not beautiful.

"Up, up," Bennie called, standing at Lena's side, grasping handfuls of her skirt and pulling with all his might. Lena looked down at him and smiled. His nose was crusty, she noticed, although his clothes were spotless. What was it about clothes and curtains around here?

She found out soon enough. Vrouw Wijman liked things clean. She had stockpiled soap at the beginning of the war and had access to fat, so she made more soap regularly on the stove in the lean-to. She wanted Lena to take Bennie off her hands so she could get back to her cleaning. Her husband, she told Lena, was off with his brother's cows. He came home at noon, filthy and exhausted.

"It's nice to meet you, meneer," Lena said.

Vrouw Wijman looked at her husband and let out a short laugh. "I told you. You're not in the big city now," she said to Lena. "And my husband is a butcher, not a gentleman. You'll call him Wijman, not meneer." She said that last word through her nose in a thoroughly disagreeable way. Lena thought that perhaps Vrouw Wijman regretted the missing pair of letters at the beginning of her title: she wouldn't mind being a mevrouw married to a meneer. Like the Klaassens. Perhaps that explained the excessively clean curtains.

Wijman looked Lena over, shrugged, nodded gruffly at his wife's brief explanation of her presence and collapsed into a chair in front of his dinner. The meal seemed wonderful to Lena—bits of beef with onions and potatoes floating in thin gravy, soaked up with bread that actually tasted like what it was supposed to be. She struggled not to gulp hers down, keeping her attention on the little boy.

Still, she couldn't help noticing the man of the house wolfing down his food, his eyes falling on her now and again, but with hardly a word for anyone. His glance was cursory, but it contained something unpleasant nonetheless. Lena was pretty sure that Vrouw Wijman saw those glances, each one of them. Every time Lena looked up from her plate, she caught them both, his gaze comfortable and pleased with itself, hers wary. Lena resolved to stick close to the kitchen, just as Vrouw Wijman demanded.

She also noticed that Vrouw Wijman did not say a word about the other girl who had arrived on her doorstep earlier. She explained Lena's arrival as if Lena had just shown up, begging for a meal and a roof over her head. No Meneer Klaassen; no Sofie Vogel. Why?

Lena was tempted to say casually, "Sofie Vogel was here," just to see what would happen. Tempted, but not very tempted.

"There's a train in today," Wijman said as he scraped up his last bite.

Lena stiffened.

So did Vrouw Wijman. "Taking our food again, are they? They've got all our young men. And now they've got to have our food." She looked at her husband, fury and contempt competing for dominance in her expression. "And I suppose you gave them a nice cow or two."

Annie looked up, her long hair skidding across her plate as she did so. "What do you expect him to do, Mother?" she said. "Hide the cows? Offer himself up instead?"

Wijman reached out and cuffed Annie on the side of her head. She glared at him and went back to eating.

His voice was tired when he said, "Actually, they took six cows, one with calf. Not many left."

"Well, eat up, then. Enjoy!" Vrouw Wijman said. "There won't be much more where this came from!"

Her voice was bright now, falsely merry. Lena shuddered.

* * *

All afternoon she played with Bennie. She changed him and put him down for his nap. She took him out for a walk, exploring the neighbourhood. The train station was quite a few blocks away, and she had to carry Bennie almost the whole distance, back through the long square and onto the long, straight road. If she was going to find the station in the dark, though, she needed to make sure she knew the route. The last thing she wanted was Sofie and Albert and Uli showing up at the Wijmans' looking for her.

She walked up the station steps and peered in the door. Then she moved back, out of view. The train was still there. German soldiers milled around. She was turning to pull Bennie into her arms and retreat when a voice spoke softly. "There you are!" It was Uli. He stood inside, out of sight of the street. "Where is Sofie?" he asked, his voice urgent.

176

Lena looked up at him and back out the door. "She's with a family," she whispered, "down that street there." She gestured in the right direction.

"We'll see you tonight." He made it a statement and Lena bridled, fear stirring her insides.

"I don't know," she said.

He stepped toward her.

"Yes," she said quickly. "We will try."

"You must do more than try," he said. "I . . ."

Lena didn't need to hear what he would say next. She must not be seen here, on German territory, chatting with the enemy.

"Bang, bang," Bennie said over Lena's shoulder as she stumbled down the steps with him in her arms. "Bad guy!"

And he kept on like that once they were home, marching around the living room, shouting things he had probably heard his parents say. It took Lena the better part of an hour to distract him.

Ten o'clock. Sofie expected Lena at the station at ten o'clock. And Lena wouldn't put it past Sofie to come knocking on the window if she stood her up. With her feet back on solid ground, a couple of good meals in her belly and a handsome man waiting for her, Sofie would have her old confidence back. Enough for both of us, Lena thought, or hoped. Or hoped not. She wasn't sure.

The alcove was tiny, but once the family had retreated upstairs to bed, Lena was alone. Truly and completely alone. Light was precious even here, so bedtime was early. By eight thirty, the house was silent. Lena sat on her narrow cot, which she had made up with crisp white sheets and two thick wool blankets. She stroked her pillow. It was soft and inviting. A single candle burned on the tiny bedside table, but it would not last long. Lena knelt to slide her satchel under the bed and paused. The cologne. She had decided to throw it away. She snapped open the latch on her bag, eased up the lid, leaned her forehead against it and gazed inside.

An idea occurred to her. She could give the cologne to her hostess as a little gift. Lena's mother had taught her few rules of good conduct, but in the books she read, guests always came bearing gifts. She rooted around in her bag, in search of the tiny bottle, and as she rooted, she remembered: the snow, the view, the cold, Albert's coat warming her, Albert holding her mittens while she discovered his small offering.

Abruptly, she pulled her hands free, snapped the bag shut and shoved it beneath the bed. Vrouw Wijman would have to take her gift in peeled potatoes and babysitting. The cologne was staying right where it was.

She ran her hands over her skirt and sweater. Vrouw Wijman had looked at her clothes with distaste. "Tomorrow you will give me all your clothes. You can wear something of mine for the day." Lena couldn't help it: her eyes flicked down to Vrouw Wijman's large body and her tent-like dress. Vrouw Wijman gave a small huff of annoyance. "Yes, I know they will be too big for you, but you can stay in for the day. By the next day, your clothes will be dry." She paused. "And you will bathe."

Lena wasn't sure why she couldn't have bathed today. She had slept in straw for two nights. She had crouched on damp, snowy ground. She had huddled up to a fire. She had sweated terror. Her hair was heavy with grease. It smelled sour.

Vrouw Wijman did allow her to take a basin of warm water into the lean-to with a sliver of soap, a worn washcloth and towel, a comb and a bit of soda to use on her teeth. Lena had done what she could, afraid to remove her clothes in case someone came in, as the door to the outside did not lock. And it was cold in the lean-to, the stove black and empty.

Now, in her grubby clothes, Lena was not going to get between the sheets, but she longed to close her eyes, just to rest for a moment before the ordeal to come. She pulled out one of the blankets Albert had given her on the train, spread it over the bed, lay down on top and pulled it around her. The bed supported her all the way along her body. She listened. Silence. When had she ever been alone like this? No one near? It was exquisite. She closed her eyes and immediately began to drift, softly, into a world of delights. There were people there—people she loved, people she had left—but they gazed at her in silence, smiling. All is well, they seemed to say, and she felt it too. All was well. She spiralled deeper. Rest had never felt this good.

Deeper. Faces faded away and sleep took their place.

She started awake to pitch blackness. The candle had burned itself out. Now that wasn't safe, was it? She should have blown that candle out before she lay down.

Then the clock struck the quarter hour. Time. She hadn't meant to go to sleep because she—Time. She was supposed to—Time. She was supposed to meet Sofie. Ten o'clock. Lena crept from her bed, pushed aside the lace curtain and thrust her face close to the grandmother clock on the kitchen wall. Ten fifteen. It was ten fifteen! Her coat and her shoes were by the front door. Fearful of creaks, she made her way down the hall, even more fearful that any second Sofie was going to knock. She reached the door, pulled her coat off a hook and pushed her feet into her shoes. The door was locked. She had wondered earlier if the door would lock with a key Wijman kept with him. It was a bad plan in case of fire, but many a man liked to keep his family secure in that way, risk or no.

The key was in the lock. She turned it, but the door would not give. Lena looked up toward the top of the door and found the bar, an extra level of security almost beyond her reach. She stretched up and grabbed the small knob that secured it. She had trouble turning the knob from that angle, but dragging a chair down the hall would make a racket. If she could just push . . . She stretched a little higher, concentrated on the muscles in her forearm and pushed again. It gave. A moment later, she had pulled the bar free. She pushed the door open a crack, peering out. If she was caught by the Germans during curfew, she had no idea what the penalty would be.

She heard a rustle and another sound. A giggle. She pushed the door open the rest of the way, her heart pounding. Please don't let them be . . . But they were. Sofie and Uli and Albert were right there, in front of the shop window, jostling one another like a trio of teenagers playing a prank. Right above their heads was the Wijmans' bedroom window. Lena had seen it from the inside when she was putting Bennie to bed. She gave thanks for blackout paper and hoped theirs was extra thick. Closing the door firmly behind her without looking at any of them, she marched off down the street toward the station.

Albert came into step beside her. "Lena, I am glad to see you," he whispered.

She ignored him.

"We turn here," he said as the square opened up in front of them.

"I know," Lena said, without meeting his eyes. Behind her she could hear the lovers' scuffling steps and quiet voices. Her fury mounted.

As they approached the far side of the square, Albert led them off to the right, to a row of buildings facing the canal. They stopped at a doorway just as dark as all the others, though it had the look of a restaurant or a pub from bygone days. The sign was gone, but Lena could see where it had been attached above the door. Uli stepped past them, turned the handle and ushered them in. The space they entered was dark and cramped, but they found the inner door easily enough. Checking that the outer door was closed behind them, Albert opened the second door. Warm light, real tobacco smoke, music and excited conversation poured over them.

Even though the room was full of men in German uniforms, and Lena had spent little time in pubs, she immediately felt as if she had entered an earlier time in her life, a happier time. The room was crowded with tables, each enjoying its own small circle of candlelight. The tables were crowded with men and covered in glasses. Smoke from cigarettes and cigars burning in dozens of hands clouded (and scented) the air. At the far side of the room, the bar glowed. Made from wood and backed with a mirrored wall, it reflected light. Bottles lined the shelves, empty—beer seemed to be the only available beverage—but still filled with promise.

Lena looked more closely at the people in the room. There were women. Several women were waiting on the tables. Older women, it looked like; Dutch women, certainly. A large man worked behind the bar, filling glasses with pale beer. And there were women at the tables. Lena saw four at first count. A pair at one table with three men, and single women at two others. One young woman at a nearby table met Lena's eyes. Instinctively, Lena looked away. She drew a deep breath. At least she and Sofie weren't the only ones.

"Hey," shouted a man from the back of the room, "it's Uli and Albert with their stowaways!"

Many of these were the men from the train. Of course they were. Three men called more insistently than the rest, pulling up extra chairs, waving for more beer, and Lena found herself quickly seated, separated from Sofie, who was practically in Uli's lap on the other side of the table. Albert leaned in close. "I'm so glad to have this time with you, Lena," he said. "I'm sorry that we surprised you back there. We were afraid that you were asleep, that we would miss you."

Hearing her name on his lips melted her heart just a little, and the fact that they had made it safely to their destination stilled her fears, but Lena was not going to let Albert off as easily as that. "And what were you going to do about it?" she said fiercely. "Knock on the door and ask my hosts to wake me?"

"Oh, no. I . . . we . . ."

"You didn't have a plan. You just marched down the street and giggled outside my door." Lena looked at Albert properly for the first time that night, and what she saw in his face melted what resistance remained. It would not have been his idea to gather outside the Wijmans' door. She allowed her lips to curl into a smile.

Albert gasped with relief and grinned. "We are safe here," he said. "And I am so glad to set eyes on you again!"

Lena wrapped her fingers around her glass and raised it, gesturing in his direction. He quickly reciprocated, and soon all the glasses at the table were clanking against one another high in the air. "To the end of this war," Lena said, and everyone, it seemed, could drink to that.

As time passed and Lena grew accustomed to her surroundings, she began to observe the mood more closely. What had seemed jovial began to take on an edge of desperation. The drink and the camaraderie were holding at bay a terrible darkness, a darkness that if given the mere whiff of a chance, threatened to overwhelm the room, the people in it, the nation, the continent, the world. Lena could feel it pressing on them right there, right then. The darkness, she thought, had a human form, or a human presence, at its helm.

Lena tuned in to the conversation again. An older man was speaking, his words slurred. "It seemed right and good, you know, before, but now it's been years, and Berlin destroyed and most of the world against us. How can we win?"

"And so many dead. What do we have to go home to?" said another.

Uli looked at Lena and Sofie. "We take your food," he said. "We know that the Dutch in the west are starving. But in Germany it is not good either. The need is great everywhere."

Lena opened her mouth to ask whose fault that was, but different words came out of her. "If I could get my hands on that Hitler of yours," she said, her words clear, confident, with lashings of bitter humour, "I would scratch his eyes out."

Silence descended on the table. Six sets of eyes stared. Six fists froze on damp glasses. Lena stared back. What had she done? Where had those words come from? Then the older man tipped back his head and roared. It was a sound of furious delight. And it spread. Soon the whole table was revelling in the glorious wickedness of Lena's words. Albert's arm snaked around her and squeezed. He leaned over and kissed her cheek.

"You're a brave girl," he said. "Too brave for your own good maybe, but good for all of us!"

For a moment, just a moment, Lena let herself snuggle into the crook of that arm. She let the sensation of Albert's lips on her face sink right inside her through her skin. Then she thought again about what Albert had done. Come to think of it, many of the men in the room had almost certainly done worse. And here she was, drinking beer with them. She shrank away from Albert. And the terrible word *collaborator* formed in her mind.

Sofie raised her fingers and made claws with them, sending everyone off again. Lena gazed around the table over her beer, trying (and failing) to reconcile these friendly, laughing men with their probable actions. And what did it mean that she could say such a wicked thing and the Führer's minions could wrap themselves up in it like a blanket? Not hard to guess. Loyalty was thin, riddled with holes, held together by many, many threads of fear. And somehow at this table on this night for this moment, fear was absent.

* * *

Lena stood with Albert in the dark doorway. Uli and Sofie were gone. He had offered to walk her home, and she had accepted. Lena had circled the table to talk to her, to convince her not to do it, to urge her to make her own way home, but Sofie had laughed and pushed her away. "We'll be careful," she had said. "No one will see us. Besides, who knows when I'll see him again?"

Lena wanted to say, "You won't see him again. At least I hope you won't. Ever." But she kept silent. Moments later, Sofie waved goodbye to her across the table, and Uli said jovial good-byes to everyone, accepting the nudges and winks with good grace. Even eagerly, Lena thought, disgusted.

She turned to Albert. "I must go too," she said, "before they miss me. Before they find their door unlocked." And he rose. "No," she said, "I will go alone. It is safer."

"Please," he replied. Nothing else. Just that, and he followed her to the door. There they were in the darkness, with dozens of blacked-out windows pressing down on them. It would only take one person to pull the blackout paper aside and peer out for one moment . . .

"Goodbye, Albert," Lena said. "Thank you for all you have done for me."

Albert's face was hard to make out in the dark. He stood before her, his arms at his sides. Lena moved closer. Silent tears were carving two wet paths down his cheeks. "I love you," he said. "I will return after the war. I will find you."

"No," Lena said. "You must not. You will find someone else."

He stood still, silent, just the occasional rough-edged breath. Lena felt a warmth in her own chest, a prickle in the back of her nose. She shook her head sharply and coughed.

"I must go," she said shortly. "I thank you. You are a good man, Albert." She rose on her tiptoes, pressed her mouth to his for a heartbeat, only a heartbeat, turned away and launched herself down the street in a dead sprint.

In the first moment of her mad dash, she heard Albert call her name. In the next moments, she heard him take off in a run after her. Then she turned into the wide-open square and kept on running without looking back. Behind her, silence.

She skidded to a stop two doors away from the butcher shop and crept the rest of the way. Only at her own door did she look back. The street was empty. Gently, gently, she turned the doorknob. Quietly, quietly, she slipped inside. On her toes, she slid the bar across. Coat on the hook, shoes on the shelf, key turned in the lock, she tiptoed down the hall, past the stairway that led up to where the family slept. She peered up and froze. Sitting on a step, right at her eye level, was a dim shape that could only be Annie. It was too dark for their eyes to meet, but a long moment after Lena saw her, Annie rose, ghost-like, and disappeared up the stairs. Lena heard the click of her bedroom door closing behind her.

Lena had to wait for a long time for her heart to stop pounding. Would Annie tell? she wondered. What if they learned where she had been, who she had been with? At last she walked on, through the living room and the kitchen, into the alcove, where she stripped to her slip, slithered out of her stockings and crawled between the sheets.

That narrow bed was a lonely place, it turned out, with nothing but a thin curtain separating it from a houseful of strangers. Lena thought of Albert briefly, of their last goodbye and her perilous journey home, but it was Bep's small, warm body that she imagined curled up in her arms as she cried herself to sleep.

CHAPTER TWELVE

"I'll need Lena with me in the morning," Wijman said to his wife at the dinner table after Lena had been with them for three weeks or so.

Those weeks had passed in a blur of hard work, hurried meals and endless hours on the kitchen floor devising games to keep one small boy entertained. After two or three long nights, Lena began to fall asleep without weeping. She put Albert out of her mind altogether, and she brought Bep and Nynke to mind less and less. As for Sofie, one day she would visit, Lena was sure. In the meantime, she waited and watched, seeking the right moment to ask if they could send a food packet to Amsterdam.

Today, Wijman's announcement took everyone by surprise. Lena looked up from her plate, caught Vrouw Wijman's eye and looked back down. There had been panic and rage in her face.

"What do you want with her?" Vrouw Wijman's voice said, fury barely contained in the words.

"I'm bringing in a cow. One of the last. We had her tucked away in a bit of a wood when they came last, so she's not in their count. But we can't expect the same luck next time. Might as well have her in our bellies."

"What's that got to do with our girl here?"

"I need her help," he said briefly, his eyes resting casually on Lena herself.

Lena stared. Help. What did he mean by "help"? Wasn't he talking about slaughtering a cow?

"You've never needed a girl's help before," Vrouw Wijman replied.

He turned his gaze to his wife, unruffled. "She'll come with me out to Bert's farm and help me bring the beast in. Bert's got enough on his hands. And his boys are gone, like everyone else's."

"There's another girl right here, if you notice," Vrouw Wijman said, nodding her head toward their daughter. "And of no use to me, that one."

Annie had been making faces at Bennie, causing him to giggle and spit out potatoes. She paused and looked up, her face a studied blank. "I won't be available," she said, and turned back to her brother.

Vrouw Wijman reached out and turned Bennie's head back toward his own plate. "That food is for eating," she hissed.

"It's Lena I'll be taking," Wijman said shortly.

Vrouw Wijman nodded her head, once up, once down.

Lena turned her own attention back to her dinner, or tried to. Instead, in her mind, four black-and-white, mud-stained legs crumpled while she watched, helpless. Behind her in the image, a man loomed, his intentions unclear. She took another bite and chewed, swallowed, and another.

* * *

Everything happened fast the next morning—or night, really, as it was still dark, curfew not yet lifted, when Lena tiptoed from the house once again, this time out the back door and this time under orders. She followed Wijman for about a quarter of an hour, but to the outskirts of town, not to the country, as she had expected.

"Where will we take the cow?" Lena asked at one point.

"Home, of course," Wijman said without slowing his pace. "We butcher her in the shed."

Lena stopped dead. The shed? He meant the lean-to attached to the house. He was going to kill the cow there? And what exactly did he mean by "we"? The bit of bread she had eaten for breakfast threatened to batter its way out of her stomach. She swallowed hard and set off at a jog to catch up.

Soon they turned off the dirt road and onto a track leading to a house that loomed suddenly out of the dark. Lena sensed that farmland lay behind the house, although she couldn't be sure from the front, as the houses were lined up close. Wijman led her off to the right, where the narrow track squeezed between that house and the next, before ending at a large shed.

The cow was inside, in a stall so small that she could not have turned around, or got up again if she had lain down.

She shifted and let out a low sound—more a groan than a moo—as they entered, plunging into true blackness because Wijman would light no light. The shed was warm, heated by cow, and the smell almost knocked Lena right back out the door. Cow manure. Fresh, though, she thought. Then she started. Wijman's hand was on her waist.

It rested there for a long moment, pressing against her through her coat. And then he said, "Oh, I'm sorry, that's you." And the hand was gone.

We've moved from eyes to hands, Lena thought, and a flicker of fear rose in her and fell away.

Minutes later they were outside, leading the cow through the narrow passage between the houses. Wijman walked well in front, holding the rope. Lena walked backwards at first, as close to the creature's head as she could, murmuring to her, stroking the side of her face.

"She must be silent," Wijman had said. "There are soldiers about."

Not our soldiers, Lena thought. Uli and Albert were long gone; Lena's midnight sprint was a fading memory. For several days after that first night in Almelo, she had waited for someone to come forward to accuse her, someone who had seen her right out there in the street. But no one had. She had avoided going far from the Wijmans' house for fear of running into a soldier who recognized her. And in all the weeks since, she had not been to see Sofie. She thought of her daily, but she did not go. Nor did Sofie appear at the Wijmans' door. She was probably too busy lapping up the luxuries of life at the Klaassens' to bother with an old friend.

"Shhh, cow. Shhh," Lena whispered, stroking the silky skin near the cow's ear. The creature tossed her head a little, but she made no sound except for her hoofs on the hard dirt. Lena imagined those same hoofs ringing on cobblestones and gave thanks for that dirt. The sky seemed a little paler now. It was easier to make their way. But still, the town was tucked up behind blackout paper or blackout boards or blackout curtains. It would have been a peaceful walk had it not been for the war, the impending death of the animal she cooed to as she walked, and Wijman's eyes resting on her so casually the night before and that heavy hand pressing down on her waist just now.

The cow balked at the entrance to the lean-to. The floor of the room was a little higher than the ground outside. The cow had to step up. And she refused. Wijman pulled on the rope and swore quietly. The cow pulled back and mooed, a long, low sound of discontent. Wijman stopped pulling. Man and girl froze. The cow looked around for a better place to go than into this room, perhaps a bite to eat.

Lena shook herself out of her trance. No one was coming. It was all right. She thought for a moment. "Can we make a ramp?" she asked. And yes, it turned out they could. The door was removed from its hinges, which made the opening wider, more welcoming. Once the door was laid on the ground, leading up and over the sill, they had only to bribe the cow with some fresh hay, and she was inside.

Wijman put the door back in place and began rummaging around on his work bench.

The cow stood and munched.

Lena backed toward the door that led into the kitchen.

Wijman found what he was looking for, turned and smiled slightly at the fear on Lena's face. He was holding a large knife.

"I used to shoot them," he said casually, "before the war. But that's too noisy now. So I stun them and slit their throats."

Lena averted her eyes from the huge animal, which did not know it was breathing its last, and said the only thing that came to her: "What about the blood?"

Wijman smiled again. "That, my dear, is where you come in. Oh, and the drain in the floor. In the end, there will be no blood." He paused. "Consider yourself lucky. I hired a boy to help before. And there was a calf in there. He had to help me deal with that."

Lena stared at him. A calf? It took her a moment to understand. When she did—he meant a baby calf inside the opened-up belly of the dead cow—she turned and fled, through the door and into the warm, bright kitchen, where three pairs of eyes stared.

But they did not send her back. And Wijman did not fetch her. Not right then. She sat down on the floor and sang softly to Bennie, pushing the cow's soft ears out of her mind, the long moo and the big eyes, the life. I eat beef when I can get it, she thought to herself. And I won't say no to beef tonight.

The door opened. "All right, it's done. Time to earn your keep."

I've been earning my keep ever since I got here, Lena thought. Without comment, she rose, walked to the lean-to door and stepped inside. A ghastly smell greeted her, a ripe, hot smell. Fear, she thought. Death. Blood. The cow lay on the ground on her side, her legs poking out like sticks. Lena did not look at her throat, where she assumed the knife had done its work. Wijman was crouched in front of her among all those legs. In a rush, Lena realized what he was doing and stepped back, tasting bile. He made an incision, and Lena saw the cow's belly spill open and her insides push out between the two long flaps of skin.

Wijman looked over his shoulder. "Get over here and help me," he barked.

The hours that followed were some of the worst of Lena's life, or at least she thought so at the time. She helped disembowel the animal. Then she had to wash out the cavity. Then she had to dispose of the innards. The liver, the heart and the kidneys, she washed and placed in a big bowl for Vrouw Wijman to cook that night. That wasn't so bad. The worst part was cleaning out the stomachs and intestines, the four sacs and one long tube that ran from one end of the cow to the other. The stomachs could be eaten—they were called tripe—and the intestines could be used as skin for sausages, but it all had to be clean first. The blood and some of the mess could be washed down the drain in the floor, but Wijman told her to bury the innards that could not be eaten in the back garden. He had already used a pick to dig a hole in the partly frozen ground.

His brother came for part of the afternoon to help him halve the carcass and hang it from the ceiling on huge metal hooks to age overnight. He took the animal's skin and her head home with him, hidden on a cart beneath bundles of clothes. He would cure the hide in his attic, he said. He didn't say what he would do with the head. Lena had let her eyes fall on it only once. It looked almost as it had in life, as long as she didn't look at where it ended.

"All right. That will do for today," Wijman said gruffly after his brother was gone. "I expect that you're needed inside."

* * *

The next day, the real butchering took place.

The meat sold as soon as it was cut to a stream of furtive customers who came directly to the lean-to from the back. Wijman had alerted them that meat was available by opening the curtain in the store window. How people still had money after all these years of war, Lena did not understand, but she had seen the black market at work in Amsterdam, and she knew that money burned in the pockets of the wealthy. Restricted from legal purchases by ration books, they found other ways to spend and acquire.

By evening, most of the cow was gone. Lena's work, however, was far from done.

Wijman waited until the next morning to take her back out to the lean-to, Bennie once again in his mother's unwilling arms. The man's hand found her waist once again, this time in a well-lit room, for the space was extravagantly lit that morning, with half a dozen lanterns strategically placed. He turned Lena's body with his hand, which meant that his whole arm curved around her, and she felt herself pulled into his side. She held herself straight, as far away from him as she could get, and tried to make her skin shrink away. But shrink though she might, his hand followed.

"See the blood on that wall?" he said, his large palm flat on her back now. She leaned forward a little to see and his hand stroked upward, almost to her neck. He pushed her head down. "And on the floor?" She looked. What else could she do? "It must be clean. You must clean this space until the Gestapo could come here with magnifying glasses and find not one drop, not a speck." He stepped away from her, swinging her around to face him, a hand on each bare elbow. "Do you understand?"

Lena took a step back, out of reach of those hands. She rubbed at the places they had touched.

"Yes, I understand. I will clean," she said.

He looked at her and smiled. "You are a good girl," he said. "A very good girl." He rubbed his hair back from his forehead and took a deep breath. "I'll check in on you later." And he was gone, out into the lane.

Lena heard a rustle behind her, turned and started. Annie stood in the kitchen doorway, still, eyes wide. Could he not have seen her? Lena wondered.

Then Annie's face split open. Her grin was wide. Her cheeks pushed up almost to her eyebrows. "Bet you weren't expecting great dead cows spattering blood," she said. "And him. Bet you weren't expecting him." Her grin was a grimace, the words delivered from between her teeth, squashed eyes unblinking.

"Go away," Lena said. "Go away and leave me to it." Annie stood for a moment, composing her face.

"He won't stop till he gets what he wants," she said. "I've seen it before."

"I said, 'Go away,'" Lena repeated, her teeth clenched.

And Annie did, then. Lena crept to the middle of the room and vomited into the drain. She pumped a bucket of water from the corner, sloshed the vomit out of sight and turned her mind to her task.

It was a miserable job, scrubbing dried blood off the wall and the floor, checking the space bit by bit for drops she might have missed. She thought of the cow clopping down the lane. She thought of the endless guts she had squeezed and rinsed, squeezed and rinsed. She thought of that man and his hands. And Sofie. How was Sofie?

Then she thought of her family. All this meat and her family starving.

On she scrubbed. On and on.

That night at the dinner table, over the tender fried liver that melted on her tongue despite its source, Lena prepared to ask her question.

"They have nothing like this in Amsterdam," she said softly.

"We have nothing like this here," Vrouw Wijman said. "We could be shot for eating this."

Annie smacked her mouthful noisily and grinned around the table. Vrouw Wijman sighed.

"Well, I was wondering," Lena said. "Might I send a parcel? Might I send some butter and some beef?"

Vrouw Wijman put down her fork.

"It's not enough that we feed you?" she said, her voice sharp. "Your family expects us to feed them as well?" It was half question, half shrill statement of injustice.

"Oh, no," Lena said. "They expect nothing. I just know how

hungry they are. And with the new baby. In Amsterdam, there is no food. People are starving to death. And they can't bury them all. They have to keep the bodies in the churches."

Wijman spoke then, around a mouthful. "Oh, Martha, be easy on the girl." He winked at Lena, and Lena's insides shrank. "She's worked hard for us, haven't you, dear?" he said, and the *dear* stuck to Lena's skin like a sticky bit of offal from her day's work. "Yes, you can send a parcel. Of course you can." He turned back to his wife. "Put one together for her on Monday. Bosse is going to the city anyway. I've given him a good-sized cut of beef. You never know," he said, thoughtful now. "One good turn deserves another. This war can't go on forever. Who knows what these people might be able to do for us."

"We've done enough for them already," Vrouw Wijman said. Her hands were on the table, unmoving, her food growing cold on her plate. She looked at Lena briefly, and then turned her gaze back on her husband. The rage of two days ago was gone, but Lena could not tell what this new look meant, except that it held a great deal of pain.

No more was said then. Vrouw Wijman ate her cold food. Dinner was finished. Lena cleared the table and washed up while Bennie played on the floor with a pot and an enormous wooden spoon. Wijman sat at the table, reading by what little daylight was left. Vrouw Wijman sat opposite him, her eyes on her lap. Annie was gone out the door, who knew where, one hour left before curfew.

Lena wanted them all to go away so she could pull out the big washtub and fill it with water hot past bearing. She was desperate to cleanse away all the blood, along with the man's unwelcome touch and the pain that came off Vrouw Wijman in waves. She longed to strip down and crouch in the tub and scrub and scrub. At least she could plunge her hands into the steaming dishwater, washing herself up past the elbows he had grasped. She concentrated on the heat and on the thought of Mother and Margriet and Piet and Bep oohing and ahhing over the parcel of meat and butter, maybe a bit of cheese too. Some flour? She had noticed that they had some flour in the pantry. Would they spare a bit?

She settled a large platter into the dish rack. What had happened at the dinner table? What had made Wijman order his wife's compliance? She remembered his wink and the feeling it provoked, as if he had dashed dirty water onto her. It was all tied up with the hands, with the strange, hungry gesture he had made just before he left her to her day's scrubbing. And everything about it was nasty. It was all nasty and dangerous, but because of it, her family would have a bit of nourishing food to eat.

Maybe she would concentrate on that, she thought, as she let the dirty dishwater run down the drain.

* * *

The next day was a Saturday. And that afternoon, Lena went all on her own to see Sofie. She hadn't planned it, but in the afternoon, Bennie went down for a nap, and Vrouw Wijman lay down as well, something she had not done before. The other two members of the household were out.

And Lena's feet led her into the lean-to. She took the bicycle that leaned there and wheeled it out the door. Annie had taken the other one, but strangely, Wijman seemed to prefer his own two feet, despite the worn state of his wooden shoes.

It took only minutes to get to the Klaassens' on two wheels, and Sofie flew out the back door and into her arms when Lena knocked. The two huddled on a bench in the back garden, oblivious to the cold. Mevrouw Klaassen brought mugs of warm milk and several cookies on a small tray. Lena looked at the food in wonder as Mevrouw Klaassen smiled and gave them their privacy. Partway back to the house, she turned, the smile gone.

"If you convince our girl here not to be slipping out after dark," she said, "it will be safer for her. We think she's met a boy—though where she'd find one nowadays, I don't know— and we're worried about her. Do have a word!" And she turned back on her way.

Before the woman was done speaking, Lena knew. "You've seen Uli," she said.

Sofie's smile was soft, filled with guileless joy. And Lena's heart clenched at itself, as if all the blood had drained away. She straightened her shoulders. Now was no time for jealousy. Now was a time for strength of character.

"You can't, Sofie. You just can't. You'll be caught. It's just a matter of time; you know it is."

"I don't know anything, Lena, except that I love him." Then her face lit up even more, and she pulled a small bundle of paper from her pocket. "And someone loves you too! I saw Albert, you know, the very next day after we got here, before the train left. He wanted to come find you, but I knew you didn't want that, and with you in the centre of town, it would be dangerous."

"You never told me."

"There was nothing to tell. Truly," Sofie said. "Only a day had passed since our night in the bar. And I never saw you. If you'd visited, I would have told you . . ."

Lena settled back on the bench, dissatisfied. "Well, I'm here now," she said. "What have you got?"

"It's not much, Lena," Sofie said, and she handed her the merest scrap of paper.

On it a heart was drawn. In the heart, words were written. *Think of me often*, the words said, *as I think of you. Yours forever, Albert*.

Lena had to force herself to look up. She hated it that Sofie had seen what was on the paper. It wasn't in an envelope. She had had it for weeks. "Why didn't you bring it to me?" Lena asked.

"I've been meaning to," Sofie said, "but they keep me busy here."

"Not so busy that you haven't seen Uli again," Lena said. And she added, "Were they together?" She could not bring herself to speak Albert's name. Jealousy and anger poisoned her.

"No," Sofie said shortly. She drew breath. "Oh, don't be angry with me, Lena. Uli came back on a train headed west this time, but he was alone. He said that Albert had been sent somewhere else; he didn't know where. Anyway, the train's been gone now for two days. And Uli didn't know when he would be back."

Lena stood up stiffly. "Thank you for telling me," she said, sarcasm hardening her words, belying them. She smoothed the folded bit of paper in her pocket. "You're welcome to visit anytime." And she walked away to her bicycle leaning by the gate.

The house was quiet when she arrived, mother and son still sleeping, father and daughter still away.

* * *

Vrouw Wijman, Annie and Bennie went to church the day after that. Annie complained that it would be cold, but the neighbour's baby was going to be baptized, and Vrouw Wijman was determined. Wijman was off with his brother and the few cows that were left.

"No need for you to come," Vrouw Wijman said to Lena at the breakfast table. "You can stay here and clean up the breakfast things. And wash this floor."

Lena thought about mentioning not working on the Sabbath, but she would rather stay home anyway. She would be alone, blissfully alone.

As soon as the front door had clicked shut behind them, Lena got to work. Moments later, the clock struck nine thirty. She suspected that church would run until eleven, in the huge, frigid stone building a few blocks away. Then they would have to walk back, plus allow for any visiting they might do. She probably had two hours. If she could only be sure that Wijman would stay away, she could bathe. She still felt tainted by that cow's blood.

By ten, the kitchen floor was spotless, or close enough, and the breakfast dishes were clean, dry and back in their places. She looked at the big metal tub on the floor in the corner, but she didn't dare. She would have to settle for a sponge bath. She could do that with little risk of embarrassment. A mixing bowl half-filled with soapy hot water and another with clear water, a washcloth and a towel and she began, starting with her face. She held the hot washcloth against her skin and let the heat soak right in. Then her neck. It was an awkward process, since she stayed fully dressed throughout, but by wringing the cloth out thoroughly and following it up with the towel right away so as not to get her blouse or her skirt too wet, she managed. She did take off her stockings, though, so she was standing at the kitchen sink barefoot, damp hair sticking to her cheeks and her neck, when the door from the lean-to opened.

She turned in time to see Wijman's eyes rake her body and settle on those bare calves. "What are you up to, girl, all alone in my house?" he asked.

"I . . . I'm just cleaning up," Lena said, trying to make her voice strong.

He crossed the kitchen in three strides, and this time there was no gentle laying-on of hands. He grabbed her and thrust her up against the sink. "No more games," he grunted into her ear.

For once, Lena didn't freeze. She pulled all her strength together and shoved, making him stumble back. "No!" she shouted. "You mustn't."

He stood facing her from halfway across the room. He walked back, and this time he took her shoulders. His face was fierce and eager at the same time.

"What about your wife?" Lena said. "I'll tell." Even as she said it, she knew that it wouldn't matter. His wife already knew.

He pulled a hand back to slap her then, but seemed to think better of it.

"I said I'll tell," Lena said again, somehow emboldened by his anger. Could it be that telling mattered still? Yes, she thought. And she said again, "I'll tell," and then added, "and she'll send me away."

Wijman stared at her, his hands in fists at his sides.

Lena shook; her teeth chattered. She moved her head slowly from side to side. "Please, meneer." He flinched at the title and lowered his eyes. "I can't do that. It would be wrong. I . . . I can't." And she turned, walked to her alcove and pulled the curtain across the opening. For long moments, the kitchen was silent.

Then a voice. "This is not over," it said. "When a pretty young girl leaves home and places herself with strangers, she'd better expect to pay her way." Silence again.

For a long time, Lena strained for the sound of foot-steps, watched to see a hand on the curtain. Instead, after more moments than she could bear, she heard the door to the lean-to click closed.

Lena sat on her bed, knees pulled up to her chest, arms wrapped tight around her legs. What she had left behind in Amsterdam was bad, but this was worse, much worse. She might have been hungry, but she had never felt in danger in her own home. Here she could eat great slabs of liver and bowls of stew, but she wasn't safe. She had lost her friend. The one girl in the house was silent and furious. Bennie. She thought of him, and then Bep wandered into her mind, smiling, holding out a small drawing for her comment, asking her to come skip in the court-yard, showing up by her bed to keep her company when Margriet was gone. Lena's heart constricted. She had left Bep all alone.

And Nynke. A tiny baby. Hungry. And Piet. He had left her first, really, but what if he needed her? She had always been there for him before.

She shook her head, lay back down and stretched her legs out. The fear was gone for the moment, but Wijman could come back at any time. He did not want her to tell. Even though they both knew that his wife suspected his desire for her, he still did not want her to tell. That was what had stopped him. That was what would keep his hands off her. For how long, though? What did the words *this is not over* mean?

Next thing she knew, the clock was striking noon, and Vrouw Wijman was rousing her from her bed, enraged by the sloppy kitchen, the stockings and damp towel on the table, and the dopy, bare-legged girl looking blankly at her from the unmade bed.

CHAPTER THIRTEEN

Wijman stayed away the rest of that day, and at breakfast the next morning, he was silent. He met Lena's eyes once, and she looked right back, willing all her strength into her gaze, before returning to her bread and cheese.

Vrouw Wijman seemed to be done with Lena's sloth of the previous day. She was full of instructions for the morning.

Lena worked hard, concentrating on the tasks at hand, on keeping Bennie quiet and on holding at bay the memory of Wijman's eyes and hands. She worked hard and watched for the right moment to remind Vrouw Wijman that this was the day of the food packet. Possible conversations ran through her mind, all of them resulting in an angry snub. Vrouw Wijman had agreed to send food to Amsterdam only because of her husband, and Lena was desperate not to involve him.

Eventually, she ran out of time. The morning was wearing down, the table already laid for the noon meal. Wijman could walk through that door at any moment. And Bennie was down for a rare snooze on Lena's bed in the alcove.

If she did not ask now, the day might not present another opportunity. Vrouw Wijman was standing at the stove, tasting the soup, seeming just about as calm as she ever got.

Lena positioned herself respectfully off to one side. "Ma'am?" she said.

Vrouw Wijman's head whipped around, alert, brows knit, soup spoon forgotten in midair.

Lena swallowed.

"What is it, girl? What are you ma'am-ing me about?"

"I'm sorry"—Lena bit her tongue; she had almost said *Ma'am* again!—"ah, Vrouw Wijman. Today's the day I'm to send a food packet to my mother in Amsterdam."

Vrouw Wijman lowered the spoon to the counter and frowned. "I thought you had forgotten about that foolishness," she said.

"It's . . . it's not foolishness. My family in Amsterdam is starving. The baby, Nynke. My little sister Bep . . ." she tailed off and watched Vrouw Wijman's face, which she thought had softened slightly at the mention of the baby.

They both heard the door from the alley to the lean-to open then, and Vrouw Wijman actually jumped. Her expression turned fierce again.

"Fine," she said. "You'll get your food. We'll send it today. But I don't want you whining about it in front of him. Understand?"

Lena was nodding her head when Wijman entered the kitchen. He looked from her to his wife and back, shrugged and pulled out his chair.

As soon as the meal was over and the man had departed, Vrouw Wijman started piling food on the table. Lena cleaned up around her, flinching every time a packet hit the wood. The woman seemed to be expressing some sort of furious, self-sacrificing generosity. A jar of butter. A canvas sack of flour.

A wedge of cheese. Half a dozen potatoes. And a piece of meat with lots of fat attached. Lena gave thanks for the cool temperatures of early March, which would keep the food fresh on what might be a long journey.

"Fetch a small box from the shed," Vrouw Wijman said.

And in minutes more, the box was packed, and Lena was taking it down the lane and thanking Bosse over and over and over. Bosse was past fifty, too old, he said, to fear being rounded up by the Germans, and his mother had refused to leave the city. He was taking food to her and would be happy to tuck Lena's box in the corner of his small cart.

"I can take another in two weeks," he said.

Lena thanked him once again and wandered back out into the lane, feeling lighter than she had in some time.

The sun shone on the early March afternoon, and the orange-tiled roofs of the nearby mansion, Almelo House, gleamed. She had seen the grounds in passing once or twice, and though the Germans had taken the house over as their local headquarters, local people still walked the paths.

I've been here for a month, Lena thought, and I've been a drudge. Nothing more than a drudge.

"I think I'll take Bennie out for a walk," she said as she strode into the kitchen.

Vrouw Wijman turned and looked at her, her gaze sharp. Lena looked back, keeping her face clear.

And so it was that half an hour later, the girl and the small boy set off.

As they walked down the lane in the afternoon sunshine, Bennie chattered. Lena responded absently and gazed at the world around her. She felt like she was seeing it, really seeing it, for the first time in weeks. Months. Maybe years.

Quickly they reached the Almelo House grounds. Bulbs pushed green stalks up through the grass, and they stopped to look at them. Bennie busied himself pushing grass aside and shouting in triumph each time his efforts revealed a new shoot. Lena sat right down beside him, cross-legged, inhaling the smell of damp spring earth, ignoring the wet seeping through her skirt. A light breeze rustled the world above their heads, and birds rushed about in a frenzy of nest-building. Lena pointed them out to Bennie, and they talked about the eggs the birds would lay and the babies they would have. No war for them, Lena thought, though she suspected that the war did take its toll even on the birds.

Some trees showed the faintest flush of green; others were almost in bloom. The spot they had found was sheltered from humans of both kinds, soldier and civilian, except for themselves.

After an hour, they went home, damp, chilled and grass-stained but refreshed.

*　*　*

The next Sunday, once church and the noon meal were over, Lena prepared to take Bennie out again. "It's a beautiful day," she said to no one in particular. Then, to the small boy playing in the corner, "Would you like to go for a walk?" and he bounded up like a puppy. Vrouw Wijman was scrubbing away at something in the dark, cold living room and seemed indifferent to their plans.

Annie looked up from her book and smiled at her brother. "I could go too," she said, startling Lena and bringing an extra grin from Bennie.

This time, Lena pulled the little wagon that usually sat in the corner of the lean-to, though Bennie refused to ride in it at first. She had a longer walk in mind.

"I would like to visit my friend Sofie," she told Annie as the wagon bumped down the rutted lane.

Annie was inscrutable as always. "All right," she said, shrugging slightly. "I know a good way to de Wierdensestraat."

"Come, Bennie," Lena said. "We're going on an adventure."

And they began. Trees sheltered the three of them as they made their way along the canal that bordered the Almelo House property. They had to stop to show Annie all the sights and sounds and smells they had discovered the week before, but eventually they reached the point where the canal met up with the tiny, almost creek-like River Aa.

"This will take us there," Annie said, "as long as you don't mind a bit of a windy route."

Lena did not mind. As they walked, she filtered out the signs of war; she filtered out the dread, the horror of what had happened the week before, the shame she could still feel sometimes on her body where that man had stared at her bare legs. Be gone, she shouted to it inside her head. It was a beautiful spring day. She was out for a walk with a lovely little boy and a rather puzzling girl, off on a visit.

She wanted to walk fast—to feel the muscles in her legs, feel her lungs expand—and get to Sofie's house sooner than soon, but Bennie was slow and cried if they tried to put him in the wagon, and Annie was the slowest of the three.

"I thought you wanted to come," Lena said at last, trying to keep her voice friendly.

Annie stopped. "I did want to come," she said. "Though I didn't know where we were going. I needed . . . Oh, it doesn't matter. Let's go."

"All right," Lena said, curious but relieved somehow. And she grasped Bennie's hand and continued on her way. Annie entered into the spirit of the thing, taking Bennie's other hand in hers. They walked along the narrow path, the wagon bumping along behind, a giggling child swinging in between.

* * *

At first it seemed that no one was home. The front walk was cluttered and dirty, and the back door went unanswered. Lena remembered Meneer Klaassen leading the way through the lovely garden, still buried in snow when she and Sofie had first arrived in Almelo almost a month ago, and the kind welcome that had followed. Nothing felt the same now.

She raised her fist and knocked again. This time, she heard footsteps and stepped back as the door swung open.

"Mevrouw Klaassen," Lena said, beaming, "is Sofie here?"

Janneke Klaassen did not smile back. "No, Sofie is not here. Three days she's been gone. And good riddance," she said.

Lena's heart pounded, and she could not get her breath down her throat. "But . . . but, mevrouw, where has she gone?" she managed to stammer after a long moment.

Mevrouw Klaassen stared at her through cold, cold eyes. "Do I care where she has gone? A mof lover like that? And she slept in my own son's bed! Her filthy skin on his sheets. She'd have had that man in the bed right with her if I'd turned my back for a moment more." The woman almost spat in distaste on the word *man,* her long nose and upper lip constricting around the sounds, lengthening them, packing them full of hate.

Lena felt as if ice water were running over her skin, inside and out. What had Sofie done? Mevrouw Klaassen's hatred spilled over her, clearly meant not for Sofie alone, but for her too. What did this woman know? This was precisely what she had predicted back on the train. Fear filled her, not only for her friend's safety, but for her own.

And all she could do was stand there, staring.

At last, Annie stepped forward. "Thank you for telling us, Mevrouw Klaassen. That must have been very painful for you," she said.

The woman's gaze shifted to Annie and the small boy half hidden behind her. Her brows pulled together.

"We'll go now," Annie said firmly, her hand on Lena's arm. "We wish you well, you and Meneer Klaassen. I hope your sons come home to you soon."

* * *

They walked in silence until they were back on the path beside the river. Bennie seemed to have absorbed some of what had happened, and he rode in the wagon without complaint. Annie pulled the wagon and Lena followed the two of them, her mind tumbling with thoughts, her body stiff with dread.

Obviously, the Klaassens had caught Sofie with Uli and sent her away. Or had they? Maybe she had gone on her own. Maybe she was long gone to Germany. Maybe Lena would never see her again. But surely she wouldn't leave without a word. Unless she didn't want to endanger Lena. Round and round Lena's thoughts went. Sofie was gone. No. She couldn't be gone. But then, where was she? She must be gone.

So caught up in her thoughts was she that Annie had to put out a hand to keep her from crashing into the wagon when they stopped. Lena drew her mind back to the present and looked at the girl before her.

"Let's stop here a bit," Annie said. "I've been wanting a chance to talk with you. Let's sit down on the grass, just for a minute. Just for one minute."

Lena had no desire to sit with this strange girl. She wanted her friend. But she walked off the path and sat down on the damp grass on the riverbank, pulling Bennie down beside her.

"No!" he said, and he was up, a stick that Lena had not noticed before in his hand, playing happily near the water.

Annie plunked herself down beside her. "I need help," she said.

"Help?" Lena echoed. What could Annie possibly need help with? She never did anything. And surely Sofie's fate was the concern of the moment, not help for Annie.

"I've seen what you've been through since you've been with us, and I feel like I can trust you."

"Trust me for what?" This was getting stranger and stranger.

"I am a bicycle courier," Annie said.

Lena took her eyes off Bennie for a moment and stared at the other girl. She had never heard of a bicycle courier.

Annie paused. Then she said, "I work for the Dutch Resistance."

Lena's mouth fell open. "You're joking," she said. "You couldn't possibly . . ."

"Exactly," Annie replied. "Who better than someone who 'couldn't possibly'?"

"But you're always just sitting around. You don't do anything!"

"Well, haven't you noticed that I often go out and 'do nothing' there?"

Lena thought about it. Annie did disappear regularly, but she had always seen it as aimless wandering. "But that's dangerous!" she said, her voice rising.

Again, Annie paused. "Yes," she said, "it is, but it is helping. It is saving people's lives."

Lena looked at her, fear grasping her insides and squeezing them. Why was this girl telling her? You didn't tell stuff like that. You kept it secret. That was safer. And even more, she wondered, why was she telling her now? "Does your mother know?" she asked. "Your father? And why are you telling me this when you've just been told that my friend is a traitor?"

Annie rose to her feet. "What do you think?" She stood over Lena, her fists clenched. "My mother is a selfish woman. She wants food and comfort, status if she can get it—which she can't, having thrown her lot in with a lowly butcher—and her curtains as white as she can get them. And Father? This war means nothing to him either, except insofar as it restricts him. Father works and works, and once in a while he goes after a girl."

Lena's eyes widened.

"Oh, don't think you're the first." She paused, as if thinking. "Though it has been a long time since one turned up at the door offering to move in. Years." Annie's smile was ugly.

"Anyway," she said, her anger gone in a moment as she sank back down at Lena's side and smiled at Bennie, who had stopped playing and was staring at them, "Mother and Father would not be the people to tell. I thought, though, that you might be different, that you might want to help . . ." Her voice tailed off, and she was silent for a long moment. Then she said, "And what I saw just now . . . I saw that you care about your friend. I saw your fear and your shock, and I saw that you care. That's who we need: people who care."

No, Lena thought, her mind clear and certain. She cared about Sofie. She cared about Bennie and Bep and Piet. And Nynke. But total strangers? It was not her job to care about total strangers.

She did not want to help.

She had gone to the country with Margriet to get food. She had crossed the Netherlands in a cattle car, fighting off the advances of a man who, though the enemy, seemed to want to protect her. She had spent a month in a house where no one loved her, except perhaps for one small boy, and where, though food was more plentiful than at home, she was expected to help slaughter animals. And where a man watched and waited. Just now, having failed to help her first friend two years earlier, she seemed to have lost her second, however misguided that friend might be.

And Annie was asking her to risk her life for people she had never even met. Would never meet. She did not want to help. She wanted to go home. She would take her greedy father and her bitter, starving mother and her absent brother over these people any day.

"What . . . what is it that you would want me to do?" she asked, her voice low.

"First, just ride with me. I will show you the route. Then you will take it over."

"Why? Why don't you do it?"

"I already have a route, and they think it's too risky for me to take on another."

"They?" Lena echoed.

"Yes, they. The leaders."

Lena thought for a minute. Bennie came and gave her a new stick he had found. She thanked him and held the stick in her lap. "Who was doing it before?"

"A man."

"What happened to him?"

"He was taken by the Germans."

Lena shifted, and the stick fell off her lap. "Taken? You want me to become a courier because a man was taken? I can't do that! I know what happens to—"

"Don't you care about anyone other than yourself? I thought you did."

Lena stared at her. Could this girl really be only fifteen? She thought for a moment. "What about Bennie?"

Bennie looked up at the sound of his name and grinned.

Annie's brows knit. Then she said, "He could go with you," her voice animated. "He'd be a perfect cover! And we have a bicycle with a child seat."

Once again Lena could do nothing but stare while her mind roamed. Annie was willing to put her brother at risk. She wasn't sure whether that showed courage or carelessness.

Her own brother came to mind, and the neighbour with the radio. That was what Piet had hoped for, she knew: to get involved. And she was pretty sure that his wishes had been granted, that that was what had clammed him up. Still, Piet was doing what he had always longed to do. She had never felt such a longing, not for one second.

And when she had had the chance to do one tiny thing— to ride through the city to the Jewish Quarter and greet Sarah after she was forced to move—she had stayed away. She *had* been called upon to do something, small though it was, and she had resisted. She had failed. How could anyone think she had something to offer now?

Bennie slid his hand into hers and pulled. "Play," he said, his smile bright.

And that smile brought other images into Lena's mind, images that changed her. The words *Rachel. June 12–Sept 17, 1943. RIP* carved into a wooden wall. A tiny baby, captive on the very train that had taken Lena where she had thought she wanted to go. A baby who barely made it past three months, who never got to smile and say, "Play!" who never rode in a wagon or made a drum from a pot and a wooden spoon.

Another child came to Lena's mind then as well. Nynke. What if Nynke was starving and no one offered her food? What if she was taken away and no stranger stepped forward to help her?

I've left my sister all alone, Lena thought, and she said, "I'll do it." There the words were, spoken. "Yes. I'll do it." And there they were again, meant.

They talked just a little more then.

Lena had a thought and pulled her identity card out of her pocket. "I'm worried about this," she said.

Annie took it and stared. "Aubrey Schulze?" she said at last, looking up. "This is the worst forgery I've ever seen."

Lena waited.

After another moment, Annie said, "Leave it with me. Our people can do better. Do you want to be yourself again?"

Lena nodded.

After that, Annie led the way toward home, the wagon bumping along behind her, its cargo singing softly to himself. Lena lagged behind them both. She had a great deal to think about.

CHAPTER FOURTEEN

Annie was first through the kitchen door, Bennie at her heels. Lena was still inside the lean-to, unlacing her shoes, in no hurry to re-enter her workaday life in the Wijman household, when Annie reappeared in the doorway, her face alight with surprise and excitement.

Lena stood and stared at this new Annie. Then her eyes took in the figure behind her.

"Sofie!" For a moment she felt nothing but joy, and she saw joy in her friend's face as well as they flung themselves into each other's arms.

"You have to make them let me stay."

Sofie's words were whispered, rushed, desperate. Lena had to play them again to herself in order to hear what Sofie had said. She looked up then and saw Vrouw Wijman sitting at the kitchen table, staring, her face hard.

"Come," Lena said. And then, more loudly, "We're going outside for a moment." Vrouw Wijman half rose at that, and her lips parted, but Lena did not wait. "Come," she said again, and they were in the lean-to, at the door to outside. Sofie was shoving her feet into a pair of oversized wooden shoes; Lena was ignoring the flopping laces on her own shoes and the fact that she had already discarded her coat.

"Lena!" They both heard behind them, but they were out; the door was closing behind them, and they were away.

Lena led Sofie back to the Almelo House grounds, to the same spot where she and Bennie had enjoyed the new shoots and the birds. The grass was dry now, and the two girls sat, shivering slightly, and looked at each other.

Sofie was fatter than she had been, but her clothes were dirty, her hair uncombed, and Lena could see remnants of sleep in the corners of her eyes.

"She said you've been gone three days," Lena said. "Where have you been?"

"What do you mean, 'she'?" Sofie said back, defiance hardening her expression.

"I went to see you this morning," Lena said, "and you were gone. Mevrouw Klaassen has nothing good to say about you." She did her best to smile.

"They acted so nice," Sofie said then. "They said I was like the daughter they never had. They loved me. I helped them bear the pain of missing their sons. She made me call her Janneke. She taught me to bake. She sent packets to my mother in Amsterdam. Two within three weeks! I met all their friends. It was like I had come home. They said I could stay with them even after the war. And I thought I might. I really did."

She stopped. Lena had seen her features soften as she spoke, and she understood. Sofie had thought she'd found a new family, a simpler, kinder, more loving one. The silence stretched on. Sofie's eyes were downcast, her lips soft. Lena hated to bring her back to herself, but at last she said, "And . . . ?"

The eyes snapped up. The lips parted, thinned. "Uli came

back this week," she said. "The first time, the time I told you about, he snuck away to the Klaassens' and threw a pebble at my window. Just as they do in stories," she said, and her face was soft again, "and I went with him. All three nights the train was here. It was so perfect. Everything was so perfect! I mean almost. They did catch me coming in late twice, like Mevrouw Klaassen said when you were there. Hours after curfew. They didn't like that. They worried and made me promise I wouldn't do it again. But then I did." She paused. "I had to, didn't I?"

She looked at Lena and went on. "But when he came this last time, I went too far. The Klaassens sleep at the front of the house, and I was at the back. I thought I could sneak him in, just once. It was cold outside, always cold. And we both thought what it would be like to be together in a bed. A real bed, like we'll have when we're married. And so I snuck him in. And Meneer Klaassen caught us on the stairs."

Her face darkened.

"Well, forget about love. Forget about family. In one second, I went from their daughter to a mof lover and a traitor, like the soldiers who practically tore their younger son right out of their arms. In another second, Uli and I were out on the street. They didn't let me get my things. I have nothing. The train was in town until yesterday, and we stayed together in the straw. He tried to convince me to stow away again, to come with him, but the train was going west, not east. I knew it wasn't safe. And I wanted to see you. I . . . I couldn't just go off like that."

"Where did you sleep last night?" Lena asked.

"In a garden shed," Sofie replied. "I have never been so cold."

Lena had pulled a tuft of grass and was shredding it, blade by blade. She would have to look up soon, look up and meet

Sofie's eyes, but she felt the judgment in her own and kept them on the ground.

At last, Sofie broke the silence. "Oh, Lena, I'm not so bad you can't even look at me. Uli is the one really good thing in my life, and I am not giving him up. I'm not." She reached into a pocket and pulled out a few sheets of paper, just as she had done the last time they met. Lena stared at her hand. "We're just waiting for this blasted war to end," Sofie said, "and we'll be together. I've got his address right here. Minden. His parents live in Minden now, since Düsseldorf was bombed last year."

But Lena hardly heard what Sofie said. "Was Albert here too this week?" she asked.

Sofie's eyes flickered and delight stole over her face. "Ah, if they only knew that good little Lena is a mof lover too!" she said.

"He's not my lover," Lena said. "You know he's not. But have you seen him?" She wasn't sure what she wanted the answer to be. If Sofie had seen him, why hadn't he sought her, Lena, out? Why hadn't he sent word somehow? He could at least have sent word through Sofie. She quailed at her own hypocrisy, but she wondered just the same.

"Well, Miss Good Girl Lena—who never longed for any man, let alone a dirty mof . . ." Her expression turned serious. "No, Lena, I haven't seen Albert again since that last time. But five days ago, when Uli arrived, he gave me this." Sofie had pulled a small envelope from among the mess of paper in her hand. She offered it without ceremony. "It is for you."

Lena snatched it. Like last time, anger surged inside her. How dared Sofie keep a letter meant for her? Had she read it? Then she noted the sealed envelope and Sofie's hurt stare. The darkness inside her was washed away by a rush of excitement. She turned her attention to the bit of paper in her hand.

My dearest Lena,

I know that you might not have wished it, but I was going to come for you. I was going to send Sofie and wait nearby or something— anything to see you again. But now I am to go far away. I hope to see Uli once more before I go so I can give him this little slip of paper to tell you that you are not forgotten.

Perhaps one day when this war is all behind us, you will send me a word. One word and I will come to you then, wherever you are. I know I am not good with language, and if you were not as good and kind as you are, you might laugh at this little note. But you have brought light and joy into my life, and I pray for your safety and your happiness.

Albert

Lena struggled a little with the German, but Albert had kept his language simple and she understood well enough. She wanted to pore over the note, the handwriting, the paper, the envelope, so meticulously folded and glued, but she did not want Sofie to see how much it mattered to her.

She folded the note, replaced it in its envelope and tucked it away.

Sofie had watched her throughout.

"It was nice of him to write," Lena said grudgingly, trying to make her voice casual. What did it mean that she was beside herself with joy over this little note? Then she noticed that Sofie's gaze had lifted. She was looking beyond Lena rather than at her.

Annie was striding toward them across the grass. "You're wanted at the house," she said. "Mother says if you don't come now, she'll come after you herself."

* * *

The scene that followed was dreadful. They started by sitting down at the kitchen table, like civilized people, but that was as far as the civility went. Sofie's answers to Vrouw Wijman's questions did not satisfy. And Vrouw Wijman was not interested in Lena's contributions.

"The Klaassens are respectable citizens," Vrouw Wijman said, more than once. "Why would they turn a girl out onto the street if she didn't deserve it? And why would we take such a girl in?"

"Please, Vrouw Wijman," Sofie said, all her charm on display, "it was just a misunderstanding. They are good people, but I never meant any harm. Please, please, can't I stay here with you?"

"She can share my bed," Lena said. "She'll work."

"You stayed with us once before, young lady, if you remember," Vrouw Wijman said. "You were a child, but your mother was not. When I saw you on my doorstep those few weeks ago, I thought, There walks her mother's daughter. And that, my dear, is not a compliment. It is not a compliment, and I suspect that you have proven the truth of it."

Sofie's shoulders had collapsed at this speech. Her eyes were cast down. Lena, however, felt as if a light had turned on inside her head. So that was why Sofie hadn't wanted to stay here! Why she had suggested Almelo at all was a whole other question. It was probably the only place she knew. So Sofie's mother and Annie's father . . . That was what it sounded like. Something terrible had happened. And Vrouw Wijman knew.

"Vrouw Wijman," Lena said, making her voice firm, "Sofie is not a bad girl. Truly, she is not. Please don't turn her out in the middle of a war. She could be hurt. Raped."

Vrouw Wijman looked at Lena. "I've a good mind to turn you both out," she said. "You made your own way here. You can make your own way home." But she looked at Bennie, snug in Lena's lap, as she spoke.

She would miss me, Lena thought. Not for me, but for the work. She snuggled Bennie a little closer. And I would miss him, she realized. I would miss him a lot. For the second time that day, Nynke and Bep flitted into her mind. Firmly, she ordered them out, inhaling the scent of Bennie's little-boy hair as she did so.

The door from the lean-to opened, startling everyone. Bennie slithered off Lena's lap and ran into his father's arms. Annie bit her pigtail. Sofie hunched deeper, if that were possible. And Lena gripped the edge of the table.

"So it's true," Wijman said. He didn't shout. He lifted Bennie off the ground, swung him through the air and put him down, his attention on the desperate girl hunkered down at the table. "Meneer Klaassen came looking for me at Bert's. He wanted to be sure I knew what that girl there's been up to." He turned his gaze full on his wife. "I told him I did not know that she was in Almelo at all. You," and he bore down on her as he spoke, "have been keeping little secrets."

Vrouw Wijman was on her feet, ready for him. "And why do you think I didn't want to mention the Vogel girl to you? Could it be because of the Vogel woman?" She squared her shoulders. "Now step away from me."

And he did, but his fury did not diminish. Instead it looked for a new target. "He said I should keep an eye on you too," he said to Lena, "and I expect he's right. None but me saw you parading around all damp and bare-legged that day. Now who were you putting that show on for? I wonder."

Bennie was crying by then, backed against Lena's apparently offensive legs. Sofie had bent right over, arms wrapped around her head as if she thought someone might hit her. Vrouw Wijman sank back onto her chair, the soft flesh of her face and neck slack, the fight gone out of her for the moment.

Lena looked at her accuser, shock and nausea like oil and water in her belly. It was sickening to be accused like that, especially by a man who had trouble keeping his hands to himself, a man who had apparently seduced Sofie's mother seven years before. Or had the seduction gone the other way? Or had it not been a seduction at all? Had force been involved? Lena's head reeled while her body recoiled.

Wijman was not done. "You'll be glad to hear that I didn't mention your display. I told him that our Lena is a good girl and a hard worker. I also told him that I know the Vogels, that they were once our guests before the war."

Vrouw Wijman's head came up again, neck stretched taut.

"So, young lady, you can stay in our house. You will share Lena's bed. You will not set foot outside or show yourself to anyone. I will give you two days. Then, Lena, you can decide if you wish to stay with us or leave with your young friend here, despite her poor judgment and wicked ways."

And with those words, he turned and was out of the house, his work for the day not done.

Vrouw Wijman was on her feet, her breath coming in furious gasps. Ignoring her son and her daughter, she came at Sofie with the force of a tank, gripped her arm and yanked her to her feet. "You," she spat, "will not do to me what your slut of a mother did. Do you understand?"

Sofie's chin remained in firm contact with her chest as she nodded.

"If I see you within three paces of my husband, I'll have you out in the street, barefoot and in your shift. And that is after I take the broom to you."

Bennie whimpered, and Lena pulled him into her arms. "It's all right," she whispered lamely. "She doesn't mean it." But it was clear to all of them that she did.

Lena took one arm from around the little boy and reached out and touched Vrouw Wijman's shoulder. The woman flinched and turned her head. Two wet lines marked her face, eyes to chin.

"Sofie won't do anything wrong," Lena said. "I'll see to it."

At that, Sofie met her eyes. Her voice was not strong, but her words were. "I won't do anything wrong," she said, "because I don't want to. I don't know what my mother did, but I'm not like that. I love one man." Her voice grew louder, defiant, angry. "One man. Yes, he is one of the enemy, but he is the man I love. His name is Ulrich. Ulrich Rauch."

Silence took hold of the room for a few moments. Mevrouw Wijman stepped away from both girls. "Good girl. Bad girl. Whatever you are, you'd better get busy helping Lena make the supper. I am going to go lie down." And she did.

CHAPTER FIFTEEN

With Sofie's arrival, Lena almost forgot about the conversation with Annie about the Resistance. When she did think of it, she was sure that Annie would do the runs herself or find someone else. How could Lena be a Resistance worker with a lover of the enemy sharing her very bed?

But the conversation had taken place, and it turned out that Annie had no intention of making other plans. Almost a week passed.

Then, on Wednesday afternoon, she walked into the kitchen and spoke. "My bed is much bigger than Lena's, Mother," she said, her voice crisp. "It doesn't make sense for the two of them to share that tiny cot. Lena should come in with me."

Sofie's two days' grace had passed with no further mention of her banishment. Lena had watched in bemused shock as Sofie put a brand-new, and perfectly selected, strategy to work. It turned out that Sofie could clean. At first, she just followed Vrouw Wijman's angry instructions, passed through Lena, since Vrouw Wijman would neither look at Sofie nor speak to her. Then she started asking questions, still through Lena: questions about cleaning, about getting out stains, about reaching those hard-to-reach spots. On the second day, she made several suggestions that drew Vrouw Wijman's brows high on her forehead and gave her eyes a glitter that Lena had not seen before.

On the third day, instead of seeing Sofie onto the street, Lena watched, surprised and pleased, as Vrouw Wijman entered deep into conference with her about what might work best to remove those grass stains from Bennie's pants.

And on that Wednesday afternoon, while Sofie scrubbed away in the kitchen under Vrouw Wijman's watchful eye, Lena packed her few things into her small suitcase and moved upstairs. Annie did not come with her, and she seemed to take little note of her through the rest of the day. Lena went about her tasks in some bewilderment, and quite unsure, as well, about whether she was pleased with this new arrangement, although she did look forward to a peaceful night. The last few nights' sleep had been spotty at best, shared as they were with a companion who kicked and wriggled and yanked at the bedding, not to mention moaning over her lost love.

At bedtime that night, Lena found out why Annie had orchestrated the change. Lena undressed shyly and tucked herself into the bed right up against the wall, determined to be no bother. Annie, on the other hand, shucked her clothes off and slithered into her nightgown with no attention to privacy, and positively bounced into bed.

"I should have thought of this ages ago!" she said.

"Why did you?" Lena asked.

"Isn't it obvious? When can we talk with you downstairs and people always about? Now, with Sofie here, it's impossible! And so I thought, Bed. That's the place to talk!"

All in a moment, Lena's brain cleared. "The Resistance," she said.

"Yes," Annie replied. "Didn't you realize?"

Lena had not.

"Hey, I almost forgot," Annie said gleefully, and she slid out of bed and rooted around on the floor for a minute. "Look what I've got for you!" Back in bed, she held out something.

Lena's identity card. She took it, and Annie brought the candle close so she could see. There she was. Herself. Lena Berg. And as closely as she peered, she could see nothing wrong. The card did not even look unnaturally new. Relief swept through her—relief of a worry she hadn't even known she was carrying.

They whispered together for a long time that night after the card was tucked away and the candle blown out. Or Annie whispered and Lena listened.

Annie explained that a large part of Resistance work involved supplying ration cards for people in hiding. Many operations existed to steal ration cards in large quantities. Then they had to be delivered to those who bought food for the hidden. Without weekly ration cards, the hidden people would starve.

"And that's where girls like us come in," Annie said. "Nobody notices us . . . most of the time."

It sounded simple enough, but Lena's determination to become a doer of good waned as the night wore on. The risk was death. Death! Perhaps she should say she had changed her mind. But she did not say that, and eventually the two girls lay down, and to Lena's surprise, she slept.

On Thursday morning, Lena awoke in the pitch dark. Annie was leaning over her, invisible but breathy. "Shhh," Annie said fiercely. "Here are your instructions."

Lena sat up abruptly.

Heart pounding, she waited.

"I'm going to show you the route today," Annie said. "I have the cards. You don't need to know anything about where they came from. You just take them from me and give them to the man who answers the door if he says, 'Hello, Elsa. What do you have for me today?' And that's it. That's all."

Lena could not see Annie's face, and Annie could not see hers. "That's it? That's all? It sounds like a lot to me!"

"Well, it's not. We'll leave right after lunch. We'll just tell Mother that we're taking Bennie for a bike ride. Then next week, you can go on your own. It's only once a week."

"But what about Sofie?"

"What about Sofie? She's got nothing to do with this. Just keep it to yourself!"

"But what if she . . ."

Annie reached out and grabbed Lena's arm. "Look. This work is important. You know you can't say anything to Sofie. And she's not allowed to leave the house. She'll just think you're off for a bike ride, that's all."

It sounded so simple when Annie said it. Lena shrugged the hand off. "Fine. A bike ride after lunch," she said, and wriggled back down into the bed. She did not have to get up quite yet.

She turned her back on the other girl and tried to go back to sleep, but it was no use. What had she agreed to do?

Vrouw Wijman was gruff that morning, more demanding than usual, if that was possible. In the first days after Sofie's arrival, Lena had seen her shake with tension when her husband was at home. He stayed away a great deal, though, and as long as he was not there, Vrouw Wijman was easily distracted by cleaning. When he was in the house, Sofie kept her distance. She and Lena and Annie took to eating their dinner early, with Bennie, and thus peace was maintained, fragile though it might be.

228

Wijman had not asked Lena for help of any kind since she rebuffed him in the kitchen, and though she had felt his eyes on her many times, he had not once touched her since then. He didn't even look at Sofie. It was almost as if Sofie were a powder keg and his eyes and hands matches. He was afraid of the explosion and took no risks.

As Lena washed windows that Thursday morning, while Bennie played nearby and Sofie scrubbed the floor, she almost wondered if she could relax where Wijman was concerned. Drudgery, she could handle. After all, she had been raised to it. But Resistance work? Lena gritted her teeth and rubbed a little harder.

While Wijman and Vrouw Wijman were eating their noon dinner that day, Sofie scrubbed at a pot that Lena had burned, Annie read in a chair she had pulled over beside the stove and Lena kept Bennie entertained on the floor near Annie's feet. A second parcel would go off to Amsterdam in a few days. She relaxed into imaginings of her mother's excitement over a bit of butter and some flour.

Then Annie looked up from her book. "Lena and I are going to take Bennie out for a ride this afternoon," she said, tossing her hair out of her eyes.

Sofie turned around from the sink, her expression startled. "A ride?" That was Vrouw Wijman.

"Yes, a bicycle ride. He'll love it!"

Vrouw Wijman stared at her daughter.

Lena watched the exchange and then shocked herself by joining in. "We had such fun on Saturday, the three of us!" she said. "We thought, Wouldn't it be nice to get out into the country?" She looked at Sofie and added impulsively, "I wish you could come, Sofie. It would do you so much good to get out of the house!"

Vrouw Wijman turned her gaze on Lena. Her husband looked up from his plate. "Sofie knows she's not going anywhere," he said. "The rest of them, why not? No need for them to stay cooped up here."

And that was the end of it. Bennie wriggled with excitement, their quiet game forgotten. Lena stood up to help Sofie at the sink.

"You never told me," Sofie whispered. "Why are you keeping secrets?"

Annie elbowed in, dishtowel in hand. "I'll dry," she said.

"They don't need you there, Sofie," Vrouw Wijman said. "You can spend the afternoon polishing silver. You know where the things are."

Twenty minutes later, Bennie was strapped into the child seat and Lena was pedalling after Annie right across the market square, illegal ration cards weighing like a lead brick inside her clothes. They passed two SS officers leaning on a car and talking. Lena waited for them to shout, "Halt!" but they did not. On the girls went, along the northeast side of the canal that ended in the square. They crossed a bridge over another canal, and town turned to country. Lena was flooded with something that could only be called joy. This was even better than Sunday's walk along the River Aa. The road along the canal stretched forever in front of them, green fields on their right. Train tracks followed the canal on the other side, but not the same ones that had brought their train to Almelo. Lena felt the sun on her shoulder. They were cycling northwest.

The breeze blew her hair away behind her. Bennie laughed and held on to her waist.

Her hunger journey with her sister flitted into her mind and out again. Maybe it was the comparatively full stomach, maybe it was the signs of spring, but this ride had fun about it. That ride had not.

Annie looked back over her shoulder, and Lena grinned. Annie grinned back. "Not so bad, eh?" she shouted.

Too soon, Annie turned onto a dirt track leading to a farm. She pulled to a stop off to one side. "Make a note of these trees," she said. "There's no sign."

Lena looked at her blankly.

"For next time," Annie said. "Come on, Lena. Think!"

Lena started at the words *next time*. She had forgotten about next time, about this time, even about the war. She was not pleased to be brought back.

"I'll wait for you here," Annie said.

Lena opened her mouth to protest, but she changed her mind.

"Fine," she said, and remounted. The bicycle wobbled as she adjusted to Bennie's weight and the rough ground. Tension flooded through her as she approached the farmhouse. It was rundown, hardly looked lived in, but she dismounted, wheeled right up to the door and knocked. Almost instantly, the door opened. A man, a very tall man, looked down at her.

"Hello, Elsa. What do you have for me today?" he said.

Lena stood, frozen. Then she said, "Oh, yes," and dug through the layers of her clothing to unearth the ration cards. She handed them over.

"Thank you, Elsa," he said as he took them. His smile was warm. "See you next week." And he closed the door, gently, in her face.

Lena could see Annie's relief from the moment she turned the bend in the track and the other girl came into view. "Did you . . . ? Did it . . . ?" she asked, wheeling her bicycle forward as Lena slowed to a stop.

"Yes, yes. It all went fine. Now let's go," Lena said. And it had gone fine. She felt a small blush of pride and exhilaration. It *had* gone fine. The ride home, she discovered, could be even better than the ride away.

The week flew by.

The second food packet, this time with no beef, went off with Bosse on Monday. He had made it safely to Amsterdam and back, and insisted that all had gone well, though to Lena he looked more worn than he had, as if he had returned from a dark place.

He brought no note from her family. Her father had answered the door, he said, taken the packet and said a curt thank you. That was all. Bosse hadn't seen anyone else. Lena stamped down the hurt as she placed the new packet in his hands. Thanks or no, she was glad that he was willing to go again. And almost glad that she had other things to think about.

Twice that week, Lena took Bennie on short rides in response to his incessant begging. Each time she felt happier, more confident. She rode by SS officers without a second glance. After all, she had nothing to hide on those occasions. She and Annie shocked both the Wijmans with their sudden friendship, and Annie pleased her mother, although Lena knew that was no part of her intent, by playing more with Bennie and lifting a dishtowel now and again. She felt the glow too, it seemed, of a genuine connection with another human being.

Lena continued to regret leaving Sofie alone each time, but she grew used to her reproachful looks. After all, it wasn't Lena's fault that Sofie was living like a prisoner in the Wijmans' house. In fact, it was thanks to Lena that Sofie had any place to stay at all.

Thursday came again. Annie handed over the envelope, and Lena made her announcement at lunch. A bicycle ride, despite the drizzle. Bennie perked up immediately. He didn't mind a bit of rain. And Vrouw Wijman didn't even glance out the window. It was fine with her.

Lena had been tense all morning, despite her newfound confidence and her joy in last week's ride. She knew that the risks were great, and that they extended beyond her to Sofie and the whole Wijman family, especially to the little boy who held up his arms with such excitement to be placed in his special seat. She pushed the tension aside. These risks were not taken without reason. This was how you helped people. This was what people did. It was a war.

I sound like Piet, she thought, and smiled.

The second ride was not as nice as the previous week's because of the rain, but it was no more eventful. Lena arrived home ready to burst. Despite the mountains of potatoes and sugar beets that she had peeled and chopped, the hours scrubbing floors and looking after Bennie, she discovered that she had never felt truly useful before this day. Not once. She and Bennie practically danced into the house, drawing a grumpy comment from Vrouw Wijman, a sad look from Sofie, who was washing pots, and a warning look from Annie, who was in her customary posture at the kitchen table, hair in eyes, book in hand.

The next Thursday morning, Annie put something else into Lena's hand, a matchbox. "They want you to take this as well this time," she said as Lena's fingers closed around the small object. "It's a matchbox, and here is a box of cigarettes to go with it. There're only two in there, so you can put the matchbox in with them. Then if you're stopped, they probably won't look inside. And here are the ration cards. Hide them well. You don't want them to find both, or else they'll search the cigarette packet more closely."

"But I don't smoke," Lena said weakly.

Annie laughed. "Don't be silly," she said.

* * *

That was the day they were stopped. It was a sunny afternoon, almost April. Everywhere the land was greening, ducks were swimming, birds were flying. And Lena was flying too, filled with joy despite the matchbox and her dangerous task.

The officer had parked his car on a crossroad out of sight, and he only stepped into Lena's view as she drew close. "Halt!" he called to her, and she had no choice but to put her foot on the brake, brought to earth in a moment.

"Where are you off to today?" he asked as he took the forged identity card that she held out to him in steady fingers.

"Just a ride," she said quietly, hoping her voice didn't shake. "Just taking my little brother for a ride." She surprised herself by calling Bennie her brother. Would he ruin everything?

"Hello, little guy," the officer said. "Having fun?"

Lena waited for Bennie to shout, "Bad guy!" or make machine-gun noises, but he just grinned widely. "Ride!" he said.

The officer flipped open Lena's identity card and glanced at the picture and the stamp. "Lena Berg," he said, glancing up and meeting her eyes. Lena tried not to think about her face, about all the ways in which it could give her away. A muscle in her cheek twitched.

"Hold your coat open," the officer said.

She did, feeling the bulge at her waistband where the ration cards were tucked. Would he notice?

He pulled off his gloves, shoved them in his pocket and went carefully through each of hers. Eventually, as she knew they would, his fingers found the cigarette packet, and then he had it out, in his hand, and was looking at her. Her heart raced, her throat dried up, her hands gripped tighter at her coat.

"A smoker," he said as he opened the packet and peered inside. "Cigarettes are hard to come by nowadays. You must be connected!" Was his look suspicious now? She couldn't tell. Then he reached two fingers into the packet and removed one of the cigarettes. "One for you. One for me," he said, and her heart, beating so rapidly a moment before, stopped.

Please don't smoke it now, she begged inside her head. Please don't smoke it now. If he did, he would need a light. She waited for those fingers to turn the packet upside down and shake out the box of matches.

They did not. He tucked the cigarette into his pocket and finished searching hers. There was nothing but her identity card and the cigarette packet. He handed them back to her, and she let go of her coat and took them. The ration cards remained undiscovered.

"Off with you, then," he said.

And she went. The tall, thin man at the farmhouse door was surprised when she asked him a question as she handed over her cargo, but he was happy enough to direct her to another way back to Almelo. Lena was not prepared to chance running into that officer again, ever.

Her exhilaration surprised her. In bed that night, she did not stop chattering to Annie until she pulled the blanket over her head and moaned.

"Sleep!" she begged.

Lena tossed and turned for a long time, and she would have done so for longer still had she known what was in store for her.

Four days later, Annie woke Lena at dawn and told her that she was to make an extra trip that very day, in the morning. And she was to go without Bennie.

The day before was Easter Sunday, the first of April, and the weather had turned cold and wet. After breakfast, Lena bundled up.

"Where are you going?" Vrouw Wijman asked.

"I'm going out for a bit," Lena said. "I need to see if Bosse is back from Amsterdam."

"Ride?" Bennie shouted. "Ride!"

"No, Bennie," Lena said. "It's too wet for you. And I'm not going far. We'll go together later."

She pried his fingers off her coat and settled him with an ancient wooden puzzle, the pattern almost entirely worn off. Sofie watched her throughout but said nothing.

"I'd best not find out you're off with some young man, like your friend here," Vrouw Wijman said, but there was little force behind her words.

Lena went through to the lean-to, shutting the kitchen door firmly behind her, hoping no one would notice that she was taking her bicycle to go such a short distance.

The rain hit her sideways as she pushed the bicycle out into the lane, and the ground was slick and muddy underfoot. She wrapped her scarf around her head and lower face and set off. The wind was stronger still in the open country along the canal, and it was all she could do to keep from being driven off the road right into the water. The weather took all her concentration, distracting her from her worries about what was to come. She arrived at the farmhouse damp and shivering.

The elderly man who had greeted her on each of the previous occasions came to the door when she knocked and ushered her inside.

"Welcome, Elsa," he said. "Please join us." And he led her through to a small room off the kitchen, where two other men sat with a girl at a small table.

"Annie . . . ah, I mean Ria!" Lena said. In her surprise, she had forgotten to use Annie's false name. The men looked at her sternly, but Annie just grinned.

"Hi, Elsa," Annie said.

If Annie was already here, why had Lena needed to come at all? What was being asked of her? Lena smiled at everyone as best she could and took the seat that was offered to her. The conversation resumed.

"The liberators are going to arrive any day. We must be ready for them," said one of the men. "They may need our help to drive the Germans out."

He sounded as if shooting a few Germans would give him great pleasure.

"All right. Let's tell these girls what we want from them." The man who had answered the door turned to Annie and Lena. His gaze was warm and a little sad, as if he wished he had something else to say. Lena wished he had something else to say as well. "Arms," he said. "We are going to ask you to carry arms."

Lena's stomach turned right over, badly destabilizing its contents. She swallowed.

The man did not appear to notice her discomfort. "There was an arms drop last night," he said, "not far from here." He unfolded a large map on the table. "I can't give you this map, so you must learn it. Do you understand?"

Lena understood nothing, and she was by no means sure that she was going to do what he was asking of her, but she peered obediently at the map.

"The drop was here." He pointed at a spot a little to the north of them. "And it was collected last night and stored in a well right here." He pointed to a spot just a bit closer. "And we expect our liberators to come from here." He pointed on the map to the south. "They are going to meet opposition, and German soldiers may well try to loot and murder as they flee. We must be ready to support the arriving troops and to send the enemy packing. We need you to carry guns and grenades from here to here." His finger jabbed down at the map in two spots. They meant nothing to Lena.

Another man at the table leaned forward. "This is not something you can do in broad daylight," he said. "Just before curfew is best. You will dress in a nurse's uniform. We have new identity cards for you that say you are nurses. You will be travelling for an emergency—a birth, I think. If you meet up with Germans, you will talk your way out of it. You will not let them search you." Lena didn't think that he really believed they could pull that off, but she granted that she might have a better chance than any of these men.

"When must this happen?" she asked, hoping he would say in a week, in a month, never . . .

"Tonight," he said.

Tonight? Lena felt herself nod. I am going to carry arms, she said inside her head. Tonight. It did not sound real to her at all. She felt a strange calm, a funny floaty feeling.

Alongside Annie, she studied the map.

"You can ride out from town just as you have been doing," he said, "but continue on past this house. You'll need to cross the canal here, but then get off that road immediately. Here is your pickup point. You'll stow the arms about yourselves and carry on. You'll skirt Wierden on the west side."

He went on talking, but Lena wasn't listening. She was staring at the map and remembering. Wierden. She had walked that road! She felt a small boost of confidence. She would be cycling at least one familiar road tonight. And she had made that other journey successfully. Why not this one?

She paid careful attention as he showed the drop-off point, and she noted with relief that the ride home from there would not be long. It was all in her head, clear as clear. Between the two of them, they were sure to find their way.

"I think that Elsa should go first," Annie said. "I don't mind going after curfew."

Go first?

"What do you mean?" Lena said. "We're doing this together, aren't we?"

The man who hadn't spoken yet laughed. "Well, that wouldn't make much sense, would it? If you go together and they catch one of you, they catch both. This way, if they catch one, the other will probably get through. And one young nurse on the road is more believable than two. Even better, Annie will take a different route."

"But you showed Ria the same route."

"No. She learned her route before you got here," the man said, an extra measure of patience slowing his speech.

Annie turned to Lena. "You can do it, Elsa. You'll be fine! We'll go over everything together ahead of time."

Lena wanted to slap the other girl.

She felt trapped as she never had before, despite all she had been through in the last two months. Tonight, she was going to be forced to ride right into danger in the dead of night with illegal weapons in her bag.

And it was all Annie's fault. Every bit of it.

The meeting wrapped up quickly then, and Lena was ushered to the door, a nurse's uniform in her bag, a new identity card in her pocket. They had kept the old card, as it would not do for her to be stopped with two different identity cards on her person. They must have copied her photograph somehow—the new card looked just as real as the old one did.

* * *

The afternoon went by far too quickly. By the time she got home, Lena had realized that blaming Annie was not going to help her to survive. Over and over again, she reviewed the plan in her mind: the map, the pickup and drop-off points, what she would say if she was stopped. She realized two weak points almost immediately. First, she had no excuse, no reason to walk out the door with a bicycle late in the day. Second, she could hardly come downstairs dressed as a nurse!

Outside, the rain and wind kept on and on and on.

The second problem was solved more easily than the first. She would have to change on the road. She had no other option. In her mind's eye, she traced the first part of the route. Yes, there was a small copse of trees well outside of town. She would simply wheel off the road, change quickly and wheel back on again. She would have her regular clothes in her bag then, but it could not be helped. She would have to find a place to change back again after she had dropped off the things.

She called them *things* in her mind, not *arms*. It was not possible that Lena Berg was going to risk her life carrying guns and grenades on a clandestine nighttime journey. No, Elsa Holst, young nurse, was going to take a few things with her to a woman outside of town who was giving birth. After all, she (Lena, that is) had helped at a birth before—a difficult but successful birth.

Lena never did come up with an acceptable excuse for leaving the house that night, so when the time came, she gave none. When Vrouw Wijman sat down to supper with her husband, Lena took Bennie by the hand and led him across the room to where Annie hid, as usual, behind her book. "Annie," she said, her voice quiet but not a whisper. "Will you watch Bennie for a few minutes?"

Annie met her eyes, and then smiled at the little boy. "Shall I tell you a story, Bennie?" she said.

Lena released his hand, turned and walked toward the door to the lean-to. Sofie looked up from the sink. Vrouw Wijman looked up from the table. Both began to speak at once. "Where are you . . . ?"

Lena half turned toward them and waved a hand vaguely. "I . . . I'll just be a moment. It's not quite curfew." And she was gone. She had the whole journey to think up an excuse for her long absence.

The heavy rain of the afternoon had let up a bit, and the evening was drizzly and not quite dark. The moon, which had been full just a few days before, showed through a gap in the clouds, so there would be light even once daylight was completely gone. Lena rode through town quickly. She needed to be in the country, alone, before curfew. And she was. The road by the canal looked different in the damp night, but it was straight and easy to follow, even with little light. She found her copse of trees and rode right in among them without looking behind her. Confidence, she had decided, was key. She must show confidence at all times, even if no one was about.

Five minutes later, a young nurse wheeled her bicycle out of the trees and onto the deserted road. On she pedalled in her new guise, her chest booming with the beating of her heart. It took another twenty minutes to reach the spot where the well was supposed to be. She crossed the canal, as instructed, turned onto the fourth small road and stopped where a long line of poplars began. She worked at catching her breath as she pushed her hood back from her head. A drop of water ran down her neck, but the drizzle had almost ceased, and the clouds had pulled back a bit from the moon.

By the light of the moon, she gazed at the trees and the looming clouds, at the grey-and-black world that surrounded her. The world smelled of earth and leaves, of spring. After all, April had begun. Somewhere near here, Resistance workers had dug an enormous hole, called a well. It was big enough, she understood, for men to sleep in if they needed to, and its entrance was covered, thoroughly disguised. She was not to see it. A man would meet her here.

A rustle and there he was. What he gave her was wrapped, and she was glad that she didn't have to see what it was. She could stick to her fantasy. The two barely spoke to each other before she was on her way again, her load a good bit heavier with the packages, the "things," tucked into her saddlebags. The drizzle turned suddenly to rain, and she was thankful for the hood on her nurse's cape. Still, through a break in the clouds, the moon cast a little light, and the way was easy to follow: a long road, almost straight.

She passed Wierden on her left, and for a few short minutes rode the same path she had walked some weeks before. But where she and Sofie had then turned left together, tonight she rode straight on alone.

Another twenty minutes, and she could drop off her package and go home. Ten of those minutes passed. The moon still helped her pick her way, though the rain fell a little harder now. Then, without warning, darkness—pitch darkness. A cloud had covered her small sliver of light. Lena rode on cautiously. She had seen the road ahead, and it was straight, she was sure. She could keep going just a little farther.

She felt a small rise and then the ground beneath her wheels changed, grew rougher. She put down her foot to bring the bicycle to a stop and found herself in the air. She just had time to realize that she was flying before she was under water, still astride her bicycle and entwined in her nurse's cape. A canal. Either the road had not been as straight as it looked, or she had not been keeping to a straight line. It hardly mattered now. The water was cold and deep enough that she could not feel the bottom. She thrashed about, felt her head break the surface and drew an enormous breath before the bicycle and the weight of her clothes and shoes pulled her under again.

The water was cold, astonishingly cold, and dark. When she opened her eyes under water, she thought the cloak in her face was blocking her view until she shoved it back and still saw nothing but black. Panic welled up in her then, and with it came the air she had been holding in her lungs, out in a string of bubbles followed by the start of an indrawn breath. Water filled her mouth, and she inhaled just a bit before she realized what she was doing: drawing death into her body. It took only that, and the accompanying realization that she wanted to live, and everything changed.

She had managed to push back the hood on her cape; now she unwound herself from its fabric and set herself free from that at least. The bicycle was more complicated. A cape, she could abandon; a bicycle, she could not. Without the bicycle, she would have a long walk in her wet clothes. She would likely get picked up long before she made it home. And she would be losing one of the Wijmans' most precious possessions. It could be years before they were able to replace it. Then there was its cargo. She didn't know if wet guns and grenades were of any use to anyone, but it wasn't her job to guess about that. It was her job to deliver them. She unhooked her leg from the crossbar of the bicycle, held on to the saddle and burst once more from the water to breathe. This time, she was able to keep to the surface, but stare though she might into the blackness, the shore was nowhere to be seen.

Well, if she swam in one direction, chances were she would get to the edge, she thought. Which edge, though? She might end up in a muddy field on the other side of the canal from the road, with no idea which way to go. She treaded water, trying to fight down panic and set her mind on a course of action.

Chill night air struck her face. That's all I need, she thought. Wind, to go with the cold.

And wind, it turned out, was exactly what she needed. That chill wind blew the clouds aside, and she could see. There was the shore, no more than a few strokes away. Legs kicking, free arm stroking, teeth chattering, she managed to get there and to get enough purchase with her feet on the muddy bank to shove her bicycle partway out of the water, far enough that it would stay put for a minute at least. Then she made her own slippery journey out. Finally, flat on her belly, every muscle engaged and many bruises incurred, she was tangled with her bicycle again, but this time on the bank, not in the water.

She disentangled herself once more, stood and took stock. The canal was wider than she had imagined. If she had struck off in the wrong direction, she couldn't say if she would have made it. She shivered violently. She was completely soaked, very muddy and missing her cloak. The bags were still attached to the bicycle's rear carrier, but she decided not to look inside. She picked some reeds out of the front tire of the bicycle, wheeled it back onto the road and looked up at the sky. The clouds were well out of the way now, and the moon was doing its best to light her path.

Lena felt tears rise in her, much as the panic had a few minutes before. She breathed—air this time—and ignored those tears. Pedalling warmed her slightly, although the breeze she created cooled her at the same time. By the time she reached her destination, she was afraid her dip in the canal might still be the death of her, but she did her best to let the cold and her fear and the steady tears be.

"I was starting to think something had happened to you," the man said as she drew to a stop where he stood in the shadow cast by few trees. She had almost ridden past, so well hidden was he until he stepped forward at the last moment. When he reached her, he stopped and stared. "And it looks as if something did!"

"I . . . I . . . I fell in a canal. I hope it didn't ruin the . . . the things," she managed.

He seemed to pay no attention to her explanation, rummaging in her bags, pulling out the packages one by one. "Well, let's hope they're well wrapped," he said. "It is oilcloth, after all." His voice was brisk. He pulled out the bulky cloth sack containing her clothes, saw what it was and put it back.

Lena's tears began to flow a little more freely. She hiccupped through her chattering teeth.

He looked from her to the collection of parcels in his arms and sighed. Bending down, he deposited the "things" at his feet, removed his jacket and placed it on top of them. Then he unbuttoned his sweater and placed it around her shoulders. "Put your arms in," he said, as if she were a small child. And he buttoned his sweater back up. "Now, off with you. I want you back in your own bed within half an hour. And be sure no one at home sees that uniform."

The sweater was wool and must have helped a little, though Lena could not imagine being colder or more miserable as she pedalled toward home. She was aware that she was in danger, even though she no longer carried guns. She was wearing a wet uniform with a dry sweater over it, and she had her civilian clothes in her bag. What possible explanation could she have for that? And it was now well past curfew. Still, all she could do was ride on, shivering, crying, and just to pile humiliation on top of misery, hiccupping as well.

Well, she had been helping with a birth, and she had fallen in a canal on her way home, and a man had pulled her out and given her his sweater. The clothes in her bag were a gift, a sort of thank-you for her assistance at the birth. A girl, small but healthy.

She thought about stopping close to home, changing clothes and abandoning the uniform, but she was more afraid of the Germans than of the Wijmans. Besides, she was worried that any extra delay, especially one that involved stripping off her clothes outdoors, might just kill her. She decided to keep the uniform on.

Puzzling out the story passed the first part of that last frigid half-hour. Imagining Nynke on her first day of life got her through the second part: the dark streets of Almelo. She came out of the fantasy when she crossed the railway, well south of where she had crossed it on foot with Sofie and Meneer Klaassen, but she re-entered the fantasy immediately. What might Nynke be like when she got home? Would she be crawling? Would she smile at her?

The moon cast its cool light. The road stretched ahead, eerie and empty; houses loomed on either side. She crossed the tiny River Aa and glimpsed the big church, the Grote Kerk, in the distance. There she stopped, put down the kickstand, retrieved her dripping coat from the cloth sack and hung the sack from her handlebars so she could easily grab it and slip it out of sight under her coat once she got home. The coat reached her knees and should obscure both the uniform and the sweater. On she went. Moments later, she turned into the lane. She was home.

And the lean-to door was locked against her.

Were they sitting inside waiting? What would they do with her? Turn her over to the Gestapo? Or merely turn her out into the street? A spasm shook her, and she leaned her forehead against the cold, wet locked door.

She heard a sound on the other side; the door opened a crack, no more, and a face peered out. Sofie! Sofie opened the door farther and pulled Lena and her bicycle inside. Lena stepped through the doorway and stood while Sofie closed it. Tears threatened then, but she couldn't cry, not yet. She had to think. Sofie must not see the uniform or the bag of clothes under her coat, nor should she realize that Annie might not be in the house.

"You can wear my nightdress," Sofie said in the kitchen. "It's on the bed. I've been keeping the fire going so I could make you some tea and warm you a brick."

Lena's stocking feet made squelching noises on the floor as she walked through the kitchen, swearing to herself that she would never think badly of Sofie, ever again. In the alcove, she pulled the curtain to behind her and went to work in the dark space. In a flash, her own wet clothes were in a heap on the floor, and the uniform and the sweater were shoved into the sack and pushed into the far back corner under the cot. Naked and shivering violently, she felt around on the bed until the found the nightdress. She yanked it over her head and collapsed onto the bed. That was when the tears came, once and for all. She did manage to make them quiet tears. If the Wijmans were asleep, she had no wish to wake them.

When Sofie came in with a stub of a candle, a cup of tea and a hot brick wrapped in a towel all on a tray, Lena was crying freely, with all of Sofie's blankets wrapped around her.

"Have you gone mad, Lena?" Sofie asked then. "Where have you been?"

"I fell in a canal," Lena said, incredulous still. "Rode right in. And it was so dark!"

"Yes, I can see that. But what were you doing? Why?"

Lena had not been certain that she was going to lie to Sofie. She knew that she should, but she hadn't been sure that she would until she did. "I was kind of frustrated with everything here," she said. "All of a sudden, I just had to get out. I thought I would just ride around a bit before curfew. I knew that it would make them angry, but I can't stand it here, the way Wijman looks at me. And Bennie reminds me of Bep and Nynke. I want to go home, Sofie! I want to go home." The tears that had only recently subsided threatened to start up again. Maybe she wasn't lying after all.

"But curfew was hours ago."

"I know. I took a wrong turn and ended up in the country, and then I took a really wrong turn and ended up in the canal!" She looked at Sofie and smiled wryly. Her teeth clanked loudly together, and Sofie reached out and rubbed her back through all the blankets. "What did they say after I left?" Lena asked.

"Oh, they're angry with you. Very angry. There was a great deal of talk about respect, or lack of it. 'Brazen,' Vrouw Wijman said. She should turn us both out into the street. You, apparently, are most likely no better than I am, off with some man. She just hopes he has the good grace to be Dutch!"

Something occurred to Lena.

"What did Annie say?"

Sofie reflected for a moment. "Not too much, come to think of it. She laughed at her mother when she started going on about Dutch men and Germans. She made some sort of joke, I think. And then she went off to bed."

"That's where I should go too, Sofie. Thank you so much for helping me. When you opened that door, I was about to shout out for help, and I hate to think what would have happened then!"

The two girls smiled at each other again. Looking into Sofie's face, Lena wondered if she suspected that there had been more to Lena's evening than she was letting on. Maybe. Maybe not. "Good night, Sofie," she said, crawling out from among the blankets and gulping the last of the tea. "Could you hang my wet clothes in the lean-to for me? I'll throw your nightdress down the stairs in a moment."

And up the stairs she went in the dark, clutching the brick. The door to the big bedroom was closed, she thought, but she could not quite tell for sure. At the top of the stairs, she shucked off the thin nightdress, dropped it over the banister and stood for a moment, cold though she was, to watch the thin white fabric float down in the darkness.

Then she went into the small back bedroom, pulled on her own nightdress and crawled into bed. She had not asked Sofie if

Annie had gone out because she knew that Sofie was not supposed to know, and it seemed that, indeed, Sofie had not known. Lena could not imagine how Annie had escaped once she, herself, had made her obvious exit. But apparently she had. The bed was empty.

As the brick warmed her frozen toes, Lena sent off one of her prayers, hoping simply that Annie was having a dryer night than she. And sometime later, when she was certain Sofie was asleep, she crept down the stairs, freezing her toes all over again, made her way back out to the lean-to and unlocked the door. After that, sleep came, fast and deep.

* * *

"It's morning, Lena," Annie was saying. "And you're wanted downstairs!"

Lena's eyelids were glued together, and her mind was foggy. She was wanted. She was pretty sure that was bad. But Annie was here. That was good! She sat up abruptly and squeezed shut her sleep-stuck eyelids as Annie rolled up the blackout paper, letting light stream in through the small window.

Annie sat down beside her on the bed. "They're furious with you, but they have no idea," she whispered hastily. "They've seen your wet things and the messed-up bicycle, so they've started making up a story themselves. Just go along with it!"

Lena put her hand on Annie's arm. "I'm so glad you're safe," she said as she swung her legs out of bed.

"And you know what else is safe?" Annie said. "Your packages. They were dry inside the oilcloth. You're a hero!"

Lena was glad to hear it, but she was not thinking about heroics. She was thinking about what awaited her downstairs.

CHAPTER SIXTEEN

The days that followed passed more slowly than Lena, even after five years of war, could have ever imagined. Her punishment was a week indoors. She was not to set foot outside for any reason whatsoever.

That it should be this particular week! Even from indoors, she could sense the buzz that was building in the streets; the liberators were on their way, people said, and now she had reason to believe it might be true. Seven months earlier, she had carried marigolds in her arms, joined the throngs at the entrance to her nation's greatest city and gone home disappointed. She was pretty sure that this time things would be different. Perhaps her dangerous journey of Monday night was helping somehow; surely the burden she had carried had made its way into the proper hands.

The hours and minutes crept by. Bennie begged to go outside to play. It was spring and he was just old enough to enjoy it, but Lena could not take him out. Instead, she moped around the house and snapped at him when he whined.

Any skills in the kitchen that Lena had acquired slipped away from her that week, and everyone complained about the food. Vrouw Wijman shouted at her about grime in the kitchen, and Sofie rushed to do what Lena failed to. On the third occasion, she stood, hands at her sides, as Vrouw Wijman held out the big cast-iron pot and pointed to crusty bits left over after Lena had supposedly scrubbed it.

"Let me," Sofie said, and she lifted the heavy pot and carried it back to the sink.

Lena's teeth ground together. "I will do it myself," she said, and she stepped forward and shoved Sofie aside bodily.

"Lena!" Sofie said. Her face looked soft, open. Lena almost felt a qualm.

Then fingers dug into her arm and she was yanked aside. "No," Vrouw Wijman said, "you will not. If you cannot get it right the first time, you have no right to step in now."

After that, the two girls did not speak to each other again for some time—not, in fact, until it was almost too late.

* * *

On Wednesday, April 4, news tore through Almelo. The 4th Canadian Armoured Division was south of the city, fighting to cross bridges into town. German machine-gunners and snipers were resisting. By the afternoon, fighting was going on right in the market square. Wijman was in and out all day gathering news, while the rest of them huddled in the kitchen, fear and hope and excitement keeping them all on edge.

By nightfall, the situation was not resolved, and neither Annie nor Lena slept much, tossing and turning, peeking out past the blackout paper into the blackness of the street and whispering to each other.

Lena felt twinges of guilt about Sofie, all alone in her tiny bed downstairs, but she squelched them. She was tired of worrying about Sofie, of being shown up by Sofie. She was tired of feeling guilty.

Annie and Lena both woke up early. It was Thursday, but there were no ration cards to deliver today. Today was a day for much larger events.

Lena lay in bed, eyes closed. Gradually, she grew aware of something going on, of something in the air, a stir. At first, when she focused her mind and tried to detect what it was that had attracted her attention, she heard nothing. But as she sustained her focus, listening with her whole being, sounds set themselves apart. Something was happening in the streets. Something new, not the battle of yesterday.

"Annie," she breathed, and she found that Annie, next to her, was rigid, listening too. The two girls slipped out of bed, padded downstairs and entered the unused shop. There was no blackout paper in the shop window, as the room was never lit at night.

The first light of day had filtered down to the streets, a pale and colourless light that made the scene into something eerie, the figures into ghosts, not people. Men—many, many men—were walking by the Wijmans' door. They were soldiers, but they were not marching. They were disordered, dreary, rushing, some hefting bundles. A great many rode laden bicycles. Once in a while, a lucky few passed in an overburdened vehicle. They were German soldiers, and they were headed north. They were going away.

Lena had seen such an exodus once before, last September, and even though that madness had not heralded the Allies' arrival, hope warmed her. Real hope. The Allies must be close behind, or the Germans would be going the other way, toward the closest route home. They were doing more than *going away*. They were *fleeing*.

Lena and Annie watched and watched.

"It's over," Lena said at last, right out loud.

Could it be true?

Moments later, Bennie trundled into the room. He gazed outside, his thumb in his mouth. Then his thumb popped out and he spoke. "Bad guys scared," he said.

And all three of them could see that it was true.

Sofie joined them next, but she stood a little apart. Then the Wijmans. No one asked about breakfast. Not even Bennie. No one moved. They watched and they watched and they watched. And the men walked and they walked and they walked.

Then the streets were empty. Empty in a way they had not been in years. Lena felt it deeply, and she was sure the others did too.

They gathered in the kitchen after that, and Lena laid out some bread and a few remnants of cheese. Sofie laid a fire and boiled water for tea, but Vrouw Wijman took the kettle from the stove and forgot it, the empty teapot standing by. Perhaps there would be real tea soon.

Bread and cheese in hand, Wijman left the house out the back in search of his brother. The others hesitated.

Then Annie said, "Lena, let's go out. Let's go and see what has happened."

"You will do no such thing," Vrouw Wijman said. "I have no power to keep your father indoors, but the two of you will stay."

Annie barely paused. "No, Mother," she said. "We won't." Then, "Come, Lena."

Lena looked at Vrouw Wijman and then at Sofie.

"It's all right," Sofie said. "I'll stay here. Go. Go."

So they did.

But first Lena said, "A minute. I need a minute." She ran upstairs, her tread light, as if she were buoyed by air. In Annie's room, she tugged a comb through her hair, an extra bit of grooming in honour of the approaching troops. She was on her way out of the room when she had a thought. She turned back and knelt beside the bed. Digging into her small suitcase and scattering her few possessions about her on the floor, she unearthed the tiny bottle of perfume, her first romantic gift, removed the lid and turned the mouth against her wrists, first one and then the other. How odd that she felt compelled to put on perfume from her German soldier to welcome the Canadian troops. Yet it felt right. Perhaps one day she would find a way to contact the man who had shepherded her across her country, who had treated her with respect when other men did not. The very first man to fall in love with her.

Back downstairs, Lena let Annie take her hand, and down the front hall they went, out the door and into the street. It was filling rapidly with people, and with the colour orange: flowers and flags. And joy. The mood was different from that mad Tuesday in September, Lena thought, because now, even if they hadn't admitted it to themselves, they had known for days that their liberators were on their way.

Lena and Annie allowed themselves to be caught up in the press of bodies, which carried them rapidly into the square. The large open space was filling from all directions with excited people, signs of exhaustion and starvation somehow lifted from them, despite their boniness and ragged clothing. Yesterday's fighting seemed a distant memory.

Shouts rang out in the distance, rang out and gathered volume like a snowball on a downward slope as the sound moved toward them.

The first tank had been spotted. Lena fought forward, letting go of her grip on Annie's hand as she wriggled her way through the crowd. She had to see it. She had to. And there it was, the metal bulk rolling into view: the first tank. A man was standing on top, the first of their liberators, his legs inside, his helmet already adorned with marigolds, a grin on his unshaven face.

Lena looked around to share her joy with Annie, but Annie was not there. They had lost each other. She scanned the crowd for a moment, but there was little chance of finding any single person among the thousands, and it was all right. They would meet up again eventually.

She was just turning back toward the tank, which had moved on a bit, and was opening her mouth to add her own cheers to the joyous shouts, when she heard a different sound, a German voice raised in fury.

She felt a lull in the happiness, a flurry of something else in the distance on the other side of the tank. She saw something fly through the air—and right in front of her, the man on the tank and everything around him exploded. Several bodies flew through the air. Where the man had stood a moment ago, a charred corpse now slumped across charred metal. And all around was screaming, wounded and dead bodies. Lena stared, her body and will separate. Nothing would tear her eyes from the smoking ruin in front of her.

Had it happened moments earlier, she would have been bleeding on the ground as well. Men and women with makeshift stretchers rushed into the mayhem. Almost without knowing she was doing it, Lena stepped forward and bent over a woman who lay on her side, clutching her knees up to her chest, but she was pushed aside by others, and she backed away a few steps and stopped.

And as Lena stood, frozen, the screams of fear and pain subsided, and the crowd's joyful noise turned to rage. She sensed rather than saw the scuffle on the far side of the tank. She heard a single gunshot.

The lone German soldier who had thrown the grenade must be dead.

After that, Lena was surprised to see how quickly the crowd moved on, despite the burnt-out tank and the wounded and dead in their midst. The crowd surged around the blackened tank, seeking the liberators, and Lena surged right along with it, although she wished she had Annie or Sofie at her side, and the sickness did not leave her for a long, long time. It was blended with fear. She sensed that the attack had set the people on edge, brought out in them a large measure of fury to temper their joy. They could turn into a mob in a moment.

But another tank arrived, and then another. Tank after tank of Canadians, making their way toward her. The mood of the crowd shifted back to joy, and a lightness entered Lena's step. This was freedom. Five years of war and she had just witnessed her first violence, her first death. And now she was walking forward, celebration pushing out what she had just seen. The images would return, over and over again, for the rest of Lena's life. But for now the war was over. The Canadians had come!

Soldiers walked alongside the tanks, filthy and exhausted, but jubilant. One, a man barely older than she was, with his hair hanging in his face and a scrubby beard trying to exert itself on his chin, grinned at her. Lena grinned back. Next thing she knew, he had stepped away from the tank and taken her hands in his. She found herself spun round in a dance for two, the first of her life.

"You are free!" he said in English. "And very pretty," he added.

Lena laughed into his face, pushing what she had recently witnessed out of her mind. "We are free," she exclaimed in English as well, "thanks to you!"

She thought of Sofie. Sofie would not stop at dancing: she would be kissing them too!

Then Albert entered her mind, unbidden. These men had arrived to free her from the likes of Albert, but shouldn't the first dance of her life have been with him?

Lena heard singing and shouts and the roar of the tanks. The air was fresh and cool, but not cold. Many of the soldiers had orange flowers woven into the netting on their helmets. The dreary, war-worn town had sprung to life. Joy filled the air and joy spilled through Lena's body.

How she would have loved to share this with Sofie! Perhaps she would make her way back to the house and share the news. Maybe Sofie could even sneak out. After all, no one would know her in this crowd. Surely she had no need to stay hidden now that they were free!

Then a different kind of shout filtered through to Lena. Someone was screaming. More than someone. "Whores! *Moffen meiden!*"

Lena turned and stared.

Two men and a woman were up on some sort of a stage, right in the centre of the market square. And they had a girl up there, a girl who had been stripped down to her grey, drooping underwear. Lena saw the girl try to wrap herself in her own arms, but two men grabbed them and spread them wide. Three other young women huddled miserably behind her.

Lena's stomach lurched. One of the men was Meneer Klaassen. Then her own hands flew to her face.

The girl was Sofie.

Meneer Klaassen was spitting in her face and brandishing something in his hand. Nothing in her head but horror, Lena fought her way forward through the crowd.

"Meneer Klaassen," she cried, "what are you doing? We're free!"

He didn't even turn. But his wife did. "No thanks to sluts like this one," she said, speaking not just to Lena but to the growing crowd, who jeered in confirmation of her words. "We took her in and she was off with the Nazis. Letting them in between her legs in exchange for this and that. Look at her." And she pinched the pale bare flesh at Sofie's waist. "She's grown fatter. If whores like this had their way, Hitler would rule the world, and Holland would be under water."

Lena stared up at them, unable to take in what she was hearing. Sofie bent her head, and their eyes met. After less than a moment, Lena wrenched her gaze away; the mixture of humiliation and terror in Sofie's face was too much for her.

Something fell to the ground at Sofie's feet. Lena stared. It was hair. A big chunk of dark brown hair. Another chunk fell. Meneer Klaassen was shaving Sofie's head. Lena grabbed the edge of the stage. Bodies pressed against her from behind. They reeked of sweat. Sweat and hate, she thought, and her stomach turned over again. Lena tried to turn her head away from everyone, and she vomited a thin stream of yellow bile onto the edge of the stage. Through all the jeers, the insults, the distant music, she could hear Sofie crying quietly—not resisting, not begging for mercy, not denying their accusations, just crying.

"Go slink off somewhere now. You won't be able to hide your shame. And don't think you'll be back with Wijman. He'll be done with you after today. We'll not be keeping traitors among us here in Almelo."

Lena looked up as Sofie stumbled to her knees. Not meeting Lena's eyes, she slithered off the stage and dropped to the ground. Lena had her coat off and wrapped around her friend without even knowing she was doing it. She pulled off her scarf as well and put it over Sofie's head. Sofie reached up and pulled the two ends close under her chin. Even in her misery, she wanted to cover her scalp. Lena tucked her arm round her friend and began to fight through the crowd. A few called insults as the two girls passed, but their attention was distracted by the degradation of the next woman who had somehow betrayed them.

Lena took Sofie straight to the Almelo House grounds, away from the crowds, where they could sit and talk. But Sofie wanted to talk about only one thing: Uli. "I know he'll come for me," she said, her voice barely audible through her tears. She looked up. "And what about Albert? Don't you believe he'll come for you?"

"I don't want him to," Lena said. "If he does, I want to be far away. And you should too."

"I want to wait."

"How are you going to wait? They won't have you here. Where will you live?"

Sofie crumpled again, sobbing, her scarf slipping to reveal the ugly stubble that covered her scalp.

For a long time, Lena sat and watched her cry. As she watched, she thought about the charred corpse in the tank, the smiling man that he had been, and the dead and wounded on the ground. She thought about the stage, the miserable women and the nastiness of the crowd. And she thought about Albert, raising a scented wrist to her nostrils. Did she want him to come for her?

Then all of it, every bit, was swept away, and Sarah was there, with her in her mind. What would liberation mean for her? Lena's shoulders sank. A thick sticky darkness filled her chest. Sarah had been gone for years. Lena was almost certain that she was dead. And that was past imagining.

Determined, she swallowed, straightened her shoulders and blinked, bringing herself back to the patch of grass and her weeping friend.

"Sofie," she said, "why did you go out? Why didn't you stay in the house?"

"I didn't go out," she said through her tears. "They took me. The Klaassens. They came for me. And Vrouw Wijman let them."

Lena had to do a lot more thinking after that. Her plan, weak though it was, had been all she had. She had planned to take Sofie back to the Wijmans' and beg for their mercy. Now she knew: there would be no mercy. None at all.

In the end, she took Sofie to the only hiding place she could think of: the home of the cow. It took a little doing to remember the way, but at last they were on the path down the side of the house, the shed door ajar in front of them. Lena hoped that the shed had remained unused since she and Wijman had taken the cow away to her fate, and her hopes were realized. She pushed on the heavy wooden door until it opened far enough to admit them, and the two girls stepped inside.

The reek of old manure was almost worse than the fresh, ripe smell had been, and no comforting animal warmth welcomed them, but an abandoned shed was a safe shed, and Lena was relieved.

A search turned up a tattered horse blanket on a hook on the back wall and a bit of fresh straw in a corner. "Back to sleeping in straw," Sofie said, and Lena noted the attempt at humour. A good sign.

"I'll bring you another blanket," Lena said, "and food and water."

"How long must I stay here?" Sofie asked, her voice small.

Lena looked at her. "Until the war is over," she said shortly.

"But it is over now," Sofie said.

"Only here," Lena said. "Not everywhere." And she walked out of the shed.

How long would it take, she wondered, for all of the Netherlands to be free? How long before they could leave this place and go back home to Amsterdam? However long it took, that was how long Sofie would have to remain hidden. She sent off a prayer: Please let the war be over, really over, soon.

* * *

The walk back to the Wijmans' was a thoughtful one. What if the Wijmans knew somehow that she had seen Sofie? How would she keep Sofie's hiding place a secret? She could only hope that the Klaassens had not returned, and that if they did see the Wijmans again, they would be too ashamed to tell what they had done to Sofie. That would mean they wouldn't mention seeing Lena either. Even in her most desperate fantasy, though, she couldn't imagine the zeal she had seen on the platform turning to shame in a single hour.

Vrouw Wijman greeted her at the door. "What have you done with her?" she asked. "The little slut," she added.

Lena's gut constricted. Vrouw Wijman moved her arm aside and let Lena pass. She walked through the lean-to, stepped up into the kitchen and stopped. Her desperate fantasy resolved itself into nothing.

Mevrouw and Meneer Klaassen were sitting at the kitchen table, sipping tea.

Lena gazed at the three adults and composed herself. Calm

seeped into her, all of her: torso, limbs, skull, face. Her heart slowed to a normal pace. She opened her mouth.

"I tried to help her," she said. "I tried. But people followed us, and they pulled her away. They took her. I don't know where. What did they do to her?" Her brow wrinkled. A tear slid down her cheek. She marvelled at herself. "You are cruel, cruel people," she said, speaking the truth now. And she marched through the kitchen and into the alcove that had become Sofie's, letting the curtain swing shut behind her.

She collapsed onto the bed, and the next thing she knew, the curtain was shoved aside and Bennie was on the bed with her, burrowing into her arms. Real tears flowed then. And she did not hear what was exchanged at the kitchen table while she wept.

* * *

The story came out at dinner that night, everyone sitting down together now that Sofie was gone. The Klaassens had left in a huff when Vrouw Wijman resisted turning Lena into the street. Lena figured that she had Bennie to thank for that.

Vrouw Wijman reported to her husband what the Klaassens had told her, and Lena repeated her own story about the people taking Sofie away. She felt the same calm again and was rewarded with the same convincing tears.

"We've got to find her," she said as they all stared at her. "What have they done to her?"

She saw doubt in their faces, even Annie's. And then Annie spoke. "I'll help you look for her," she said.

"You'll do no such thing," Vrouw Wijman said. "She may have been good with the silver polish, but she was a bad girl and we're well rid of her."

"Yes," her husband said. "You will stay in the house tonight, both of you." And he looked at Lena in a way that she did not like.

If only she could run away too, to stay in the shed with Sofie and wait, but she could not. This house was their source of food. They could not both go into hiding.

She got up and started to wash the dishes, her thoughts tumbling. Annie joined her. As Lena reached for a plate, Annie thrust her hand out at the same time. She touched Lena's wrist. Lena turned and met her eyes. Annie's brows thrust upward in a question. Lena gave a single nod.

"I'll help you with that," Annie said loudly, brightly, as she lifted a platter into the dishwater. Lena knew that she did not mean the platter.

Almelo was alive with excitement far into the night. The noise was mostly joyful and now and again just a little scary. Lena quailed at the thought of venturing out into the dark, but it had to be done. The thought of Sofie alone in that shed appalled her.

The Wijmans, it seemed, were not big on celebration. They went to bed early, claiming exhaustion. Annie led the way up the stairs. Lena was already in Bennie's room, telling him his favourite bedtime story. She left the softly snoring body, whispered goodnight through Annie's doorway in what she hoped was a suggestive tone and made her way down to the kitchen. Earlier in the evening, under Vrouw Wijman's instruction, she had moved her suitcase out of Annie's room and back into the alcove. She had already bundled up the two spare blankets from the train, along with a skirt, blouse and sweater, and had thrust the bundle under the bed. Sofie still had Lena's coat and scarf, and luckily, when they humiliated her up on that stage, they had not removed her shoes or stockings.

Lena got the bundle, pushed the curtain aside and started. There stood Annie, candle in hand. "I'll get a basket for food," she said. And Lena nodded.

For the next ten minutes, they worked almost without speaking.

Thus began a nightly routine. When she could, Lena visited Sofie during the day as well, but she brought little food at those times. At night, she and Annie packed only what would never be missed. They squirreled away bits of their meals into pockets, scooped bits of stew into jars, sliced scraps off loaves of bread. Any hint that food was disappearing would instantly reveal what they were up to; Sofie would be discovered, Lena would be turned out and they would be run out of town.

Lena could not imagine Sofie's hours in that shed. She and Annie worked also at alleviating her boredom. They brought her books, one at a time, and paper and pencils. Lena never saw her write, but she imagined the love letters mounting into stacks, the writing smaller and smaller as Sofie tried to make full use of the bits of paper Lena brought her. And she hoped and prayed that Sofie would have the sense to stay put.

Thus two weeks passed.

"I could go for a walk," Sofie said one day as Lena sat opposite her idling away a spare hour.

Lena jumped to her feet. "No, you could not," she said, her voice almost a bark.

"I . . . I need to get out of here. I can't—"

"You need no such thing!" Lena was shouting now. "It's not safe. You know it's not safe."

"Easy for you, going to a nice warm house every day, and a bed." Sofie's voice dwindled, and she mumbled something that Lena did not understand.

Lena collapsed back onto the straw. "What?" she demanded.

"I need Uli," Sofie said, her voice a whimper now.

"If it wasn't for Uli, you would have the warm bed and the nice meals. If it wasn't for Uli, the evil Klaassens would be your sweet new mummy and daddy!"

Sofie mumbled again. Then she looked up at Lena, opened her mouth and spoke. "I'm pregnant," she said.

And that brought silence.

At last Lena said, "You are not. Or at least, you can't be sure."

"I'm pretty sure," Sofie said. "I'm late, and I just feel it, you know?"

"No, I don't know."

"Well, I don't feel any of the normal things. No cramps, for one."

Lena had no response to this news. It was too much. She just would not respond. She could not. She would not.

"I have to go," she said.

"But, Lena."

"I said I have to go. I'll be back tonight. And NO WALKS!" With that, she strode out of the shed, almost tempted never to return.

She did return, of course, that very night, with Annie, although she did not share Sofie's news, not then. They brought Sofie food and drink, chatted for a few minutes and made their way home. Annie commented on Lena's silence, and Lena shrugged.

Back in the house, Annie whispered goodnight. Lena stood and listened to her quiet footsteps on the stairs. Then she pushed aside her curtain, stepped into her alcove and sat down on the bed. The air felt different in there somehow, she thought, and the bed was lower or something. She had no time to make sense of these thoughts before her mind exploded in terror as a hand clamped down on her mouth.

"Do not make a sound," Wijman said into her ear, and he removed his hand.

Instinct made Lena do as she was told, but she lunged off the bed, intent on escape, only to find that the grip on her mouth had shifted to an iron grip on her arm. She was yanked back to her spot on the bed, now with Wijman's body right up against hers.

"So where are you keeping her?" he asked, again right into her ear.

Lena shrank into herself.

"I said, where are you keeping her?" he repeated, his voice sharp and breathy, his fingers twisting her forearm.

"I . . . I don't know what you mean," Lena said. Her voice shook, but she could not help that.

He let go of her arm and turned from her to light the candle beside the bed. She did not try to flee. Where could she go?

In the flickering light of the candle, he turned back to her. "You don't have to tell me. In fact, I don't even want to know." He paused and she watched him, disgust and terror warring with that calm place inside her that was busily forming a plan. "I want something else," he said.

"No," she said. "You can't. I can't . . ."

"Yes," he said, "you can. Either that or we'll go together and get Sofie and turn her over to the authorities. I don't know where you've got her, but I doubt she would prefer prison."

Lena looked at him for a long moment. She let her shoulders drop. "All right," she said, and she put her hands over her eyes and let out a small whimper of fear.

He reached for her.

"No, wait," she said. "Let me . . ." She stood and began to unbutton her sweater, keeping her eyes downcast. From under her lashes, she saw him sink back onto the bed, his back against the wall, watching her. She undid another button.

Then she turned and shot from the alcove, across the kitchen, down the hall and up the stairs, silent and fast. Behind her, Wijman grunted in surprise and anger, and she knew he was following, but once she was on the stairs, what could he do? She slid into Annie's room and knelt beside her bed.

"I need to come back in with you," she whispered to the sleeping girl, and Annie mumbled and moved over. Lena crawled in beside her. She listened then and heard his step on the stairs. The footsteps stopped outside Annie's door, the door opened and Lena sensed him peering inside. After a moment, the figure in the doorway withdrew and the door closed.

"What happened?" Annie whispered, still not fully awake.

"I'll tell you tomorrow," Lena said, then she shocked herself by falling asleep in minutes, Sofie's pregnancy and Wijman's lechery turning to the stuff of dreams.

* * *

Lena did not tell Annie what had happened, not in words. "I need to sleep with you again," she whispered the next morning when they found themselves briefly alone in the kitchen.

Annie looked at her. "Did he hurt you?" she said at last.

Lena pushed up her sleeve and held out her arm.

"Only this," she said, and they both gazed at the bruises his four fingers had left behind. She flipped her wrist, revealing the larger thumb-shaped mark on the other side of her arm.

Annie met her eyes. "It's not safe for you here," she said.

"I know, but we need to eat, Sofie and me. The war's got to be over soon, everywhere. It's got to."

The smallest nod and Annie turned back to peeling potatoes. Vrouw Wijman was on her way down the hall, Bennie in tow.

Lena watched Wijman closely after that on the rare occasions when he was in the house, and she took roundabout routes to Sofie's hiding place. He pushed past Lena roughly whenever he had the chance, muttering obscenities at her, but Vrouw Wijman, Lena noticed, was watching him too. Lena was pretty sure that his threat to turn Sofie in was words, nothing more.

* * *

With her pregnancy more certain every day, Sofie talked of nothing but Uli and the coming baby, alternating between enraptured imaginings of the family she would soon have and terror that Uli would come for her and be captured or leave without finding her.

Over and over again, Lena and Annie promised to be on the lookout, to bring him to her or her to him the instant he was spotted. Once, Lena ventured to suggest that he might not be able to come. "He could be a prisoner," she said, "or he could have been sent far away. There's still fighting in Germany, you know. And in the west," she added, thinking once again of her own family.

Those words brought glares and fierce denials, all the fiercer for the knowledge in all their hearts that the baby's father could well be dead.

"He loves me," Sofie told Lena more times than she could count. "He will come."

269

* * *

Lena had other things to think about. For her, liberation meant an end to her barely begun Resistance work. Annie took her out one day to meet the tall, thin man at the house in the country. Two Jewish families were there too, on their way back to what was left of their homes. They had benefited from her ration cards, she learned, and she felt pride and humility all mixed together. The matchbox, it turned out, had contained tiny rolled-up bits of paper with signals in code to be communicated by radio to Britain. If she had known that when the German officer was taking his cigarette, she was sure she would have fainted from fear, although she was glad to learn that the message was concealed under a false bottom in the box, which did contain matches.

She thought about Piet. Was he all right? Resistance work had to be more dangerous in Amsterdam. And freedom was so slow in coming to the west. She imagined the corpses piling higher every day. She imagined the German soldiers, cut off, angry. What might they be doing to people? She woke up from dreams of gunshots and bomb blasts. It was as if she were really hearing the guns and bombs, not dreaming them.

In late April, they heard of food drops near Amsterdam, and then, within two days of each other, the two dictators were dead, Mussolini shot in Milan and Hitler killed, many said by his own hand, in Berlin.

Five days after that, it came. The end. The war was over. Amsterdam was free.

Wijman showed little expression when he heard the news on the wireless. He had come home with the radio the day after Almelo's liberation, so they heard daily reports of the progress of the war. Now, as joy blossomed in her heart, Lena observed

Wijman's indifference. His own freedom was what had counted. And he already had that, or thought he did.

He looked at Lena across the table. "You'll go," he said.

She held his gaze. "Yes," she said. "May I have a day to prepare?"

He frowned and looked at his wife.

"Come on, Father. You can't just put her out on the street." That was Annie.

"We can and we will," said Vrouw Wijman. "But you have your day, girl. Beyond that, it's up to you."

"I will leave first thing tomorrow," Lena said firmly, while her mind screamed, What about Sofie?

* * *

She left through the lean-to and wandered alone to the Almelo House grounds. Excitement was everywhere, people rejoicing at freedom for their nation and for the world. May had arrived, bringing warmth and sunshine. Everywhere was a riot of flowers, the earth itself in celebration.

Lena lay down on a warm, grassy slope and thought. She must return home. She longed to see Piet and Margriet and especially Bep and Nynke. Surely the food parcels had arrived safely and her family had all survived.

But what was Sofie to do, marked by the stubbly growth on her head, pregnant, longing for her German soldier? What was Lena to do about Sofie?

Minden, Sofie had said. That was where Uli's parents were. It had not been bombed like Düsseldorf. If Uli did not come for her, Sofie was determined to go to Minden. But how? The Allies were taking control of all of Germany. Minden might not have been hit directly, but the whole country was in ruins, with everyone starving, desperate. They had just lost a war.

Sarah flashed into Lena's mind. Lena sat up abruptly and hunched over, her hands knotted between her knees. She could not hold Sarah and Sofie together in her mind. Was she supposed to accompany Sofie to Germany where Sarah and her family likely died? To stay in hiding with her here? Or should she drag her, kicking and screaming, back to Amsterdam?

She smiled wryly through her tears. Sofie was beginning to feel more like a millstone than a friend! Lena hoisted herself to her feet and set off for the shed. One decision had mostly settled itself in her mind: she was returning to Amsterdam, with or without her millstone.

* * *

Lena stared at Sofie. They had opened the shed door and ventured out into the sunshine, just out of sight of the road, where they sat, side by side, backs against a stone wall.

Sofie, it seemed, had it all worked out! "It's not so far, Minden. Straight east. There's been bombing near there, Uli told me, but not the town itself. I'm to go to his parents, he said, and he'll meet me there when he can."

"Sofie, you have no idea. They've just lost a war! Minden could have been bombed since you saw Uli. There's been a lot more bombing since then. Haven't you heard the planes?" Lena said.

Sofie paused. "I know," she said. "I know. But it isn't far, and his parents know I'm coming."

She was gearing up to start babbling again, Lena could see. "You don't even know if they'll let you across the border," she said.

"I'll show them Uli's letter. He wrote it all down for me, you know. I . . . I'll just keep trying. Or I'll sneak across. I'm just one girl. There've got to be lots and lots of people on the move now. Don't you think?"

"I don't know, Sofie. I don't even know what it will be like to travel back to Amsterdam!"

Lena thought about Albert for a moment. She tried to imagine going east into the unknown, the defeated country of their enemy, on the chance that she would be able to find him and build a life with him. Her memory of Albert was warm, and she thought it might be nice to hear from him one day. But she did not feel the burning passion that drove her friend. Sofie might weep and whine a lot, and she didn't think about others much, but she did have courage—courage and commitment.

At the moment, Lena was most excited at the likelihood (she hoped it was a likelihood!) that she would soon see Bep and Nynke. Every moment she spent with Bennie had made her long for the chance to show the two of them just how much she loved them. Romance would have to wait.

"Well, if you must, you must," she told Sofie, just as Annie came pelting around the corner and hunkered down beside them.

"What are you planning?" she said, gasping for breath as she spoke.

"I think a parting," Lena said quietly.

Sofie stopped breathing for a moment. "A parting," she echoed.

Annie nodded. "I can help," she said, "with bicycles. One for each of you. It turns out that bicycle you pulled out of the drink is going to come in very handy for you!"

Lena choked on a sob. "Oh, Annie, I'll miss you," she said.

"Well," Annie said brightly, "I may be only fifteen, but you never know when I might show up in Amsterdam! And Sofie," she went on, "I do believe that I can lay my hands on a map for you."

Lena looked from one to the other. "We can all write," she said. "At least, I know you can, Sofie. When Uli gets home, he's going to have to read for a week just to catch up!"

She thought for a moment about the next morning: Bennie staring at his wooden toys on the kitchen floor, struggling to understand why the most loving person ever to enter his life had just given him a big, damp hug and gone away; Annie grumbling as she washed the breakfast dishes and watched over him, maybe laying a hand on his baffled head and blinking a tear or two out of her eyes; and Lena and Sofie setting off on laden bicycles, together only to the nearby square, where one would turn east and the other west. Maybe, just maybe, Sofie would carry a note in her pocket, a sweet little note for a certain young German who made his living pasting pretty paper onto people's walls.

At the moment, grief at parting eclipsed fear of the dangers of the road, which Lena imagined would be plentiful, especially for Sofie. Then something eclipsed even that.

When she was younger, Lena had not been a good friend. She knew that. And though she would try, once she got home, she would never learn Sarah's fate, and she would never forget her own terror and how it had made her turn her back on her first real friend.

Now, though, with warm stone at her back, and a girl on either side, Lena realized that she had changed. Sarah had not been able to count on her. But Annie and Sofie could.

And best of all, she could count on herself. Imminent parting or no, that was something she could hold on to.

EPILOGUE

The magnolia was in full bloom.

Sunlight streamed through the massive white blossoms and cast dappled shade on three young people who sat together on a wooden bench in a courtyard, breathing in the sweet scent. At their feet, a toddler busily gathered thick white flower petals into the bowl of her skirt. The eldest of the three young people, a tall woman with blonde hair, held a letter in her hand. A boy, almost as tall as she was, sat close beside her, and a girl of perhaps eleven nestled under her arm on the other side.

They were happy, those three, glad to be together, and they were glad to learn that another girl, the eldest one's friend and writer of the letter, was safe. Her husband was a prisoner of war, but his parents were kind to her (though there was little to eat and she had to work hard) and her baby was healthy. She had named the baby Lena. That made all the young people smile.

The eldest was smiling for a more private reason as well. Deep in the pocket of her skirt was another letter from a different prisoner of war.

She would read that letter later, when she was alone.

ACKNOWLEDGMENTS

Many people helped in the research for this book and gave me invaluable feedback on it once it was done. My thanks to the following:

Lin Stevens, who shared her story with me, answered all my questions willingly, and listened and responded when I read parts of early drafts aloud, while accepting with grace the deviations between the fictional story and the real one.

My father, Jan de Vries, who shared maps and information about the major events of the Second World War, went through old family papers and shared those with me and put me in touch with Jan and Iny Slomp.

Clea Parfitt, who travelled with me to the Netherlands and walked, rode trains and pedalled bicycles with me, seeking out the sites and information I needed to move forward in my writing.

Jan and Iny Slomp, who welcomed Clea and me into their home in Leusden and shared Jan's father's story. The Reverend Frits Slomp was a key figure in the Dutch Resistance, and his story provided useful background for me. The Slomps also lent me an important book: *To Save a Life: Memoirs of a Dutch Resistance Courier* by Elsa Caspers.

A family friend, Ria Orr, who lent me books of photographs and other material.

The research librarians at the Vancouver Public Library, who went out of their way to support me in my first research for this story when I was writer-in-residence there in 2005. They put into my hands a book I read over and over: *The Hunger Winter: Occupied Holland 1944–1945* by Henri A. van der Zee.

Lynne Missen, my editor, who saw promise in the story I submitted to her and guided me through major revisions, without which *Hunger Journeys* would be a mere shadow of itself.

And all the others at HarperCollins who worked on this book: Sarah Howden, whose insights made their way to me through Lynne; the designers who created the beautiful cover; Noelle Zitzer, Janice Weaver and Debbie Viets, who refined my words and caught my errors; Inge Siemens, sales rep for BC and Alberta, whose keen enthusiasm for this story bolstered my confidence; and everyone else who worked the miracle of turning my imaginings into a real book.

Any errors that remain are, of course, my responsibility alone.

I gratefully acknowledge the British Columbia Arts Council for a grant that assisted in the writing of this book.